PRAISE FOR *UMAMI*

'This book is such a gentle and sensitive deep dive into the cycles of mourning and loss o~~ut of which~~ ~~fam~~ ~~il~~ ~~y~~ ~~ties are u~~nmade, terrifying and uncanny  ~~the perso~~nalities of hearth and home an~~d the memories th~~ey serve.'

~~Literar~~y Hub

'*Umami* offers the enti~~re experience of the Mexico Cit~~y ~~me~~galopolis being opened up.'

Independent

'The best Mexico City novels find a way to incarnate that city's crazy protean energies, every sentence lifted from its psychic sidewalks and rooftops, and with a dashing charisma all their own. Roberto Bolaño's *Savage Detectives* did this, and so does Laia Jufresa's extraordinary, utterly enchanting and brilliant, multi-everything *Umami*.'

Francisco Goldman, author of *Say Her Name*

'Ms Jufresa: Where the f*#! did you learn to tell a story so well?'

Álvaro Enrigue, author of *Sudden Death*

'*Umami* is a debut novel that I am afraid has been criminally under-read, a slim book about community and loss that somehow doesn't feel as heavy as it could... Laia Jufresa magically layers the [stories] on top of each other, illuminating the secret sorrows that connect them all. It's beautifully translated by Sophie Hughes, a tall order because of the different kinds of language all of the characters use. In the end, *Umami* isn't resolved in the ways a traditional novel would be – but it's satisfying and moving.'

NPR, One of the Best Books of 2016

'Luminous.'

Le Monde

'*Umami* surely signals the arrival of a major new talent... In prose that is dazzlingly inventive, funny and tender, Laia Jufresa immerses us in the troubled lives of her narrators, deftly unpicking their stories to offer a darkly comic portrait of contemporary Mexico, as whimsical as it is heart-wrenching.'

Nudge

'In *Umami*, language itself is a character. The talents of Sophie Hughes are displayed in Marina's constant wordplay which comes alive in her sensitive and playful translation. Jufresa's talent for neologism and her inventive structure give the novel a lightness of touch that never undermines its revelations, but rather enhances them.'

Culture Trip

'Fans of contemporary literature are in for a treat.'

Press Association

'Grief, though, is neither defined by culture nor constrained by time. Yes, Jufresa could have written *Umami* the "normal" way – a single perspective in chronological order with first person the whole way through – instead of this backwards telescope, alternating voices and switching perspectives between first and close third. That version of *Umami* would be a dark, bitter thing, like molasses in the coffee grounds. Instead, Jufresa and Hughes offer a version that is complex without weight, a saffron purée. Dynamic and delicate, *Umami* draws our attention without pretense.'

Rumpus

'Jufresa directly appeals to any reader who was once a 12-year-old girl obsessed with Agatha Christie (*cough* me), but also, and truly, this is a gorgeous book that meditates on loss and grief, healing and redemption, and also offers an enchanting look into life in contemporary Mexico.'

Nylon

'A tale of five lives in one block in Mexico City's inner city – in a complex designed with human tastebuds in mind – this sad and funny novel has already snagged awards, and was dubbed an "international hot property" by PW when the English rights were sold.'

Flavorwire

'Presents an evocative and sensory insight to its central American setting... The five voices and the jumpy timeline require a little patience, but perseverance pays off.'

St John's Wood Magazine

'The people of the neighborhood are dealing with different types of grief in private. But as each story unfolds, an astounding sense of community (and healing) begins to take place. Yet it's quite clear that the novel's dire warning is that those who do not pay attention to the losses around them suffer in silence. Jufresa's non-linear storytelling is challenging to read, but the humor in the book makes the effort worth it.'

Rigoberto Gonzalez, NBC News Online,
Great Latino Books Published in 2016

'Whimsical and inventive... [its] heart, charm and originality are a welcome addition to Mexican literature.'

Emerald Street

'Jufresa, an extremely talented young writer, deploys multiple narrators, giving each a chance to recount their personal histories, and the questions they're still asking. Panoramic, affecting and funny, these narratives entwine to weave a unique portrait of present-day Mexico.'

The Millions

'I couldn't put this book down, and when it did end, it left me in tears. An extremely charming novel... Jufresa's disarming, unabashed tone and interest in the intersection of languages and cultures reminded me of Chloe Aridjis' wonderful *Book of Clouds*, while Sophie Hughes' translation stands alongside the original as a dazzling feat in its own right. A beautiful and surprising meditation on community, absent maternity and growth of all kinds.'

Three Percent

'Thoughtful, eccentric and heart-wrenching… Jufresa crafts a story with warmth and tenderness but also gives insight to the uncanny human talent of engaging in cruel and awkward behavior. Some of the stories told are playful and light, others are tragic. *Umami* is quirky, insightful and ultimately tells the stories of humans coping with living next to one another in order to feel less isolated and alone.'

World Literature Today

'*Umami* is true to its whimsical premise, the narrative a little sweet, a little salty, by turns bitter and sour. Very umami, and very funny at times despite the tragedies that mark each household. The setup could admittedly become tired over 250-plus pages, but Jufresa also works an innovative structure that leaves the reader questioning until the end.'

Globe and Mail

'*Umami* dives into a grief-soaked corner of Mexico City, where five houses gather around a courtyard. Ana, a 12-year-old girl still haunted by the mysterious drowning of her young sister, looks for answers and relief in Agatha Christie novels, barely glancing up from her books. Her neighbors share their own losses and tragedies, and Laia Jufresa jumps between them, drawing out the pain and secrets weighing down the neighborhood.'

Minnesota Public Radio, Best books of the Fall 2016

'This book was one of my favorites this year. Set in Mexico City, where Jufresa lives, it focuses on a group of neighbors that all live in houses named after flavors – Sweet, Salty, Sour, Bitter, and, of course, Umami – and is about the loss and light in each of their lives. I cried a bunch of times while reading this book – it's not shy about emotional gut-punches, but they never feel cheap or hollow.'

Alejandro Olivia, Remezcla,
#1 Book Written by a Latinax in 2016

UMAMI

LAIA JUFRESA

Translated by Sophie Hughes

ONEWORLD

A Oneworld book

First published in North America, Great Britain and Australia
by Oneworld Publications, 2016

This paperback edition published 2017
Reprinted, 2022

Originally published in Spanish as *Umami*
by Penguin Random House Grupo Editorial, 2015

ISBN 978-1-78074-892-4
ISBN 978-1-78074-893-1 (eBook)

This book has been selected to receive financial assistance from English PEN's
PEN Translates! programme. English PEN exists to promote literature and our
understanding of it, to uphold writers' freedoms around the world, to campaign against
the persecution and imprisonment of writers for stating their views, and to promote
the friendly cooperation of writers and the free exchange of ideas. www.englishpen.org

Typeset by Tetragon, London
Printed and bound in Great Britain by Clays Ltd, Elcograf S.p.A.

Oneworld Publications
10 Bloomsbury Street
London WC1B 3SR
England

For Tod, por todo

If poetry could truly tell it backwards,
Then it would.

– Carol Ann Duffy

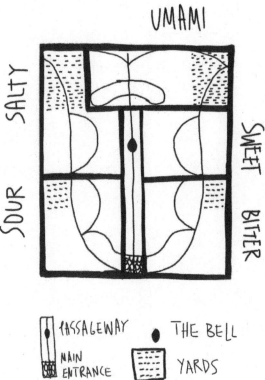

UMAMI

SALTY

SOUR

SWEET

BITTER

PASSAGEWAY • THE BELL

MAIN
ENTRANCE YARDS

I

2004

'A *milpa*,' I said.

I stood up on my chair in the dining room and said, 'A proper, traditional *milpa*, with corn and beans and squash. I could plant it myself, right next to the picnic table.'

I drew a great circle in the air with my hands and proclaimed, 'Like our forefathers.'

The three of us looked out of the sliding door to the yard where the picnic table lives. Once upon a time it was folding and portable. The benches on either side slot underneath like the retracting feet of a turtle, and the whole thing transformed into a neat aluminum travel case. Not anymore. It'd probably still fold up, but no one seems keen on picnics these days. Around the table there's just gray cement (dirty gray), and a row of flowerpots full of dry soil, the remains of some bushes, a broken bucket. It's a colorless, urban yard. If you spot something green, it's moss you're looking at; something red and it'll be rust.

'And herbs,' I told them. 'Parsley, cilantro, tomatillos, and chili for the green salsa Dad makes when we have people over.'

Dad bought into the idea straight away. He asked for some of those knobby tomatoes he once ate on tour in California. But Mom, the one who supposedly loves plants, wasn't having any of it. She went to her room before I'd even got off the chair, and only agreed to the deal three days later. We wrote the full agreement on a napkin, then signed it, making one small change to appeal to Mom's gringo sensibility: 'a *milpa* with some grass on it'. A *milpa*-garden, if you will. There's a history of *milpas* in our little development, Belldrop Mews. I'm not the first to try it. But anyway, now it's official: 'In exchange for plowing, planting, and tending the yard, Ana is excused from summer camp and may spend her vacation at home.'

My own home, I might add. Doesn't this essentially mean I'm paying rent? Other people might see it that way. Not my parents. They're really into fair trade. Fair trade and nature. Mom grew up next to a lake. She gets nostalgic about dragonflies.

In Mom's head, summer camp = privileged childhood. But in this case camp is just a coded way of saying that my siblings and I spend two months with her stepmother, Grandma Emma, swimming among the weeds and feeding pebbles to the ducks in the lake by her house. Mom equates a passion for these kinds of activities with a healthy constitution; something like drinking a glass of milk a day or waking up with the birds. She brought us up in Mexico City, and yet she doesn't want us to be city-kids, which is exactly what we are. She's been living here twenty years and still ties a hippie scarf around her head: her personal take on the national flags other expats hang from their windows. Uprooted. This is how Mom refers to herself when we have visitors and she's drinking red wine and her teeth and tongue start turning black. When I was little, I imagined wiry roots growing out of her feet, filling her bed with soil.

Protestant is another way Mom describes herself. And the word comes with a specific gesture: a slow flick of her wrist, a kind of curtsey of the hand; as much to defend as to mock herself. Within the family the mere gesture has come to mean Protestant. It's our way of laughing at Mom's neuroses: for a job well done; for punctuality. When someone flicks their wrist it's like they're dusting off the invisible cobwebs of Mexico's Catholicism. Or it means it's time to go to the airport, even if it's too early. No matter who does it, the rest of us will translate the wrist-flick as 'Behold, the Protestant ethic.'

The truth is there's a Walmart next to her childhood lake now. But it's not wise to bring that up. Neither that nor the suggestion that she too could go visit Emma. Mom tends to forget that the uprooting was her own doing. Sometimes I think I should do the same. Pack my things and get out of here the moment I hit fourteen. But I won't, because she would just love that: her eldest daughter following in her footsteps. That'd be the family's interpretation, no doubt about it. Mom twists things with the same firm delicacy she uses to fold our clothes and wring out the mop. I've seen pictures of her from when she was fifteen, with her cello between her legs and no shoes on. It was easy to vanish when you looked like that. Easy to float up and away. When I sit down my thighs meet, and there's always something spilling out from the waistband of my pants, or my chair, or my mouth. And I'm a lost cause when it comes to rhythm. Same with adventures. I suspect if I ever ran away, I'd only end up coming back.

*

Now we have two sacks of 'optimized' soil. The owner of the garden center convinced me that our soil, the stuff that's already there in the yard, won't do. He told us it's contaminated with lead. He told us that throughout the whole of Cuauhtémoc, the whole of Benito Juárez, and the whole of the city center, there are 1,300 micrograms of lead for every kilo of soil. I'm not sure I believe him, but in any case I bought some of his. Really I bought it so that my best friend Pina and I could get the heck out of there. He didn't stare at our titties or anything, but he did sink his hands slowly into the sack of soil, all the way up to his forearm, while lecturing us about terrains and fertilizers. At that point, Pina, who'd only come on the condition that I buy her a half-liter of *horchata* afterward, dug her elbow into me.

'Buy the soil,' she said. 'There's enough shit in our tuna already.'

After we left, we hung out at La Michoacana, an establishment that by all appearances survives solely off our business.

'You think he was a pervert?' I asked Pina.

Pi licked her lips, stroked one of the sacks and moaned, 'Mm, soil.'

Then she put her hand between her legs.

'Mm, a little lead worm!'

Sometimes I truly resent having to be seen with her in public. The rest of the time I just feel jealous. I don't know how to say no to Pina. When we were in fourth grade she made me play a game where you scratched your hand until it bled. Then we did a blood pact to be sisters. But lately we're not so similar: everything she does, everything that happens to her, makes me jealous. It's all so much more exciting than anything going on in my life. And I don't know when this started. Actually, I do. It started when her mom reappeared. Before that we each had our own ghost: she had her mom and I had my sister. But three months ago her ghost contacted her online. It's not the same, obviously, your mother leaving or your sister dying. But what's worse: a mother that reappears out of nowhere, or one that never leaves the house?

Pina has stopped moaning.

'Don't say "pervert",' she says.

'Why not?'

'It's what assholes call gay people. It's a discrimatry word.'

'Discriminatory.'

'Whatever.'

*

'Shall I just throw the new soil on top of the old soil and forget about it?'

We're in my yard. Pina's got one arm raised, with her head turned in toward her armpit. With the help of some tweezers, which she's holding in the other hand, she slowly plucks out the hairs. When her neck gets stiff, she changes side. She looks like a heron: beautiful and twisted. I stare at the sacks of new soil but they're not hiding any answers. My current favorite word is 'ennui'. This is ennui: that time of the day when even the flies are sleepy. Everything is still. Everything stinks of dust and cement. I don't know about lead, but I did find a flip-flop in the old soil. And some bottle tops. And my cuddly toy dog who disappeared a zillion years ago, clearly buried with malice aforethought. If my brothers weren't at camp, I'd be taking my revenge.

'You have to take off the old soil first,' says Pina, who doesn't have a clue what she's talking about.

'And what am I supposed to do with it then?'

'You sell it to Marina. Or give it to her, so she can plant something and eat it.'

'With lead in it?'

'It's a mineral, Ana. She could do with it.'

'Maybe she could do with reading *Umami*.'

'What's that?'

'Alf's book. I lent it to you a zillion years ago.'

'I gave it to someone else. Was it a novel about pedophilia?'

'Not even remotely. It was an anthropological essay on the relationship between the fifth taste and pre-Hispanic food. Do you even know which mews you live in?'

'Yes, Ana, I know what umami is, but why would he write a book with the same name as his house?'

'You are so dumb.'

'You're the dumb one who doesn't know what to do with your dirt.'

Dad comes out through the sliding door. He got rid of his beard a couple of weeks ago and I still haven't got used to it. He looks younger. Or maybe uglier. The other day I turned up at one of his rehearsals so he could give me a ride home and I barely recognized him. Throughout his entire career he's always sat at the very back of the stage, but even then I never had trouble picking him out. Obviously, this was because of the beard. But now's not the moment to bring it up. I hand him the twenty pesos left over from the garden center.

Dad sits down on a bench with a beer and props his feet up on my sacks of soil. He puts the money in his wallet. I promised him the project would be 'a sound investment', but the truth is, I don't even know what that means.

I explain about the nitrogen in the soil first: about how the corn will absorb it and the beans will replace it again. Then I explain about the lead, maybe exaggerating a little bit. ('Toxic,' I say. And, 'carcinogenic.') He seems interested so I go on. I tell him we're going to nixtamalize our corn ourselves, the way Mexicans have always done, and unlike the Europeans, who took our corn but not our wisdom and went on to die of pellagra for centuries without the slightest clue of what was killing them.

'It was the lack of niacin, in case you're wondering.'

Pina rolls her eyes. Dad is watching Mom through the window. She's wearing an orangey turban and her lips are moving as she washes the dishes. She looks like a Japanese carp. We agree not to tell her the bit about the lead because she's one of those people whose heart breaks at the mere mention of pollution and/or progress.

I propose to Dad that we buy a hose. He makes some calculations. Fretting about money is one of his tics. It makes him go cross-eyed. I list off all the different types of tomatoes to distract him.

'Some of them will be green,' I promise him, 'and others deep purple.'

Pina helps. She raises her tweezers and traces vertical lines with them.

'Some of them will be stripy,' she says.

Dad perks up at this. He goes into the kitchen for another beer and we watch him try to convince Mom to come out.

'Tiger tomatoes,' he's saying to her. 'Quality time,' he adds in English, with his Mexican accent that used to make her laugh. But Mom doesn't come out. She doesn't believe in yards. In her head a yard is something pathetic and wasted; something that wallows in its own filth; something constricted.

'Don't you think she's too skinny?' asks Pina.

'Who?'

'Marina!'

Dad comes out and announces that he's not going to buy me any tools. I'll have to borrow some. I'd put money on this being Mom's fault: she's always telling him he spoils me. I ask him who exactly he thinks is going to lend me tools, but he just crushes his empty beer can with his foot. He's played timpani in the National Symphony Orchestra for twenty years: when he makes a sound, he knows how to let it resonate. He looks up after a while and sits gazing at Pina.

'Doesn't that hurt?' he asks her.

'Yeah, it does,' she replies.

'Then why not just shave?'

'Because then they grow back quicker,' I explain through gritted teeth.

Dad takes the hint and doesn't ask any more questions. Pina puts the tweezers in her shorts pocket, crosses her arms and clutches both hands under her armpits.

'I better go pack,' she says, getting up and giving us each a kiss.

'Aren't you staying for lunch?'

'I can't, I'm going to see Chela tomorrow and I still haven't got sunblock and blah blah blah.'

'Tell her I said hi,' Dad says.

But I don't know what to say and Pina leaves. Through the window we watch her hug Mom: Japanese carp, Chinese heron.

*

An email arrives from my brothers, who have just landed in Michigan. We always get our plane tickets courtesy of the airline that my granddad, the one we can't remember, worked for as a pilot. When I was little, there was nothing in the world more exciting than flying with them, as if we were all part of one big, brilliant extended family, where there were blue washbags full of goodies for the grandchildren of pilots, infinitely better than my friends' party favors. At the airport they'd hang a badge around my neck, and I'd take charge of my siblings. Back when there were still four of us, we didn't all fit in one row. I would sit on the other side of the aisle and pretend I was traveling on my own. Emma didn't even have Internet in those days. Now she can't stop forwarding things. She sent us an email recently about skin cancer; one of those PowerPoint slideshows that get shared endlessly online. And this probably explains why in the photo attached to the email Theo is wearing a baseball cap, Olmo a visor, and Emma a conical Asian hat, no doubt from Penny Savers where she buys everything in threes because she knows they'll fall apart. All three of them have the unique phantasmagorical skin tone of cheap total sunblock, and Emma has a cigarette between her fingers. There's not a PowerPoint in the world that could convince her to give those up.

Last year, Theo tried to explain to Emma that it would make more sense for her to buy one decent-quality flashlight, let's say, than three crappy ones. Emma let him finish then said, 'Well, you obviously never lived through a war.'

Theo was too slow to react, because by the time he'd said, 'Neither did you!' Emma had already wandered off in the direction of the detergent aisle, her trolley packed with triplicate items. Whenever anybody tries to take her up on this habit of hers – so inconsistent with the rest of her so-called off-the-grid and, as she would have it, antiestablishment ways – Emma defends herself, arguing that by shopping in Penny Savers she's doing her bit for the Burmese economy.

'Or Taiwanese, or one of those countries in the process of expansion.'

'The universe is the only thing expanding,' Theo tells her.

And she says, 'Alrighty, then.'

*

Mom cries at the email, and the photos. She gets worse in summertime. Like a dirty river carrying trash, the summer drags the anniversary of my sister's death to our door. She was the youngest.

'The dumbest, you say?' a deaf aunt asked me one day during those weeks when family kept crawling out from under stones, like insects that only live for one day (the day of condolence).

'NO!' I shouted back. 'I said she was the YOUNGEST!'

12

Luz was almost six when she drowned. That's what she'd say from the day she turned five: 'I'm almost six.' Mom hasn't gone back to the lake since, but she insists on sending us. To her mind, if you fall off the horse you have to get right back on again. Or if not you, at least your kids.

'Is there anything you want to say to your children?' the psychologist asked, the one time we went to group therapy, not long after Luz died. Dad, Theo and I had been talking for an hour, but Mom hadn't said a single word. Nor had Olmo, who was really little. The doctor raised her eyebrows, as if to remind Mom that our future was in the balance, our mental health at stake; all those things she had spent the last hour repeating. In the end, Mom gave in. She looked at us one by one, her three remaining children, and, so slowly you could make out the foreignness in her accent, she said, 'Kids, you are very brave, and I am not a fish.'

2003

An evening in July. The crisp, seemingly clean mist left by the afternoon downpour – a daily occurrence throughout Mexico City's fake summer – drifts along the central passageway of Belldrop Mews. The floor gleams. It smells of wet terracotta. The puddles reflect a peculiar, unseen light show. It's coming from Bitter House, where Marina Mendoza lives. She always leaves the lights on, but tonight something strange is going on with them. They keep flickering, moving from very dim to very bright. Not rhythmically, like when the TV is on, but in bursts. First they even out, then they change again. There are no neighbors around to notice any of this, but nor would they be surprised if they were: it's just Marina Mendoza, once again unhappy with the atmosphere.

Bitter House is the first one on the right, and overlooks the road, but the front door and most of its windows face onto the connecting passageway. The six square meters in front of her house change more than any other corner of the mews. Marina shuffles plants around, finds things on the street, stacks them up outside her door. There is a giant, black acrylic M which she picked up when they dismantled the signboard of an old cinema a few blocks away; a string of burnt-out Christmas lights; a stool with one leg missing; a forty-centimeter-tall brontosaurus given to Marina by Olmo, the little boy from next door; a wooden mobile that hangs from the window railing; and an aloe vera plant sitting in fake bloom, some little red ribbons tied around its leaves. But tomorrow, who knows. Tomorrow the brontosaurus might be mounting the aloe vera, and the M positioned to guide the creeping ivy. Marina lets the dust build up for weeks and then, one day, in a burst of self-reinvention, she redecorates.

Directly facing Bitter House is Sour House.

On the right when you come out of Bitter is the bell that gives the mews its name, and which is surrounded by three other houses: Sweet, Salty and Umami.

The main entrance to the mews is to the left of Bitter. It's covered by a low, tiled roof that is all but useless against the rain, but which gives the place a certain rustic *je ne sais quoi* appreciated by all of its residents, especially in spring when the jacaranda tree on the street lays a carpet of flowers over the roof and sidewalk. The landlord meant to paint the central passageway – that is, all five houses' facades – the color of the jacaranda flower. Instead, in the shop they came up with an insipid pale purple, which he didn't have the heart to refuse. Marina detests the color. It reminds her of the bed sheets in the hospital where she was. She calls it asylilac.

In fact, Marina hasn't ever been in an asylum, it's just she sometimes goes through periods of not eating, and every now and then she has to go to a hospital to get intravenous sodium, potassium, chlorine, bicarbonate, dextrose, calcium, phosphorous and magnesium, that's all. Or that was all until the last time. Last time they made her stay a few extra days for a bit of brain-washing. And boy is her brain spotless now. Or at least that's how she pictures it: swollen and pale, like a peeled, hard-boiled egg.

With a view to getting rid of the asylilac, Marina founded a Neighborhood Association, with capital letters and everything. Well, everything apart from members. She does, on the other hand, like the color of the inside of her house. It's white. In fact, it was precisely for the whiteness of Bitter's walls that Marina wanted to rent Bitter. And for their smoothness. Because textured walls, especially the kind with big damp stains, vividly represented everything she wished to leave behind. It was the first time she'd left her parents' home, where she'd lived all nineteen years of her life, in a city just far enough away from Belldrop Mews for Bitter to hold some promise.

The day Marina first visited the house they had just painted it. It still smelled of thinner and the sun shone through the window, casting a bright rectangle on the back wall, which is where she saw her promised land, her this-must-be-the-place. The color, then – this sunlit white on the smooth wall, a hue that seemed to spell endless possibilities and promise – she named whomise.

The owner of the mews, Doctor Alfonso Semitiel, showed her around that first day. He had a very particular manner about him, which reminded Marina of the mother of an ex boyfriend, a woman who would reel off her child's virtues only to finish each round of compliments proclaiming, 'I made him.'

Alfonso crowed on about the mews, which apparently he built himself over the ruins of his grandparents' mansion.

He laid it on especially thick about the house names, which he had chosen in honor of the five tastes recognizable to the human tongue. Marina needed to make a good impression on Alfonso because, even though she had a copy of her parents' deed, she wasn't sure he would accept it as a guarantee, or if he'd insist on calling them to verify her identity. She didn't want her family to know where she was, not yet, so she mustered all her charm and said she found the house names to be very original, which was true, only she omitted to say that they were also ridiculous, not to mention counterproductive, because who'd pay to live in a place called Bitter?

Well, her. Bitter was the perfect house. Upstairs it had two rooms and a bathroom. Below, a good-sized living room, a kitchen, a small bathroom and a yard almost entirely taken up by an enormous water tank. Marina liked the impossibility of the yard. Any other outdoor space, anything more picturesque or less cluttered, would have reminded her of her parents' house. For someone who up to that point had only ever desired impractical things, Marina felt a fiercely pragmatic desire: to have that house for herself. She immediately devised a plan to sleep in one of the upstairs rooms and use the other as a studio. She wanted to paint every day, cook perfect rice and actually eat it, learn how to use an airbrush and a pyrography machine and a drill and a dildo. No more transfusions or guilt or damp stains, never again would she go back to the dilapidated fake Athens that was Xalapa, Veracruz, her city of birth. She had left. She was going to start over again. Bitter would be her blank canvas. But for this, she was going to have to impress the landlord. She improvised, telling him she'd been an art teacher (withholding, of course, the minor detail that they fired her for fainting in front of the children). She did mention she'd graduated from high school, just not that she'd done it through home schooling because she'd worked simultaneously at her father's restaurant. And she lied. She said she'd come to the capital to go to college. The real masterstroke was her use of the informal *tú* to address her new landlord. Wasn't that how people in Mexico City spoke to each other? She then asked him coquettishly if he was married. He blushed; she even more so. He told her he was a widower, an only child, and an anthropologist. They had a coffee at a nearby bar and she stole her first object for Bitter: an ashtray. She placed it in the middle of the empty living room, then spent hours splayed across the floor, repositioning herself in line with the advancing sun, smoking and staring at the dust, rapt, convinced her life was about to start.

It's the color scheme of that first afternoon – that white panorama of full potential, that threshold white – that Marina understands as whomise. And that's what she's trying to rec-reate now, a year and a bit later, with a series of expensive light bulbs. 'White Light', the packaging promised. She fits them one by one throughout the house, and unbeknown to her, choreographs the slow dance of light-over-puddle in the passageway.

*

Marina did actually start college after she rented Bitter. She chose the degree herself, but not the timetable. Something about the word 'design' inspired a vague but firm hope in her – perhaps there she'd learn that most basic of things, the thing she saw in other people: an instinct for planning, for self-preservation. But the only thing she knows for certain up until now is that, as a direct result of attending morning classes, she's never at home at the time of day when the sun paints the wall whomise. According to her theory, this is where it all went wrong, what set her off, what made her burn out again. A deficiency. Just as some people lack sunshine, she happened to lack this particular color. It got so bad that the usual serum shot wasn't enough, and her mother had to be called for. Señora Mendoza came flying to the rescue, then disappeared again. You can still make out her fleeting presence in the spotlessness of the grout between the tiles, somewhere it had never occurred to Marina to scrub. There are new habits since the mother's visit, too. Marina is medicated now. Marina is in therapy.

She left the standing lamp in the living room till last, and now it burns to the touch. She switches it off, slips her hand under her T-shirt and, using it like a glove, unscrews the bulb. So long, oppressive yellow light! (What's that color called? Yellowoeful? Yelldown? Yepressing?) She screws in the new bulb and points the lamp at the wall. Instead of the desired whomise, a hard, futuristic light appears, as pristine as the pills she takes. This one, she decides, is called whozac. If whozac were a person it would have perfect teeth, wear a hospital gown, and roam the world preaching against hope: 'There's nowhere to run! There's no way out! Filter your pain through our new Prozac-infused light!'

A design idea. The first she's had in months: anxiolytics should be packaged like breakfast cereal, with Sudokus on the box to pass the time during that first month you wait for them to kick in, until at last you forget you're waiting, and the only sign they're working is the muffled hum of anxiety, as if someone were pressing their foot on the mute pedal. Even so, Marina takes her pills. Almost every day.

She unplugs the lamp and tests it on the other side of the room, but it doesn't give the desired effect. Frustrated, she lashes out. Then, after a clunk and a flicker, the bulb casts a cone-shape of whozac over the rug. The light bulb just isn't the sun. She might never recapture the whomise, and God, how frustrating the whole thing is. How ironic that every morning the very essence of wellbeing pours into her living room while she's not at home; while she sits in a lecture hall doing her best not to think about anything at all.

'What a waste,' she says to herself, rolling the lamp across the rug with her foot. Marina despises waste. She sits upside down on the sofa and rests her feet against the wall where there's no sunlight because it's nearly ten.

'I haven't even eaten,' she thinks.

Her trousers slip down and she looks at her legs: much wider than her arms. Damn asymmetry. Why can't everything be the same size? She lies there for a while. She's so tired it's almost like being calm. She wonders if she should just quit school, and she thinks about Chihuahua, too, the man she sleeps with from time to time, but who she hasn't heard a peep from in weeks. The last time she saw him, he'd been getting dressed after sex while she lay stock-still staring at the ceiling, and just before walking out he said, 'This is too much for me.' As if their relationship were a carrier bag he was holding, with Marina inside it. As if the weight of that tiny waif were cutting into the poor guy's fingers.

*

Marina is never home for the hours of whomise on the weekend either because she works looking after Linda Walker's kids. They live on the other side of the passageway, which means the sun doesn't hit their house in the same way. They don't get any sun at all, in fact, except in their backyard. Their yard is three times the size of hers, and doesn't have a giant water tank in the middle, but it's so crammed full of stuff it puts you off going out there. And yet, go out Marina does, to smoke in the rare moments when the three siblings settle down together in front of the TV. She has to hide because the eldest – a chubby little twelve-year-old who talks as if she's swallowed a diction- ary – is on a permanent anti-smoking campaign.

'When I was your age I was already out paying my way,' Marina wants to say when she sees her poring over some 600-page tome.

There used to be four siblings in the Pérez-Walker clan, but the youngest died a couple of years ago. Despite having never met her, Marina suspects that once upon a time the house did get some sunlight, but that the little girl took it with her to the other side, or to the grave, or to the bottom of that gringo lake where they say she drowned. They found her little body floating, caught up in the weeds. Olmo, now the youngest, told Marina all about it while he was busy with his crayons, drawing something else; a cow, or maybe a plane.

Marina charges for her babysitting in English lessons. She studies with cool but genuine interest.

'It's a healthy drive,' she told her therapist when he sug- gested that Marina was taking on too many activities. 'They're just English lessons,' she reasoned, 'so I can understand the lyrics of the songs I sing along to.'

'And the work itself?'

'I like the work,' she'd told him. 'The kids are fun.'

But really it's the kids' mother Marina likes. Every Tuesday and Thursday, Linda comes to her house and they do two hours of English. Teaching materials exist in the form of CDs that Marina has in a standing bookcase. It's a small but lovingly amassed collection, which began on a cobbled street in Xalapa, in Tavo's Rock Shop (the sole line of communication with their era for many Xalapans in the nineties). Marina used the modest wage her father began to pay her at thirteen (after she plucked up the courage to suggest that her brother and she were poster children for child exploitation) to buy one CD, then another, and another. She liked the little shop because nobody she knew ever went there. They sold T-shirts with blood on them. American blood, silk-screen printed. Fake, of course, but sufficiently convincing to foster myths about the place: 'Tavo's Rock? They practice satanic rituals in there. They're child abusers. Everything they sell's come off the back of a truck.'

Blood which, now that Chihuahua tells her so many things about the north, and now that she's stopped thinking of her country as a simple yin and yang of Xalapa and Mexico City, doesn't seem right to Marina. These days, if she sees someone on the street wearing an offensive shirt it gets her back up. Marina knows violence begets violence, and she opposes it in principle, but the problem is that, beyond taking offense, it doesn't occur to her what to do about it. In spite of herself, she has always been more impressed by the military than militants. Marina sees a lot of het-up people at college, lots of banner waving, and she doesn't know what's more shameful: her absolute ignorance of the situation, or her absolute indifference. So she picks up her chin, pulls a face that says that she too suffers, makes as if she's in a hurry and walks on by. She has coined the color redsentful.

Linda Walker is wild about Marina's album collection. She has a deep fascination – as passionate as it is patronizing – for popular Mexican music, but she hasn't sat down to listen to American pop since she left the States twenty years ago.

'But this isn't pop,' Marina insists. 'This is alternative rock.'

The truth is Marina doesn't have a clue about music genres. Her criterion is strictly aesthetical: she picks CDs for their covers. She didn't take any of hers when she left for Mexico City, but her mother brought them when she came to get her out of hospital. Or, in the words of Señora Mendoza, 'out of that little pickle'.

English has the same effect on Marina as meditation. Not that she meditates, but she's been hypnotized before, and there's this thing that happens to her when she's been painting for hours and then stops: you only realize you've been somewhere else once you're back. And English takes the edge off things, makes them feel less serious, a bit like scribbling mustaches on photos. For example, once translated, the names of her favorite groups changed from abstract poetry to random nouns: the cranberries, smashing pumpkins, blind melon, red hot chili peppers, fool's garden. Translation simplifies, it schematizes: something that seemed potentially profound falls from grace and lands on its head, turning out to be nothing but a doodle. For Marina, this law of gravity dictating bilingualism confirms what she's always suspected: that if gringos were drawings, they'd be drawn with markers.

And confirming a suspicion provides you with a foothold, some solid ground to stand on, especially when that suspicion divides the world into segments, thereby neatly marking out the part that you yourself occupy. In other words, it takes the lid off and lowers expectations. It's not that Marina believes the prejudices she confirms, but confirming them calms her down anyway.

If she doesn't entirely buy her own marker-pen theory, it's because of Linda. Linda is a gringa drawn in pastels or coloring pencils: her lines are permeable, fluid. The more Marina knows her, the less defined she becomes. What's more, Marina has started to make out the traces of past lines, from before Mexico, before Víctor, before the death of her daughter. Pentimento, they call it in drawing: those strokes the artist tried to erase but which are still faintly visible. Linda transforms according to her hairstyle and the time of day. When she's in a playful, word-game kind of mood, she's bright green; if she lets her hair down, she's peach. Some nights Marina wonders: Is this love?

It's not attraction exactly, but you might call it an infatuation. Marina has placed her neighbor on a pedestal, and she can't come up with another noun for the feeling. She spends all day comparing herself with Linda. She even makes herself eat porridge because Linda eats porridge. But it's not for her place in the National Symphony Orchestra that Marina admires her, or for her rock-steady relationship with Víctor (no carrier bags there: it's heavy-duty baggage all the way; matching, part of the same set). It's not for the fact that she's a mother of four children, or that she's lost one. And nor does Marina's admiration spring from Linda's mystifying way of being both ugly and beautiful at once, or from how, every now and again, she seems drunk in the middle of the day. Marina doesn't admire her for her long, long hair which she insists on piling up on the crown of her head like a nest; nor for the headscarf which she wraps around her bun and forehead as if dressing an invisible war wound. Or perhaps it is. Perhaps it's the complex combination of all these things that Marina worships. But most of all, she respects Linda for having renounced the product mentality. For having said, 'Enough is enough.' Or at least that's how Linda explained it:

'One day I just said enough is enough to the product mentality, you know? It's not that I'm giving up playing, I just don't need to package it. I devote myself to the music now, not the orchestra. I'm all about the process now.'

'And the orchestra lets you?' Marina had asked, for the sake of saying something.

'They gave me unpaid leave,' Linda said. 'And you know what? For not one of my pregnancies did I get that. Musicians don't believe in babies, but in mourning, sure. I blame Wagner.'

2002

A maranth, the plant to which I've dedicated the best part of my forty years as a researcher, has a ludicrous name. One that, now I'm a widower, makes me seethe.

Amaranthus, the generic name, comes from the Greek *amaranthos*, which means 'flower that never fades'.

*

I've been a widower since last Mexican Day of the Dead: November 2 2001. That morning my wife lay admiring the customary altar I'd set up in the room. It was a bit makeshift: three vases of dandelions and Mexican marigolds, and not much else, because neither of us was in the mood for the traditional sugar skulls. Noelia adjusted her turban (she hated me seeing her bald) and pointed to the altar.

'Nah, nah, nah-nah-nah,' she sang.

'Nah, nah, nah-nah-nah, what?' I asked.

'I beat them.'

'Beat who?'

'The dead,' she said. 'They came and they went, and they didn't take me.'

But that afternoon, when I took her up her Nescafé with milk, Noelia had gone with them. Sometimes I think that what hurts most is that she went without me there. With me downstairs, standing like a muppet by the stove, waiting for the water to boil. The damn, chalky, chlorinated Mexico City water, at its damn 2,260 meters above sea level, taking its own sweet time to make the kettle whistle.

*

Noelia's surname was Vargas Vargas. Her parents were both from Michoacán, but one was from the city of Morelia and the other Uruapan, and at any given opportunity they'd publicly avow that they were not cousins. They had five children, and ate lunch together every day. He was a cardiologist and had a clinic just around the corner. She was a homemaker and her sole peccadillo was playing bridge three times a week, where she'd fritter away a healthy slice of the grocery budget. But they never wanted for anything. Apart from grandchildren. On our part at least, we left them wanting.

By way of explanation, or consolation perhaps, my mother-in-law used to remind me in apologetic tones that, 'Ever since she was a little girl, Noelia wanted to be a daughter and nothing else.' According to her version of events, while Noelia's little friends played at being Mommy with their dolls, she preferred to be her friends' daughter, or the doll's friend, or even the doll's daughter; a move that was generally deemed unacceptable by her playmates, who would ask, with that particular harsh cruelty of little girls, 'When have you ever seen a Mommy that pretty?'

Bizarrely, my wife, who blamed so many of her issues on being a childless child, would never get into this topic with me. She refused to discuss the fact that it was her mother who first used the term 'only a daughter' in reference to her. And it occurs to me now, darling Noelia, that your obsession may well spring from there; that it wasn't something you chose exactly, but rather that your own mother drummed into you.

'Don't be an Inuit, Alfonso,' says my wife, who, every time she feels the need to say 'idiot', substitutes the word with another random noun beginning with i.

Substituted it, she substituted it. I have to relearn how to conjugate now that she's not around. But the thing is, when I wrote it down just now, 'Don't be an Inuit, Alfonso', it was as if it wasn't me who'd written it. It was as if she were saying it herself.

Perhaps that's what the new black machine is for. Yes, that's why they brought it to me: so Noelia will talk to me again.

*

I have a colleague at the institute who, aged fifty-two, married a woman of twenty-seven. But any sense of shame only hit them when she turned thirty and he fifty-five, because all of a sudden it no longer required any mathematical effort to work out the age gap: the quarter of a century between them was laid bare for all to see. Something more or less like this happened to us in the mews. Numbers confounded us when, in the same year my wife died, aged fifty-five, so did the five-year-old daughter of my tenants. Noelia's death seemed almost reasonable compared to Luz's, which was so incomprehensible, so unfair. But death is never fair, nor is fifty-five old.

I'll also make use of my new machine to moan, if I so choose, about having been left a widower before my time, and about the fact that nobody paid me the slightest attention. The person who showed the most concern was our friend Páez. But Páez was more caught up in his own sorrow than mine. He would call me up late at night, drunk, consumed by the discovery that not even his generation was immortal.

'I can't sleep thinking about you alone in that house, my friend. Promise me you won't stop showering,' he would say.

And then the inconsiderate ass went and died too. Noelia always used to say that bad things happen in threes.

They couldn't have cared less at work, either.

'Take a year's sabbatical,' they told me. 'Languish in life. Rot away in your damned urban *milpa*, which we never had any faith in anyway. Go and wilt among your amaranths.'

And I, ever compliant, said, 'Where do I sign?'

A first-class howler, because now I'm losing my mind all day in the house. I don't even have Internet. I'm sure the black machine should hook up to Wi-Fi but so far I haven't made any attempt to understand how that works. I prefer the television. At least I know how to turn it on. These last weeks I've got into the mid-morning programming. It is tremendous.

I hadn't heard anything from the institute since the start of my year's sabbatical. Then, two weeks ago, they came and left a machine. I'm told it's my 2001 research bonus, even though that god-awful year finished six months ago and was the least productive of my academic life. Unless 'Living With Your Wife's Pancreatic Cancer' and then 'First Baby-Steps as a Widower' can be considered research topics. I imagine they were sent an extra machine by mistake and that they can't send it back because then, of course, they would be charged. All the bureaucratic details of the institute are counterintuitive, but the people who run it act as if it were perfectly coherent. For example, they tell me that I have to use the machine for my research, presumably to get to grips with online resources and move into the twenty-first century, but then they send a delivery boy to pass on the message. That's right, along with the laptop, the delivery boy brought a hard-copy agreement. Because nothing can happen in the institute unless it's written in an agreement and printed on an official letterhead with the Director's signature at the bottom.

The kid pulled out a cardboard box from his Tsuru, not so different from a pizza box, and handed it to me.

'It's a laptop, sir. In the office they told me to say you gotta use it for your research.'

'And my sabbatical?' I said.

'Hey, listen, man, they ain't told me nothing more than to make the drop and go.'

'So "make the drop" and go,' I told him.

He put it down and I left it in there on the doorstep in its box. That was two weeks ago.

Then finally today I rented out Bitter House. It's gone to a skinny young thing who says she's a painter. She brought me my check and, by way of guarantee, the deed to an Italian restaurant in Xalapa. I know it's Italian because it's called Pisa. And this is a play on words, according to the girl, who told me that beyond referring to the famous tower, it's also how Xalapans pronounce the word *pizza*.

'Although, strictly speaking they say *pitsa*,' she explained, 'but if my parents had called it that, it would have been too obvious we were jerking around.'

'Ah,' I replied.

I only hope she doesn't take drugs. Or that she takes them quietly and pays me on time. It's not much to ask, considering the price I gave her. She was happy with everything save the color of the fronts of the houses.

'I'm thinking of painting them,' I lied.

The funny thing is that after signing – which we did in the Mustard Mug, because it's next door to the stationary shop and we had to photocopy her documents – I left feeling good. Productive, let's say. Or nearly. On my way back I bought a six-pack and some chips, and took The Girls out onto the backyard's terrace. Having positioned them so they could preside over the ceremony, I opened the box – the one now propping up my feet, and a very comfy innovation, I might add – and went about setting up the machine. I have to say I felt a bit excited as I opened it. Only a little bit, but even so, the most excited I've been so far in 2002.

The machine is black and lighter than any of my computers to date. I'm writing on it now. I was particularly proud of how swiftly I set it up. Set it up is a manner of speaking. The truth is I plugged it in and that was that. The only work involved was removing the plastic and polystyrene. For a name, I chose Nina Simone. My other computer, the old elephant in my office where I wrote every one of my articles from the last decade, was called Dumbo. In Dumbo's Windows my user icon was a photo of me, but someone from tech support at the institute uploaded it for me. My expertise doesn't stretch that far. In Nina Simone's Windows my user icon is the factory setting: an inflatable duck. Microsoft Word just tried to change inflatable to infallible. Word's an Inuit.

Dammit! Noelia used to come up with a different word beginning with i every time. I'm just not made of the same stuff.

I'm an invalid, an invader, an island.

*

When she was little, Noelia didn't want to be a doctor like her dad, but rather an actress like a great aunt of hers who had made her name in silent movies. After high school Noelia signed up to an intensive theater course, but on the second week, when the time came for her to improvise in front of the group, she turned bright red, couldn't utter a word and suffered a paroxysmal tachycardia. A bloody awful thing: it's when your heart beats more than 160 times a minute. It's certainly happened to me, but never, in fact, to Noe. Noe was just self-diagnosing: she had a flair for it even then.

After her disastrous course she enrolled at the National Autonomous University of Mexico, where, after a number of grueling years – even today, having spent my whole life around doctors, I still don't know how they do it – she qualified as a cardiologist. Noelia would say, 'That's consultant cardiac electrophysiologist to you.'

Noelia told me all this the first time we had dinner together. It seemed strange to me that public speaking could be more frightening to her than being confronted with someone's insides.

'Why medicine?' I asked. 'Why not something easier?'

It was 1972 and we were in a restaurant in the Zona Rosa, when the Zona Rosa was still a decent sort of neighborhood, not like now. Even though, truth be told, I don't know what it's like now because it's been years since I ventured out there.

'I had this absurd idea that in medicine you get to really know people, on a one-to-one level,' said my wife, who that night was no more than a girl I'd just met.

She downed her tequila.

'I suppose I've always been a bit naive.'

And that was when the penny dropped that she was a flirt, something you wouldn't have guessed at first. And naive? You bet. But only about certain things, and with the kind of ingenuousness which didn't remotely diminish her razor-sharp mind. She was naive when it suited her. Noelia was very practical but a little scatterbrained. She was openhearted, cunning and gorgeous-looking. She was also, on that first night and for the following three weeks, a vegetarian.

She liked one-to-ones. She liked going out for coffee with people. She liked to sneak out for a cigarette with the nurses and get the latest gossip on, as she put it, 'everyone and their mother'. She stopped being vegetarian because she adored meat. Even raw meat. Steak tartare. She always ordered Kibbeh on her birthday. I haven't gone back to the city center because it stirs up too many memories of our birthday trips to El Edén. Nobody warns you about this, but the dead, or at least some of them, take customs, decades, whole neighborhoods with them. Things you thought you shared but which turned out to be theirs. When death does you part, it's also the end of what's mine is yours.

Noelia didn't mention on that first evening that her father had been the top dog at the Heart and Vascular Hospital in Mexico City before opening his own clinic in Michoacán. Nor that it was there, at the tender age of twelve, that she learned to read holters, which means detect arrhythmias. Nor did she mention over dinner that she was one of just five (five!) specialists in her area in the entire country. She told me the following morning. We were naked on the sofa in her living room, and before I even knew it I'd knocked back my coffee, scrambled into my clothes and hotfooted it out of her apartment. I didn't even ask for her number. In other words, as she accurately diagnosed it the next time we saw each other almost a year later, I 'chickened out, like a chicken'.

To say I chickened out is an understatement, of course. In reality, and using another of Noelia's expressions, I shit my pants. I was petrified, and only came to understand the root of my panic later, when I began to analyze who I'd spent the sub-sequent twelve months bedding: all of them well-read, highly educated young women. Basically, my students. I was even going to marry one of them: Memphis, as Noelia nicknamed her years later when they finally met (I think because of the boots she was wearing, or maybe it was the haircut, what do I know?). Mercifully, just before the wedding I had a dream. I was a bit macho, yes, a chicken, certainly, but before either of those things I was superstitious as hell: having received the message, I knew I had to heed my subconscious, so I turned up unannounced at Noelia's apartment. For a minute she didn't recognize me. Then she played hard-to-get for a while, like two weeks. But as time went on we became so inseparable, so glued at the hip, that now I can't understand. On my job at the National Institute for History and Anthropology, on my grant from the National Organization of Researchers, on all those qualifications which supposedly mean that I know how to deal with complex questions, I swear I don't get it. I don't understand how I'm still breathing if one of my lungs has been ripped out.

The dream I had. Noelia was standing in a doorway with lots of light behind her. That was it. It was a still dream, but crystal frickin' clear in its message. Threatening even. When I woke up, still next to Memphis, I knew I had two options: I could take the easy route, or the happy one. An epiphany, you might call it. Incidentally, the only one I ever had in my life.

*

Noelia had a soft spot for sayings and idioms. If ever there was something I didn't get – which was often – she would sigh and say, 'Shall I spell it out for you?' I remember one time Noe sent me flowers to the institute for a prize I'd won, and on the little card she'd written, 'You're the bee's knees'.

But sometimes the sayings and idioms were home-grown, without her having consulted anyone. For example, she tended to come out with, 'A scalpel in hand is worth two in the belly.' And I always thought this was a medical saying, but Páez assured me that he'd only ever heard it come from Noe's mouth and that no one in the hospital really knew what it meant; some thought it was something like 'better to be the doctor than the patient', while others understood it as 'better to take your time while operating than to botch it in a hurry', et cetera, et cetera.

On the other hand, Noelia couldn't abide riddles. Or board games. And general-knowledge quizzes were her absolute bugbear. They put her in a flap and she'd forget the answers then get all pissy. We once lost Trivial Pursuit because she couldn't name the capital of Canada. She also loathed sports and any form of exercise. She had a fervent dislike of dust. And insects. For her, the very definition of evil was a cockroach. And she didn't clean, but rather paid someone to clean for her. Doña Sara stopped working for me a few months ago with the excuse that she'd always planned to move back to her home village, but really I think seeing me in such a state depressed her. I paid her her severance check; she set up a taco stand. She did the right thing. Hers really were the best tacos in the world. And it's a good thing too, I think, for me to deal with my own waste.

For much of my life I really did believe I was the bee's knees, because unlike my colleagues I liked to get my hands dirty actually planting the species we lectured on. I always kept a *milpa* in the backyard because, in my opinion, if you're going to say that an entire civilization ate such-and-such thing then you have to know what that thing tastes like, how it grows, how much water it needs. If you're going to go around proclaiming the symbiosis of the three sisters, you have to grab a hold of your shovel and take each one in turn: first the corn, then the beans, and after that the squash. But now I see my whole agricultural phase differently: I had time on my hands. Time not taken up by youngsters. Time not taken up folding clothes. It's so obvious but only now do I fully understand that it's easier to get your hands dirty when you've got someone to clean everything else for you. But there you go, I was always the most bourgeois of anthropologists.

These days, when I hit the hay, quite often the only productive thing I've done all day is wash the dishes I used, or clean up the studio, or take out the trash. I suck at it, but I give it my all. Once The Girls are in the stroller, I push them to whichever part of the house is messiest. I like to have witnesses.

'Look at me,' I tell them. 'Sixty-four years old and my first time mopping the floor.'

Noelia did like children, but from a safe distance. She'd never wanted her own, and then when she did finally want them it was too late. She wasn't into drama. Or rather she was, but other people's. She liked fried food but hardly ever let herself indulge. She liked the smell of spices – cumin, marjoram, lemongrass –, pressed clothes, and fresh flowers in the house. She paid one person to come and iron and another to bring the fresh flowers. She liked to pay well and tip on top. She liked earthenware, as long as it wasn't fussy. She refused to keep the best china for special occasions.

'Every chance I get to sit down to eat is a special occasion,' she used to say. 'At least till my beeper goes.'

The arrival of the beeper was such a momentous event in our lives that not even its evolution into snazzier, more compact devices stopped us calling everything that interrupted our meals or siesta the beeper. Above all the siesta, because traditionally it was the time we would make love. I preferred the morning (when she was in a hurry), and she preferred nighttime (when I was tired), so the siesta was the middle point that always worked for us.

Noelia smoked Raleighs until her younger brother had his first cardiac arrest and the family learned that even cardiologists can be touched by heart problems. I only ever smoked the odd cigar, but her smoking didn't bother me, and when she gave up I felt like we'd both lost something. I never told her that, of course. Each year, or at least for the first decade of her abstention, we'd put on a party in celebration of another 365 days smoke-free. That we lost something is perhaps not the right way to put it. We left something behind, I mean. We turned a page, no looking back, as the boho poets from the Mustard Mug would say.

*

The Mustard Mug is the bar around the corner which I dip into when my body so demands. Nobody knew about these trips until one of my tenants, the gringa who lost her daughter, also started going. I used to call her gringa to her face but with hindsight it sounds a mite assy. The thing is, I never felt too kindly toward that family. They're a noisy bunch and form a majority in the mews because they rent two houses: Sweet and Salty. They live in one of them and use the other as a studio, teaching piano and drums and God knows how many other instruments. Everyone in the family knows how to play at least two. The eldest daughter is the only one I get along with, perhaps because she's notoriously tone deaf, or perhaps simply because she was born right in the middle of the brief period when Noelia regretted not having children and we found ourselves cooing like idiots over every baby that came our way. But it's also true that I started to take a shine to Agatha Christie, or Ana, as she's really called, as she got older, because she was a misfit, and because she liked me. While helping me out in the *milpa* in the evenings, she would explain – as if they were puzzles – the various dilemmas faced by Poirot and Miss Marple in the pages she devoured. I never solved a single one, by the way, and not for lack of trying. Sometimes I didn't want to open the door to her, because I preferred to be alone, but the more time I spent with her at my side, the more I grew to like myself. It doesn't take a rocket scientist to work out that my empathy toward Agatha Christie is a form of self-affection, because she is who I once was: a young kid left to her own devices in this exact same nook of a huge city. Seeing her reading huddled in corners made me mad at the parents, who went on making more babies instead of paying her the attention she deserved.

Noelia, on the other hand, loved the whole family. She nicknamed the mother Lindis and forgave all the late rent on the basis that Lindis and her husband were artists and had many mouths to feed. When the mouths were very small, we used to do things together as a group: long discussions over drinks in the evening, barbeques. Linda used to toast my amaranth and sell it all over the block, and one time they organized a string-quartet concert on my *milpa*, a real sight to behold. But later on, the tenants started keeping themselves to themselves. Or maybe Noelia and I grew too old and frumpy for their liking so they stopped inviting us. It was around that time that I took to calling her the gringa. Only last year did she go back to being just Linda, one day when she turned up at Umami with a selection of scarves.

'I've come to teach your wife how to make a turban,' she said.

The hair loss from the chemo had floored Noelia. What did I tell you before, Nina? Noe was a real coquette, and she couldn't bear anyone seeing her bald head, so she insisted on covering it with beanie hats, caps and god-awful wigs that made her scalp itch like crazy. And her silly self-torture drove me crazy in turn. Agatha Christie must have related some of this private drama to her mom, and at first I didn't know how to react to Linda's unsolicited call. I worried that Noelia would take offense. But, as I've proved on countless other occasions in my life, I don't possess a scrap of the female intuition that men these days are supposed to have, and Linda's crash course turned out to be a hit. The rags, as Linda called them, were a real relief to Noe, and for a time, if the two turbaned women happened to cross paths in the passageway, the mews looked like some kind of spiritual retreat.

Then, one day Linda turned up at the Mustard Mug and sat down at my table. From that day on we've held a tacit pact not to mention our meetings to anyone. She too had been signed off work. Apparently that's the way that our cultural institutions deal with loss; perhaps it's their way of debunking the stereotype that in Mexico we know how to live hand in hand with death.

Linda orders vodka in the Mug, out of discretion. I drink tequila, since I no longer have anybody to smell it on me. Every now and then the barman pulls out all the stops and serves me my tequila shot with a chaser of delicious spicy *sangrita*, which Linda then eats with her finger, dunking then sucking it. I've tried hard to find something erotic in this gesture, but my best efforts are hampered by an overriding feeling of tenderness toward her. She's also a tall lady, and I like my women compact: Noelia was as short as a toadstool.

We never have more than a couple of drinks each. Me because I've always been a lousy drinker, and her because she has to go afterward to pick up the kids from school. Linda stays till one thirty at the latest, and the vodka always sets her off. She has deep-set green eyes, and when she cries they go puffy and pink. Some days we talk, and others we don't even get beyond hello. Every now and then I well up too, in which case Linda will ask for some napkins and we'll sit there blowing our noses. If we do talk it's about old times: her gringo childhood, my Mexico City youth, our lives before our lives with our dead. Or we talk about operas we remember. Or food. I give her recipes for exotic sauces. She explains how to make fermented pickles.

*

Now that I think about it, marriage isn't all that different from mid-morning TV. In the end, to be married is to see the same old movies – some more treasured than others – over and over again. The only things that ever change are the bits in between, the things tied to the present: news bulletins, commercials. And by this I don't mean that it's boring. On the contrary, it's awful what I've lost: the cement that held the hours together, the comfort of Noelia's familiar presence which filled everything, every room, whether she was at home or not, because I knew that unless she had a heart attack on her hands she'd be home to eat and have a siesta, then back again for dinner and to watch TV, finally falling asleep with her cold feet against my leg. The rest – all the world events, falling walls and stocks, personal and national disasters – was nothing. What you miss are the habits, the little actions you took for granted, only to realize that they were in fact the stuff of life. Except, in a way, they also turned out not to be, because the world goes on spinning without them. Much like amaranth when they banned it. What must the Aztecs have thought when the Spaniards burnt their sacred crop? 'Sons of bitches,' they must have thought. And also, 'Impossible! Impossible to live without *huautli*.' But they were wrong and so was I: Noelia died and life goes on. A miserable life if you like, but I still eat, and I still shit.

*

'Those bugs,' my wife would say.

I never got my head around how anyone could see something ugly in a butterfly, especially someone from Michoacán, the land of monarchs.

'They flap around you!' she argued.

Then she'd come out with far-fetched theories, tall tales from her childhood.

'If moths hover close to your eyes their powder can blind you.'

'What kind of scientist are you?'

'A paranoid one. That's very important, listen: you must always make sure your doctor's a believer, or at least that he somehow fears the final judgment, because the rest of them are nothing but butchers.'

*

Here the top-ten nuptial movies reshown in this household over the last thirty years:

> *Tough Day at the Clinic – Pour Me a Tequila*
> *A PhD Student Calls (I'm Not In)*
> *Procreation (The Prequel)*
> *Amaranth and* Milpas
> *The Tenants*
> *Belldrop Mews*
> *For Whom the Beeper Tolls*
> *Only a Daughter*
> *Umami*
> *The Girls*

*

Noelia constructed an entire oral mysticology around the term 'only a daughter', which I'll do my best to reproduce here, both from what I remember and with the help of Nina Simone. I'm a son too, only a son, and now an old son, but I never identified with all the things Noelia insisted were symptoms of our chosen condition as nobody's parents.

Noelia named this state of being only a daughter 'offspring-hood'. I told her that the concept was flawed because it was the same as the state of being 'human' or even of 'being': we're all someone's offspring.

'I don't care,' she said.

Then I suggested that, seeing as we have maternity, paternity and fraternity, it might make more sense to call it 'offspringity'. But she wasn't having any of it.

'Mysticology' isn't a word either, of course, but after three decades, one person's bad habits stick on the other, so now it's my turn to make up words at whim. When all's said and done, no one's going to pass judgment on Nina Simone. I won't let an editor near her, nor would I dream of sending her into the rat hole that is the peer-review system.

I was saying: while I myself didn't identify with the characteristic features of 'offspringhood', Noelia diagnosed me with all of them. I strongly denied the accusations held against me, at least in my inner courthouse. Because the same defects she branded me with (and which I acknowledged, sometimes), I also noticed in my friends with children. Especially as we grew older. We could all be impatient, irritable, intolerant, inflexible, spoiled, ailing, and pig-headed. Very pig-headed in fact: Páez had three kids and became more and more pig-headed with every one. Noelia said that it was because I didn't have kids that I was the way I was sometimes:

'If you'd had kids, your concentration and memory would be better, and you'd be more tolerant and disciplined,' she'd say to me.

'What's any of that got to do with children, woman?'

'If you have children you have to go to school every day at the same time to pick them up, and if you forget it hurts *real* bad.'

'Well, it does hurt me when I forget things.'

'Nuh-uh, Alfonso. It can't hurt *real* bad unless there's someone to remind you that you forgot.'

*

It was Noelia Vargas Vargas's job to let me know when someone was teasing me, because I didn't ever catch on. We had a code for it. She would tilt her head forwards, and I'd proceed to defend myself. Once or twice I tried to work out exactly where the gibe had come from, but it never worked so I learned that it was better to wait for her signal, then object.

'Guys, quit messing with me, will you?' I'd say to everyone. Often the culprit was Noelia herself, and in such cases, once we'd left wherever it was we were, she would amuse herself spelling it out for me. She always thought me naive. She used to say – in a friendly way, as if it were just another of the quirky upshots of having married an anthropologist (if we were among doctors), or of having married a Mexico City *chilango* (if we were among her folk from Michoacán) – that I had three basic failings: I never learned how to mess with people, drive, or swim. If you ask me, the last one isn't quite true because I can doggy-paddle just fine, thank you very much.

The point is that Noelia certainly had it in her to be more bitch than beauty. Especially at the beginning, when she was often defensive (according to her because she worked solely among men, but who knows). The first time we fought badly she told me something I never forgave her for, despite all her efforts to make it up to me. Her words were succinct, and arguably valid: 'You fuck like a rich kid.'

*

Now I feel like the inflatable duck. So let him be my alter ego. Why not? I'm going to sign everything I write here under Widow Ducky, Lord Amaranth. Let's see if I remember how to save things. At what point, I wonder, are they going to change the symbol for saving files from a floppy disk?

By the way, Ms. Simone, I should probably clarify that I'm not on a real sabbatical. On paper it might be a sabbatical, but let there be no mistake: in mind and in spirit I've retired. If I gave up work officially, on my measly pension I'd starve to death. Starve! Me! The world expert on sacred amaranth. The man who introduced the concept of umami into the national gastronomic dialog! Starve! And all because the old fool hasn't tended his *milpa* since 2001: corn is hardy stuff, but it's not invincible. Even corncobs need their little drops of water. Even a widowed duck needs love. Come on.

What else?

Laptop. Triceratops. Doo-wop. What's the research topic for the new machine going to be?

It's going to be Noelia.

2001

I 'm crawling around under the trees singing 'camu-flash flash flash'. I want to find mushrooms. I do *not* want to find any slugs. I just learned the word 'camuflash'. It means no one can see me. I'm like the mushrooms and the slugs, hidden under the leaves. The leaves fall off the trees. They're brown like nuts. The green balls with little spikes that Grandma Emma says have nuts inside fall off too. They only fall off once, then they stay there on the ground until they go brown and rotten and camuflashed with the mud. A family of trees is called a grove. This grove is Grandma's neighbor. Kind of. In Mexico our neighbors all live in the mews, but here neighbor is anyone who lives more or less near. Near you or near the lake. You have to go everywhere in the car here, and everything is camuflashed. For example, Granddad is camuflashed in the lake. Well, his ashes are. And Grandma chats to them when she goes walking along the shore, and she flicks her cigarette ash in the water, to keep him company. I don't remember Granddad but my sister does. She says he had a really red nose and said our names like this: Ann, Tee-yo, Olmou, Loose.

Before he was ashes, our Granddad was a pilot and that's why we get free tickets and that's why we fly a lot like birds, but without the feathers or the fun. Well, it's a little fun because you can watch movies and they bring you these cheese triangles on your food tray. Mama says that when her dad the pilot died, Grandma cut up all his sweaters and sewed them back together again until she'd made sweaters for all of us. Olmo calls them our woolly dead pilot sweaters.

Mama starts whistling and squeaking her boots together to make music. The song makes Grandma laugh. Mama has a basket hooked on one elbow and Grandma hooked on the other. And she has a white rag wrapped around her head. She calls them rags, those things she puts on her head. Mama's basket is full but that's because she collects everything she finds, which is cheating. Grandma doesn't approve of Mama's picking technique. Those are the words she said and that's why she won't let go of her arm, no matter how pretty her squeaky song is. Every time Mama collects a mushroom, Grandma says:

'That one's poisonous,' or, 'That one's OK, but it tastes awful,' or, 'Don't even touch that one, please.'

She doesn't say anything to me because I'm not cheating. When we got to her house this time, Grandma called me Peanut.

'Last summer you were just a peanut,' she said.

I liked that. But then Ana said, 'She means you were still a baby.'

I didn't like that.

'I'm almost six,' I told Emma.

'Five is a lucky number,' she said.

Today, the boys went camping and us girls stayed behind to pick mushrooms. Emma gave us baskets and plastic bags and told us which mushrooms we were looking out for: black trumpets. In Spanish they're called *las trompetas de la muerte*, death trumpets, even though black and dead isn't the same thing. You just can't trust English: it translates stuff all wrong. And they're not even really black; more like very dark brown. I know because Emma gave me a trumpet all of my own in a sandwich bag. I've been dragging it along behind me and the bag is so covered in mud already that you can't see anything inside. My death trumpet is camuflashed. It's happy, too, I can tell. Emma said that it's my guide specimen. A specimen is something that's like a mention of its species.

The boys are my dad, Pina's dad Beto, and my two brothers. They took the canoe and they're going to sleep on an island in the middle of the lake. I wanted to go with them, but then I saw Theo putting a bunch of straws in his backpack and I thought best to go with the girls. Yesterday, Pina made us breathe through straws with our heads camuflashed under the water in the lake and it felt horrible. Only Theo lasted a long time, and now he thinks he's king of the straws and he wants to play at straws all day long.

The grown-up girls are my mom and Emma. The little girls are me, my sister Ana, and her friend Pina who has a woolly dead pilot sweater that doesn't belong to her tied around her waist. She doesn't have her own one because she's not part of the family. We call her Pi, and when she annoys us we call her Pee-Pee and Ana gets real mad. Pi is sad because her mom left her a letter. If my mom left me a letter I'd be happy, but when I said as much to Ana she said, 'That's because you're dumb.'

Ana is ten and she thinks she's the queen of the forest.

When my mom lent Pina the sweater I instantly wanted mine. Mama said that I could only put it on if I took everything else off. That's why under my sweater I'm only wearing my swimsuit, and that's why the mud feels scratchy against my knees as I crawl along. And that's why I try to stick to the mushy parts, where I can slide along and nothing hurts.

I find a river of mud and follow it, even though it leads me off the track, even though there isn't really a track because the trees in the grove are planted in rows, and if you look at them from the right spot they hide behind each other, and between the rows everything that's not a chestnut tree is empty space, and everything that's empty space is track.

My woolly dead pilot sweater is yellow and tickly, but the sleeves are too long for me and I have to fold them up to my shoulders like an accordion. This morning Theo said that there's such a thing as a giant slug, and they're yellow and black and called banana slugs. He said I look like one in my sweater. I liked that. But Olmo said if anything I look like a rotten banana. I told him he has the face of a porcupine and Theo said, 'Luz *está* right.'

They all start talking weird when we come to the lake. And that's why I'm not going to speak English. I'm never ever going to speak English. English makes you weird.

I sit down at the end of the sort of river and rub mud in my face, because everybody knows mud-masks make you pretty. Mud-masks and also drinking tomato juice, but tomato juice is trick juice because it isn't sweet at all. Then, just next to my foot, I spot something, and that something is a black trumpet. I don't move. Apart from my eyes. I spot another one, three, four, seven, all together. I take out my guide specimen to check and yep, they're like twins. According to Grandma, when you find one you've found a ton. I turn around, get on all fours again and start singing to them even faster so that more appear.

'Flashy flashy flashy flash.'

And it works.

Where before there were none, suddenly I can see millions of them. It's like the Magic Eye pictures in Olmo's book where if you just stare at the page you don't see anything, but if you make yourself go cross-eyed you see a dinosaur.

'Trumpets! Truuumpettts!'

I shout until my mom appears, springing out from between the trees.

'Where?' she says.

'Kneel down,' I say. But she only crouches down. I point and it doesn't take long before she spots them too. They're all over the place, the same color as the dirt. Black trumpets are the real queens of camuflash.

Pina and Ana turn up to pick my trumpets, and I want them to go away but I don't say anything because they are saying how good I am at this and how excellent my mask looks on me. Emma picks a few and smells them. She says we're going to do spaghetti with black trumpets, garlic and white wine and, 'didn't I tell you five was a lucky number?'

'I'm a lucky peanut,' I say.

'You're my little truffle hog, that's what you are,' says Mama, and she rolls my sleeves back up.

I don't know what a truffle hog is, but I guess it's a pig made out of fancy chocolate. I get up and my legs are totally brown, just like my hands and my face, and I guess that's why she said it. I'm a chocolate-covered peanut.

'Wanna go shower?' Grandma asks.

'Not now,' I tell her.

'Okey dokey,' she says.

Ana and Pi take the trumpets to the house because in the end we've collected a ginormous paper bag of them. The rest of us go on walking because now Grandma wants us to find another mushroom, a chanterelle, which is yellow, but it's not like any of the yellows that Mama has in her basket, or like my sweater, or even like the yellow of the banana slugs which she says only exist on the other coast.

'Of the lake?' I ask.

'Of the country,' Grandma says.

I want to find the chanterelle. I'm going to find it. We walk. I've got so much mud on my knees it's like there are two cow patties sitting on them. I like them. I like walking with the adults because they talk without whispering secrets to each other and don't make you do anything with straws. One time, Pina and Ana tried to put a straw up my front bottom because they said that all of us women have a little hole there to make children. But they couldn't find it, so they told me I don't have one and that I'm never going to have children, which is fine by me because children can be so dumb and nasty with their little sisters, even when the little sisters are really nice and pretty.

My mom picks a mushroom for her already very full basket.

'That's a magic mushroom,' Emma tells her.

'Really?' I ask.

'She just means it makes you sleepy,' says Mama.

'And giggly,' Grandma says.

'And it makes you see things,' says Mama.

I say it doesn't sound so bad, but it doesn't sound that magic either.

'Which one is it?' I ask, and they point to one in Emma's hand, but they won't let me touch it. Emma collects chestnuts and I see her putting them in her sweater pockets which are now all big and bulgy like the stockings she hangs by the chimney at Christmas when we come to see her, and which she fills with trick presents for us, like fruit and pencil sharpeners.

'Are you going to eat them?' I ask her.

'I'm going to paint them,' she says.

'What color?' I ask.

'I'm not going to paint on top of them. I'm going to paint them in a still life.'

'Emma's *Pickings: A Still Life*,' my mom says.

'A minimalist still life, this year,' Grandma says, and they both laugh, and I laugh too so they think I get what they're talking about, but also because it's like a choir and if you don't laugh it's like you aren't singing, and it you don't sing it's like there's a lake in front of you and you've got your swimsuit on but you won't dive in. Like Ana, who never wants to swim. She says the mud is gross. But really she's embarrassed to be seen in her swimsuit, and I miss before, when she wasn't embarrassed by every little thing and she wasn't so mean.

Emma makes us hold her chestnuts while she looks for a lighter in her giant pockets. I drop a few, but she doesn't mind. She's got a long neck like a giraffe and she always seems sad until something makes her laugh out loud and she throws her neck back. She's got yellow teeth and red hair, apart from the hair that's closest to her scalp, which is white. She has an old truck filled with so many blankets you could live in there, and she keeps hot things in colorful flasks: milk, tea, soup, coffee. She always has a cigarette in her right hand, with her left hand holding the right elbow, which reminds me of the music stand where my mom and dad rest their music when they practice. When I grow up I want to be like Grandma but in Mexican. But my mom says that's genetically impossible: Emma is only my grandma because she got married to my mom's daddy. Genetically is when you generally look like someone else. Mama doesn't look like Emma, but she calls her Mom anyway. Emma is only ten years older than her but she calls Mama Kiddo. She calls us all Kiddo. My dad, too. But she calls Beto Beddo.

'I wasn't ever married to your father,' says Emma. 'Not technically.'

'*Arrejuntada*,' my mom says in Spanish. 'Shacked up with him, whatever.'

Emma tries to say the word *arrejuntada* but the r comes out all floppy.

'When I grow up I want to shack up with a pilot, too,' I tell them, and then I get back on all fours and leave. I'm a banana slug on stilts.

56

2000

Pina's mom told her how babies are made. Now Pina is trying to explain it to her friend, but she keeps getting muddled. Ana assures her that she doesn't have any hole for any penis. Pina is going to show her that she does; that her mom isn't a liar. Ana pulls down her pants and knickers. It's Ana who says knickers, because that's what they call them in England where Agatha Christie comes from. Pina calls them panties.

They lay Ana's clothes out on the stone wall that surrounds the hotel's mini playground and Ana lies on top of them. She lets her feet dangle on either side. Pina inspects her, fully concentrated. It occurs to her that since she doesn't have a penis she'll need some kind of tool to find Ana's hole. She hops off the wall, opens her backpack, and finds a BIC pencil. She clicks the end and pushes the lead nib down: she doesn't want to draw all over the inside of her friend's vagina. Her mom told her that's what you have to call it, 'Not your peepee, not your girly bits, and definitely not your flower.'

Pina has second thoughts about the BIC. What if a bit of nib somehow broke off inside Ana and stayed there for ever, and then when she had children they came out all shiny and gray? Perhaps she should use the rubber end? Pina doesn't say any of this to Ana; it was hard enough trying to convince her to take her clothes off. Ana thinks she knows it all. She says babies are made when mommies and daddies make love, because that's what *her* mom told her. This theory really bugs Pina. Firstly because it's plain dumb, and secondly because that would mean that Ana's parents, who had four children, love each other more than her parents, who only had her. As if they ran out of love to make. Pina wants to show Ana once and for all that she's wrong. Having children doesn't have anything to do with love. It's a physical, mechanical thing: the man slots his penis inside the woman. Her mom explained the whole thing with the proper words for it all: the man's penis shoots out some tadpole thingies, which are actually baby seeds.

Ana and Pina are looking after Luz while the other kids swim and the grown-ups drink beer by the pool on the other side of the hotel. There are some swings between the stone wall and Pina's backpack. Luz is sitting under one of them and Pina pats her on the head: her ringlets bounce at the slightest touch. Then Pina climbs back onto the wall where Ana is now standing on tiptoes pretending to walk across a balance beam like a gymnast. Pina pushes her gently and Ana loses her balance but regains it straight away.

'Quit it, Pina. I could have fallen like Humpty Dumpty and they would have put you in jail.'

Pina doesn't ask who Humpty Dumpty is. She never asks Ana to explain her gringoisms.

'Lie down,' she says.

Ana lies on top of the clothes.

'Open your legs wide.'

Ana opens them but she won't stop jiggling about, and Pina can't find any way in.

'Stay still!'

This, or something, amuses Luz, who starts chuckling. Pina glances over at her. She's pushing an empty swing. Ana and Pina had also been pushing each other on the swings before they'd got onto the baby-making hole. Now, if she puts her hand up to her face, Pina can smell the rust of the chain.

With her BIC, Pina carefully combs Ana for an entry point. She imagines the baby-making hole has a secret hatch: you have to press the exact point with a penis or the pencil rubber to open it up. A bit like the barely visible hole on the back of the alarm clock which you have to poke with a pin to set the time.

Ana gives up hope.

'I don't have a hole,' she says, her lip quivering.

Pina carries on her search. It's not that uncommon for her to make Ana cry, and she always gets over it in the end. This time, though, Ana shuts her legs.

'Maybe if you're chubby you don't have a hole.'

'Don't be a ninny,' Pina says. 'All girls have a hole. How else would the pee come out?'

This is what she says, even though she knows that what Ana wants to hear is that she's not chubby. But she is. A little bit. In fact, Pina's mom told her that the pee hole isn't the same as the baby-making hole, but she imagines they're similar: they're neighbors, after all. It's like they live in the same mews.

'Maybe if I pee you'll be able to see where it comes out,' Ana suggests.

'That is gross,' Pina says, wielding her pencil threateningly. 'You will not pee on me or I'll tell on you for leaving Luz by herself on the swings.'

Luz is singing a lullaby to the empty swing. Maybe she can see a ghost there. Pina and Ana have discussed this possibility before because Luz is always talking to an invisible someone or another. That thought barely finished, Pina hears the dull thump of the swing hitting Luz on the forehead. The little girl screams, drops to the floor and starts to cry.

'Hey, Luchi, Luchi,' Pina cries. 'Hey, come over and help me out.'

But Luz doesn't even seem to hear her. Ana jumps off the wall, goes to her sister, lifts her onto the swing and pushes her gently.

'We haven't finished,' Pina says.

'Why don't we try on you?' Ana says.

'I'm embarrassed to take off my panties.'

'I took off mine!'

Pina throws her panties at Ana from the wall. Luz laughs. She's got a lovely laugh. When Luz laughs Pina thinks how she'd like to have brothers and sisters. Luz puts the panties on her head like a hat, but Ana snatches them off and throws them back in the direction of the wall; they land on the grass. Ana can be pretty snappish with her sister sometimes. All four of them can be pretty snappish with each other, and when they're snappish Pina thinks how she doesn't want brothers or sisters, especially not four.

'I've tried a thousand times at home and never found it,' she says.

'How can you really try if you don't even know what a penis looks like?' Ana asks.

'Do so.'

'How?'

'OK, I don't,' Pina admits. 'My dad wouldn't show me his even though my mom yelled "It's natural! It's natural!" at him. But he didn't want to so that was the end of that.'

'I see my brother's all the time. It's just like a pinky. How about we try on Luz?'

'What if she tells on us?'

'We'll tell my mom she wet herself and that we had to change her knickers,' Ana says, lifting her sister off the swing.

'Alright,' Pina says, and she proceeds to take the lead refills out of the BIC. She counts them, then puts all eight in her pocket. She doesn't want to risk them breaking inside Luz. Then she has another idea. On the ground near the swings there's a drink with a straw in it. Pina puts the pencil in her pocket, grabs the straw from the can and wipes it on her shorts.

Between them they manage to lie Luz down on the wall on top of Ana's trousers. Pina tries to take off her swimsuit but she gets in a twist. It's not the same as undressing a doll. But even so Ana knows how to do it. Watching her maneuver the straps, it occurs to Pina that the secret is not to be afraid; it occurs to her that people with brothers and sisters are the least afraid of all. Luz is still giggling and singing, 'on the swing, a-wing, a-wing there's a little swinging lady'.

'What's she talking about?' Ana asks.

'That is so creepy,' Pina says.

But Luz carries on singing her song, making it up as she goes along. Ana holds down her knees and joins in the chorus to distract her.

'On the swing, a-wing, a-wing…'

'Stop it,' Luz says. 'My song.'

This vagina hatch turns out to be even harder to open than the last one, and Pina's job is made more difficult still by Luz, who squirms the second the straw goes near her. Luz laughs at first, but then starts to cry. Ana pins her down by the wrists. But Pina gives up almost immediately. Nobody has ever really punished her, but she has a hunch that what she's doing is worthy of serious punishment. They let go of Luz and tickle her until she rolls and almost falls off the wall.

'Maybe Luz and I don't have holes,' Ana says, 'and that's why we're sisters.'

'You don't get it,' Pina says, now not so sure about anything. She jumps down from the wall.

'If you don't have holes, you're never going to have children,' she says, then stands up on one of the swings and thrusts her pelvis forwards and backwards, rocking herself furiously. She's thinking that neither the hole, the penis, nor the tadpoles exist, that it's all a story for dumb kids; another one of those stories her mom tells her, like when she says she's going to pick Pina up from school and instead her dad shows up. Like when she told Pina she could go along to her dance class and then just went without her and without saying anything and Pina was left standing in the kitchen in her leotard.

They hear a whistle. Luz recognizes it and starts to clap. A few seconds later Linda turns up at the swings. Pina is on edge. She's scared Aunt Linda will tell her off. She stops rocking herself but remains frozen on the swing. She clutches hard onto the chains and her eyes bore into her feet, into her shadow on the grass, into Ana's panties lying there like a dead butterfly. Linda announces that they have to go back to Mexico City. It's an emergency: Grandma Emma turned up to surprise them and nobody's there to open the door.

'Get dressed, all of you!' she orders. She means all of them bar Pina. Pina is the only one who's fully dressed. Pina will have to stay there all weekend.

II

2004

It's midday when I set off for the tools. Mostly I go so I don't have to be around my emotionally disturbed mother. She's completely *loca*. This morning she burst into my room screaming, 'Go back!'

'Eh?'

'Go back to that song,' she said, sitting down on what used to be Luz's bed but is now my chaise longue. 'Pass the remote.'

I passed her the remote. The stereo was playing a CD I barely know. Mom went nuts with the rewind button and hashed the song as if she were slicing an onion. *Look at this big-eyed fish swimming... You see beneath the sea is where a fish should be... You see this crazy man decided not to breathe...*

'What is wrong with you?' I asked when she finally threw the remote on the bed and let the song play on.

'Did you ever play this to Luz?' she asks me.

'No siree, Marina just burnt it for me.'

Mom went on staring at me, I laughed, and then she got up and took the CD from the stereo.

'I forbid you to listen to this song,' she said, already by the door. And then, looking at the CD cover, 'I forbid you to listen to Dave Matthews! Or his band!'

'Yeah, right,' I told her. Mom has never forbidden me to do anything.

'And don't say no siree,' she said before disappearing down the hall.

'You're messing with my mental health, you are!' I screamed, but she had gone. When I went down for breakfast, I found the CD broken into pieces in the kitchen.

*

I go out into the mews' passageway and the salmony light hurts my eyes. Last night I stayed up reading. I got through an entire novel, but an easy one, not like the ones Emma sends me. The charactress was fifteen and had a brain tumor. Her titties, according to her, look like bananas. Now it's my favorite book, because usually in metaphors they look like apples or melons or oranges. Or rather similes. But when I bend over, my titties hang down as if I was forty not thirteen, and that's why I never have a bath at Pina's anymore, even though she has a big bathtub. Pi likes to chat while I'm washing and I don't like her seeing me naked. She's got pointy, pert titties. If it were a simile I'd say: like Grandma's hat. On the end of each one sits a dark nipple like a hazelnut. But me, I have flat nipples and my skin's so pale that my sad blue veins show through like a bad omen. Anyway, I don't want to think about this anymore. The Girls are sunbathing in a corner of the passageway. Sometimes Alf leaves them outside for hours. I go up to their double stroller.

'Charactress isn't a word,' I tell them, 'but it should be.'

I have the red trolley with me so that I can bring back whatever I manage to wangle off the neighbors. I start with the house across the street: Daniel and Daniela live just out in front with two Pugs, a baby and another on the way. They're not so bad, but they're not especially nice either. Their house has white tiled floors in every room that make the whole place feel like a giant bathroom or a spaceship. All the furniture is made of dark, fake leather, except for the baby's stuff, which is yellow because they refuse to buy anything blue or pink. Some afternoons, Pi and I look after the baby and root through their half-empty bookshelves. It's mostly manga and then this one book about how men and women come from different planets. One thing they do have going for them is their giant TV – bigger than anyone's in the mews – and while the baby sleeps we watch the random shows Daniel downloads and warns us not to touch.

As I might've guessed, they're not at home. I take out one of the pre-prepared notes I brought with me and write their names at the top (Daniel, Daniela, Baby). The baby is called Baby because they haven't given her a name. They think you should get to know your kid before naming it, because if you do it the other way around you force it to take on the personality of that name, not its natural one. My dad says, though not to their faces, that everyone will just keep on calling her Baby forever. But D and D don't want that, they just refuse to give her a name without taking her feelings into consideration. They're waiting till Baby is old enough to have an opinion on the matter. Pina's dad reminded them that what they're doing is in fact illegal in Mexico. But Daniela won't listen to him. The way she sees it, a name can make or break you. She says that in her high school there was a guy called Abel who was run over by his brother.

'On purpose?' I asked her.

'By accident,' she said, 'but can't you see? It was his fate.'

I shove the note under the door, then kneel down to see if it went through OK. There's a pair of feet standing still in front of me. My heart starts pounding. I scramble up and sprint back to the mews, the red trolley making a racket against the cobbles. Once safely inside the mews, I pounce on the first door I come to. How creepy, those feet standing there right next to the door but not opening. It must be Daniel, I tell myself. He must have another woman.

*

Bitter happens to be the first house. Marina lives there. My brothers call her Miss Mendoza, which is what she wrote on her mailbox, but she's told me before that 'this whole Miss thing' makes her feel 'old and saggy', and that she's 'only' twenty-one, which in my eyes practically makes her the local spinster. She's definitely the token single tenant. Pina and I are also technically single, but Pi has no intentions of staying that way beyond fourteen. She swore she's going to find a summer fling (those were her words) in Matute, or whatever her mom's beach is called.

Sometimes Marina lives alone and sometimes she lives with a boyfriend. There's always some new guy hanging around, and they're usually so good-looking that if I bump into them in the passageway I have to recite poetry in my head just to stop myself from blushing (*Brown and furry caterpillar in a hurry, take your walk upon the beach. I have heard the mermaids singing, each to each*). It never really works though: I always turn bright red. And maybe good-looking isn't the right word either. Let's say: tall. And when I say Marina is the 'local' spinster I mean inside Belldrop Mews, which is where everything that happens in my life takes place, apart from the way too many hours I spend at the school around the corner and in La Michoacana on the next block. What measly perimeters us city-kids are dealt.

A few months ago, the Neighborhood Association got hold of several liters of a horrible rosy red paint that the hardware store on the nearby avenue was selling off cheap. It was Marina's fault: she's obsessed with colors, particularly their names, so she chose it because the tins said Coral. I guess she thought coral would bring her closer to her marine-a habitat or something. We all had to take turns painting. Even my mom came out of her little bubble to paint for a while. Now, if you happen to be walking along the street when someone opens the door to the mews, it looks like you're peering down a larynx: like the long passageway is made of a living tissue, and the dew-like sunlight dappled across the textured walls is saliva.

Marina opens the door to me in jeans and a white blouse. I reckon I've spent more time observing her style than any other fashion trend. I don't really get it, but I love it. When she first came to the mews, Marina babysat us while Mom grieved for Luz. She would make us sit down with the instruments in Sweet House, where my parents have their music school, and we would spend whole afternoons drawing and painting. It was boring as hell, but from the window we could

71

spy on the cortège of women processing through the mews
to visit Mom. Slowly and deliberately, they'd file along the
corridor, which was purplish back then, a shade Marina
used to call 'asylilac'. And that's what they looked like, the
women; a line of loony asylum runaways, always on edge, in
a rush, fresh out of a traffic jam or just stopping by between
errands. Some would spot us through the window and pop
into the school to deliver death-grip hugs. Then they made
their way over to our house, and if they were lucky Mom
would drink wine and tea with them, in which case they'd
leave all serene, my sister's death like a pill that put their
own mini-dramas into perspective. Other days, she wouldn't
even open the door to them, so the deeply distressed cortège
would come back to Sweet House, and we'd have to make
excuses for Mom.

'She's at a rehearsal,' we'd say. And sometimes she really
was.

'What about your dad?' the women would insist.

And I'd tell them the truth, which amounted to the same
thing: 'Rehearsal. He has a concert coming up.'

Sometimes it feels like they spent that entire first year
locked away in a permanent rehearsal while we sat among
the untouched instruments in their silent music school, the
hallway piling up with gift baskets. Something I understood
then is that the Mexican gift industry may be well and truly
gringofied at Christmas, but when it comes to death, our
own comfort foods trump everything. I've never received so
many bags of Mexican sweet treats – *pepitorias*, *palanquetas*,
jamoncillos – as I did when my sister died. I found it dumb
and pretty insulting, them bringing us candies. Not that that

stopped me eating them. My mom and Marina also used to meet up for wine or tea, until last year when they stopped talking to each other. I never found out why. When I ask Mom she says Marina's a traitor, or that she sided with the enemy or something along those lines. But the last time I tried to get her to dish the dirt she stood there thinking for a while and then said, 'Because I'm like Corleone, you better don't mess with my people, or…'

'Or…?' I asked, but she just stuck out her tongue at me.

I don't dare ask Marina what went on, but once she let it slip that she thinks Mom is 'rancorous'. She also said it's 'pathological' that she's still mourning, and that she lives 'shut out from the world'. But she doesn't, really. Mom still rehearses and she's gone back to teaching in Sweet, and if we put on a play or show at school she always comes. She doesn't play in concerts anymore, though.

'So why rehearse?' people ask her.

'Because it keeps my head above water,' she answers, as if the lifeline music throws her were material and evident: a big, fat buoy at the base of the cello, keeping her from slipping under. As if we weren't all wading in the river of shit that Luz's death left in our home. Except that it's not even quite a river, our sadness: it's stagnant water. Since Luz drowned, there's always something drowning at home. Not everyday. Some days you think that we're all alive again, the five remaining members of the family: I get a zit; some girl calls Theo; Olmo plays his first concert; Dad comes back from tour; Mom decides to bake a pie. But later you go into the kitchen, and there's the pie, still raw on the wooden countertop, half of it pricked and the other half untouched, with Mom hovering over it, clutching the fork in midair. And then you know that we too, as a family, will always be 'almost six'.

*

Marina greets me like she greets everyone: by grabbing you by the back of your head and planting a kiss on your cheek (and if you don't know her, and if you're as dumb as my brothers, you might think she's going in for the mouth). From this angle, I can see her black bra. Maybe I need me one of those. Thirteen is definitely the age for one's first black *brassiere*. It's too embarrassing if Dad takes me, but maybe Pi will want to come along when she gets back. I go into Bitter. It's always a surprise when you step through the door. Firstly, because it's different every time, and then because there's something over-the-top about it. Something bubbly. The décor consists of piles of cushions on a chicken-yellow sofa, the only constant in the whole place. Some of the cushions have tiny little mirrors that twinkle depending on where you stand. Marina donated me some cushion covers, which now take pride of place on my chaise longue. I filled them with plastic bags, just like she showed me. Luz would say Marina is the queen of recycling. She gets all those clothes I like second-hand. With her hands on her hips she says, 'Yes, miss?'

Before they clashed, my mom used to teach Marina English. She tried to teach Dad too, back when they met, but his pronunciation still sucks. According to him, on principle you should distrust any language that uses the same word for *libre* and *gratis*. When he's around she speaks

to us kids in Spanish. He says she doesn't want us to turn
out like foreigners, which is exactly what we are. Or, at
least, we have two passports. Even Luz had an American
passport. She's a baby in the photo, just a few months old.
Mom is holding her in her arms and Luz looks serious, sort
of startled, as if even then my sister foresaw the gravity of
the trip she would come to take. Four by five centimeters
of portentous ID.

*

The only thing I tell Marina is that I designed a garden. I
don't feel like explaining that my parents still feel the need
to send me to the epicenter of the tragedy each year to wallow
in seaweed and memories under the now obsessively watchful
eye of Emma, and that to avoid going, I had to make up some
form of tangible compensation. She wouldn't appreciate the
word *milpa* either: too native for her liking. Design, on the
other hand, is one hundred percent her thing, I think.

'And now I'm actually ready to build it, so I need tools,'
I go on.

But before I've even finished my sentence I realize how
absurd my request is. The most useful thing I'm likely to
find among all this velvet is a spoon. And if there is a spoon
then it's probably from the cutlery set my mom gave her the
day she discovered Marina ate exclusively out of recycled
yogurt pots.

Marina puts her hands on her hips, raises her elbows and
curves her spine, her breastbone backing away from me.
Her collarbones stick out. She always does this when she's

thinking. She looks like a mandolin. Then, quick as a flash, she straightens up again and leaves the room. I don't know what this means, but I stay put. There's a new lampshade above my head. It's made of a series of solid, sheer droplets which hang in semicircles around the bulb, like a ghostly spider. The correct word would be 'ethereal'. It must be made of plastic because Marina doesn't use glass. My mom explained that this is because Marina saw her father break a glass of wine with his teeth when she was a little girl. It gives me goosebumps just imagining it. In fact, when I want goosebumps I think of exactly that: my mom calmly biting her wine glass and chewing on it.

Marina comes back, takes a little bow and hands me the prettiest, tiniest, most ridiculous hammer I've ever seen. It's half the size of a normal hammer and has an elaborate, flowery, leafy pattern printed on it. Marina unscrews it and shows me how, inside the handle, it has a spade hidden on one side and a brush on the other. I laugh.

'The land,' she says, 'belongs to she who decorates it.'

'I'm going to get it dirty,' I say, 'maybe even get lead on it.'

I say 'lead' slowly and deliberately, to impress her. Marina squints.

'Keep it,' she finally rules.

'You sure?'

'It was a gift from a total waste of space. You can cover it in mercury for all I care.'

'Lead.'

'Whatever.'

Very gently, Marina pushes me toward the door.

'Thanks so much,' I tell her, 'I like your lampshade.'

She takes me by the neck, kisses my forehead, and just before closing the door behind me points to the ceiling and clarifies, 'It's called a chandelier, darling.'

*

By the time I leave Bitter House, The Girls are nowhere to be seen, which means I'll find Alf at home. His mailbox says Doctor Alfonso Semitiel. I've known him since I was born. His wife was the doctor really, but ever since he retired a couple of months ago he's been supplementing his pension selling the prescriptions she left behind. He doesn't skimp on diagnoses either. No matter what time of day you pop by, he always insists on giving you an *alegría* (which are kind of like cereal bars, only made of amaranth, 'So not a cereal bar, Agatha Christie, but a seed bar!') from the basket he keeps in the hallway. He says amaranth is the food of the future. And of the past. Above all, the past. Alf is my friend. In fact, Alf is the inspiration behind all of this: it's thanks to him I know how to grow things. I spent my entire childhood sowing amaranth and other Mesoamerican pseudo-cereals: quinoa, chia, acacia. And real cereals, too: wheat, barley, oats, millet, corn (naturally); and corn's two sisters: beans and pumpkin. He called it his MM or Modern *Milpa*. Over the last years almost everything we planted was destroyed by the toxic summer rains, but some of them did OK. The MM used to be in his yard, but he let it die when his wife died. Now, in its place, there's a built-in jacuzzi. My dad, who is the least medically minded person in the whole mews, diagnosed Alf with depression. But when I go over, Alf's always soaking in the jacuzzi and reading. He says he's learning to swim or, at the very least, to take little dips. Missing the MM; wanting to bring it back to life, for Alf and for all! These were some of the arguments that helped me finally convince Mom that the whole yard-renovation thing could really work.

Alf seems pleased to see me when he opens the door (looking like a dog fresh out of the water). He is wrapped in a pinkish robe that looks like it might have belonged to his wife, but I have the goodness of heart not to comment. I follow him to the yard, skipping over his wet footprints. I don't need to explain my plan to him because he already knows it. In fact, it was to him and not to Pina that I took the serviette contract the day we signed it. Pina is my best friend, but for her the word agriculture might as well refer to the superstore around the corner. Or La Michoacana. Her idea of a harvest is when she buys herself two *horchatas* in a row.

We sit down on the rocking chairs on the terrace looking out over the jacuzzi. The Girls are sitting on a bench, one looking at us and the other out to the horizon. I explain to Alf that I need tools.

'I'm so frickin' proud of you, Agatha Christie.'

He's always called me that, and coming from him I like it, because Alf is an investigator. Not a private investigator, but definitely a research investigator something or other. Alf is actually a doctor too, but in anthropology not in curing people. It could be I'm the only person who knows this because hardly anyone goes into his study where he keeps all his diplomas and books, some of which he wrote himself. His doctoral thesis is about umami, the fifth taste, which wasn't at all known except in Japan, and it was him who helped to spread the word about it in the West. Or at least in Mexico. Mexico is in the West. I don't dare tell him, but I'm proud of him, too. He carries his grief better than my mom. He doesn't act like a ghost, or go totally nuts over songs. At least not in front of me he doesn't. I guess I'd have to ask The Girls what they think about it. But The Girls don't think.

Alf starts pulling tools out of a mini-shed, which he keeps locked, as if someone might come steal his shovel.

'Where's your friend?' he asks.

'Pina? She's with her mom.'

Alf scans my face to see if I'm lying.

'She turned up, didn't she?' I say, then try to think of something to change the subject quick because I don't want him to ask me any questions. I don't know if Pina wants Alf to know her mom has resurfaced after all these years, and that she's living on that Mazuzzy beach, which isn't even that far from Mexico City.

'When was the very, very first time you heard anyone talk about umami?' I ask.

'I never told you? I was at a conference dinner where I got lumbered sitting next to a grouchy Japanese man, one of those people who make waiters miserable for sport. He complained that his food didn't have enough umami in it, and of course I had no idea what he was talking about. It was 1969. Is this any use to you?' he asks, holding up a microscopic hose, which I immediately recognize.

'A Dampit?' I say.

'A what?'

'A Dampit. It's a guitar humidifier.'

'Really?' he asks.

'I think so, let me see. Yep.'

Alf laughs, 'I always thought it was to keep cacti and other things you don't need to water from going dry; I found it one day out in the corridor!' He's really losing it now: 'I suppose one only sees what one wants to see.'

'It was probably my brother's.'

'Well, in that case, take it.' He takes a couple of deep breaths and manages to stop giggling. 'Tell him I nicked it off him.'

'I haven't seen you laugh like that for ages,' I say without thinking. He sighs and his face relaxes into a smile somewhere between stoical and serene, and which makes me feel older than I am. Emma always says I have an old soul, and sometimes I think she's got that right.

*

I leave Umami with a loaded trolley. Aside from Marina's dainty hammer and Theo's useless Dampit, I have: a shovel, a rake, a pair of enormous, mucky gloves, an extension hose and some garden shears which Alf uses to prune the little tree on his porch. It's a lemon tree that has never given lemons. I've only just started to appreciate the huge amount of plants in his house. Before, I always focused on the MM, never on the pots inside, which I thought were more his wife's territory. Her name was Doctor Noelia and she always offered me sugar-free candy because she was worried I would get fat. It worries me too now, a little bit, but I can't consult her anymore because she died three months after my sister. When I ask my mom if I'm fat she says no, that it's only baby fat and that I'll grow out of it.

'So, what you mean is that I'll keep growing till one day I burst out of my fatness and leave it behind like snakes shed their skins?' I ask her.

'Calm down, Ana,' she says.

'I'm not a baby,' I say.

'You've got such beautiful eyes,' she says, and I get mad because she's always trying to change the subject.

Growing the *milpa* is a matter of principle, but the house-plants inside are more like Alf's pets. That's what I think as I leave Umami. He looks after them lovingly. Not as lovingly as he looks after The Girls, but almost; a lot like the other old folk in the neighborhood look after their dogs. Normally I like to hang around Umami for hours, but this time I left quickly because ever since I let slip about Chela I feel bad. Sort of like a traitor. This reunion with her mom is going to be the weirdest thing that Pina's done in her life, and it's going to happen without me. I didn't even help her pack. I decide I'm going to call her tonight. I hope her cell works in Macuque, or whatever that beach is called. Me, I don't have a cell. One day I asked Dad for one and he said, 'If you lived in the nineteenth century, what would you think of a thirteen-year-old girl who spent all day glued to the mailbox waiting for a letter?'

'I'd think she was pathetic,' I said.

'Exactly,' he said, 'end of discussion.'

I'll ask again when I start high school. Safety first, Dad.

I leave the trolley by the bell in the passageway and head out of the mews again. Then I cross the street and poke my nose under the door of the house in front. The feet are still there, and I bolt it again. It's only when I'm back at home arranging the tools out in the yard that I realize two things. One: I'm as stupid as stupid can be. Two: the feet under the door are a pair of shoes.

*

A week later I'm finally ready to throw out the old soil. Since you can't do any work in the afternoons because of the dumb summer rains, I've been waking up earlier, pretty early in fact: around ten!

I emptied the planter with the shovel. It took me the best part of the week. Then I put the mega-loads of mud in trash bags, which I stacked in a corner. Now I'm hauling the bags through the mews out onto the street. One of them snags on the bell, splits open, and covers the passageway in soil. Bah, the rain will wash it away.

I'm just putting the last bag out on the street when Beto pokes his head out of a window of Sour House.

'You're polluting the planet, my girl,' he calls down to me on the sidewalk.

'*Au contraire*,' I tell him. 'This soil here is full of lead, whereas the one in my yard will have plants and the plants will produce oxygen!'

'Right on,' he says.

My mom has called Pina Pi her whole life. Pina calls my mom Aunt Linda. I also used to call Pina's mom Aunt Chela, and she would call me Ananás, which means pineapple in French. But she doesn't call me anything anymore because she disappeared when we were nine, and even though she's back now, she still hasn't shown her face around here; instead she wrote Pina an email and sent her a ticket to go visit her Mitsubishahi beach. Anyway, Beto is just Beto, and he calls us kids 'my girl' or 'my boy', even though we're not in any way his.

'How's the plantation coming along?' he asks.

'Come down and see,' I say. 'Come over for a beer later. My dad always has a beer in the yard around eight.'

'You got it.'

I think I'm pretty generous for having invited him. He must miss Pina. Although not more than I do. Beto shuts his window and I head back into the larynx feeling like a breath of fresh air: light and magnanimous.

*

I've got soil in my nails and hair. The new stuff is a lot softer and almost black, and as much as I try to spread it out evenly, I can't. It's a bit like trying to pour flour from its packet into a jar. If you squeeze the sack you can end up squashing it into clumps, and then only one side of the planter gets any soil and you have to go back and fluff it all up again with the rake. The one thing I'm really not keen on is the worms; where the heck do they all come from? Once I'm done I'll clean the plaster around the planters. Soap, bucket, scouring pad. Mom watches me from the window, frowning.

'What?' I ask.

'You're so pretty,' she says.

'No I'm not,' I say.

But that night, after my bath, I inspect myself in the mirror. Maybe I'm not so ugly these days.

*

I spend the next three weeks sowing, by which I mean that I spent one day pressing seeds into the soil and now I spend my mornings reading aloud to them, to cheer them along. That's what Daniela did with Baby, and now she does it with the new one inside her, which we've already begun to call Baby II. I miss Pina like crazy, and then I don't miss her so much. I miss my brothers too, but only because now that they're not here to distract Mom she spends hours on the sofa with a book in her hand never turning the page. I make her iced tea with fresh mint and she takes a few sips, leaning on one elbow and barely lifting her chest, as if she were sick or something. Then she leaves the rest untouched. The ice melts. The glasses sweat. Dust has started to build up all over the house. The beds are unmade. It rains every afternoon and I really want a cat or a turtle, but when I bring it up Mom says, 'You're just nostalgic for camp.'

Beto often comes round to see us. I often go see Alf. Sometimes the three of us coincide in Umami and we dip our feet in the jacuzzi, eat peanuts and chat about what Beto should read to understand our obsession with *milpas*; about what Alf should do with his yard; and about what I should plant in mine. Sometimes Alf wets a flannel and washes The Girls while we chat. Summer isn't too shabby at all for grown-ups. Maybe it's because Pina's missing out on this that I'm not so jealous of her anymore. Some of my seeds sprout.

One day I finally ask Mom, 'Why did you break my CD?'

She answers with a strange motion of her hand. It's a bit like the Protestant flick, only this one ends in great big thumps on her chest.

'What's that supposed to mean?' I ask.

'It means Catholic.'

'Who's Catholic?'

'Me, maybe, since I can't sleep for the guilt.'

'It was only a CD.'

2003

Marina gets up off the sofa and walks to the kitchen, determined to eat something. Ever since the landlord explained to her about umami and protein, she's been thinking she ought to eat more chicken and tomatoes. That's what healthy people eat: chicken breasts. But the meat aisle never fails to intimidate her. It all looks too raw, too shiny and demanding. When Marina does buy food, it's precooked and all neatly packaged: tear along the dotted line and consume before the doubt creeps in.

Her kitchen has a screen door that leads out onto the yard with the water tank. Salty and Umami have a decent sized yard, but Sour and Bitter got this sad substitute instead. And poor Sweet got no outdoor space at all, nor is it compensated like Sour and Bitter by facing out onto the street. Perhaps that's why nobody has ever lived there and it's only used as a music school.

A broom and the ossified dusters her mother bought, and which Marina hasn't touched since she left, lie scattered around the water tank. There are some beer bottles, too, which Marina has every intention of taking to the bottle bank before the world comes to an end. Chihuahua's bicycle has been there for months, propped up vertically, its flat tires removed and left draped over the axle, drooping like the titties of some emaciated old lady. Marina tries to shake the image. She'll be sure to mention this in her next session: 'I've noticed an improvement, Mr. Therapist: the idea of someone emaciated sets my teeth on edge.' He'll be pleased; he's a good person.

Marina makes some calculations, leaning against the water tank: a half-plate of oats in the morning, a Yakult mid-afternoon.

'Damn it,' she thinks.

Then:

'Listen.'

And then:

'Cheese.'

Blue cheese.

Roquefort! Boy, was she into Roquefort! She used to eat it with tortillas, spread it on Wonder Bread, let it melt on spaghetti straight out of the pan in the teeming kitchen of her father's restaurant.

'It to-ta-lly reeks,' her brother would say with that affected authority that made him string-all-his-words-together-very-slowly, as if by going any faster his message might be missed; as if by pausing the whole act might fall apart.

'Go-back-to-your-room,' he'd tell Marina those nights her dad didn't come home, at the same time grabbing their mother's hands to stop her from biting her fingers and nails.

It used to be her favorite thing, blue cheese. Once, at the height of his happy hour, her father put his arm around her mom's waist and they swayed in a kind of clumsy waltz while

Marina ate her spaghetti, her brother ate his – with nothing but butter on it – and her dad sang, 'Blue cheese, you saw me standing alone…' Mom giggled and Marina, who didn't know the original or even understand the lyrics, felt more in awe of her dad than ever: on top of everything else, he was also a gifted composer.

This childhood memory soon smothers her little craving. ('Be alert to the signs,' the nurses told her, 'salivating, rumbling tummy…') Unlike appetite, she can recognize anger now. Her mouth tastes sour just thinking about the restaurant kitchen and the sweet smell of her dad's happy hour.

'Unstable childhood?' repeated Marina, genuinely surprised by her therapist's question.

Not unstable, no. Everything was timetabled; everything had a name. After Happy Hour came Client Time – the orders, the smells, the sound of conversations bouncing off the walls, her father treating the cooks like crap, the dirty plates, the leftovers. When the clients left it was Closing Time – the waiting staff turning the chairs upside down, her father singing, doling out tips and little pats on butts, the cooks changing into their normal clothes, and some of them, on more than one occasion and while the others kept guard at the door, flashing Marina parts of their anatomy that she'd rather not have seen. Then, every single day, at around eleven p.m., they would all leave and Dad would get out his hipflask, which he carried around in his apron, and serve himself what was left in a highball glass. It was His Time, 'because he'd earned it'. Apart from on Mondays. On Mondays he was 'going to change'. There was even stability in his broken resolutions.

The sour taste in her mouth makes her feel a certain pride for being alert, for noticing these things. Before the brain-washing, she didn't even know where her sternum was. More than once she'd punched herself there; a beneficial punch, but purely intuitive. Now everything has a scientific name. The place where the knot is is called The Sternum, and if she feels she wants to cry but can't, she is to massage it firmly: 'No need for punching, Miss Mendoza.' The sour taste is caused by Stress Hormones. Then again, it may just be her cigarette. She drops it in a bottle and goes back into the kitchen. Attempt number two.

'Cravings are discreet, you have to be alert to them,' the nurses would say. 'The brain is like a puppy.'

One of the nurses didn't shave her armpits and secretly Marina longed for her to be fired, to confirm that she wasn't the only one to fuck up everything through physical self-neglect.

In fact, what those 'alternative' nurses were really saying was, 'The brain is flexible: we can train it!' and it was Marina who would automatically think, 'Like a lapdog!' But ever since she came home and her mom left her on her own again, little by little she's been softening, trying out the advice she always rejected. She wants a Play-Doh brain, one that lets her imitate the self-respect she recognizes in other people, the same way she already imitates their way of talking and laughing and dressing. A 'chewing-gum personality' is what she calls this tendency of hers to mimic whatever or whomever she has in front of her. She talks like her classmates and gesticulates like Linda. If she spends a few nights in a row with Chihuahua she wakes up with a little northern-Mexican lilt, drawing out her syllables at random. Then

Saturday comes around and she has to go and look after the kids, and by Sunday she's talking like Olmo, who has a new habit of saying everything twice: 'yes yes', 'no no', 'why why', 'I know I know'.

Marina distrusts her own malleability and is attracted by the possibility of its opposite: the fascinating and at the same time terrifying prospect of being someone. Someone complex yet clear-cut. Like Linda. Like her landlord. An adult, if you like, although she knows it's not exactly that. It's something else: to have an incontestable persona. To be someone about whom people say: 'typical', 'of course she did', 'that's so Marina Mendoza'. But no one has ever said those things about her, because she is many people at once, and all of them go equally unnoticed. It annoys her that her therapist doesn't understand this basic deficiency of hers, this absolute absence of definition. It's something he should help her to work through, not urge her to ignore. Instead, over and over again, he asks her to be herself. He says it as if 'herself' were something solid, unequivocal, a marble bust in a park somewhere.

There's certainly something stony about the concept of selfhood; something that leaves Marina cold. Not indifferent, but insensible. She finds nothing in her swampy insides to connect 'selfhood' with. The only thing she's come across to gain some mastery of the whole issue is to think about it in English. Yes, instead of the Spanish *yo misma*, 'self' works for her. Succinct and detachable, in English the term sounds like somebody else's name: 'Marina, meet Self.'

*

Lately, some nights, before falling asleep, Marina tries out some of the affirmations suggested by her therapist. She tends to stop after a minute because she struggles repeating the same thing over and again, and all too soon the affirmations turn into something else entirely.

'I am a beautiful and productive woman; I am an artist. I am a fruitful and defective woman; I am an artiste. I am a fearful and resentful zoo-man; I am a sadist. I am a dutiful representative of batshit; I am batshit, I am zoo shit. I am a fruity loopy arsonist.'

Affirmations were obligatory at the 'alternative' hospital and had to be performed out loud for the ever-supportive staff. They made it sound easy:

'Now all we're going to do is simply repeat the same positive thought ten times before bed.'

And by 'we' they meant 'you'. Not wanting to give in to those enlightened nurses, Marina prayed instead. She didn't know any others apart from the Lord's Prayer, and only bits of it at that, but that's what she repeated. By the second round the whole thing would start to degenerate into free verse: 'Our Father, who art in Devon, halloweened be thy name. Your whiskey gone, you will be prone to bursts of laughter and rage. Give us this day our daily taste of fasting, and forgive us our thefts as we forgive your bad taste. Our Father, who art incompetent, hollowed be thy name, your fiascos come, give us each day our daily fail, and forgive us our lack of hunger, forgive our breath if it comes out stale. Your wisdom come, I will be gone...'

The night nurses made sure to praise Marina's creativity, and then proceeded to recite her affirmations for her, in a whisper.

'You are an artist,' they'd repeat ten times, and Marina would cover her ears like a little girl. Although every now and again, once they'd left, a little smile would spread across her face.

Since then she's realized that she actually enjoys affirming things, and making them up even more so. It's just repeating the same thing over and over that seems unbearably sad to her.

'I'm a blue cheese,' she affirms. 'I'm a blugheese.'

'Third time lucky,' she affirms. 'You have to lure the cravings with details.'

The flavor. The flavor was so rich it would go straight to her brain, like a chili, though not spicy. She liked the texture, like butter but better, slower in the mouth, with more lumps, smooth and explosive. She pictures the cheese for so long it starts to repulse her. Then she goes out to the yard, takes a deep breath, leans against the water tank and looks up to the sky.

'Go-back-to-your-room!' some part of her drawls.

Where was he now? In the restaurant, maybe, or holding Mom's hands: 'Don't-bite-your-nails-Mother.'

She breathes how they showed her to. She looks up to the sky how they showed her to. It's a stubborn dark gray color: it's never fully night in the mews. Years ago, Marina invented the word graycholy. It might be the first color she ever invented: a bit gray, a bit melancholy. And yet, that wasn't the shade of a fake night like this, but rather of a foggy afternoon in Xalapa, one of thousands. This big city's sky is something else, with its blanket of electric light emitting a sort of sonic-luminous fusion: a low, droning 'brrrrr'. What's it called, then? Darktric, maybe. Is it ever really night in Mexico City?

Marina never goes far enough out of her comfort zone to be able to confirm such a thing. Maybe if you go up one of those skyscrapers they say exist in the business district you can escape the darktric, leave it all below, look up to the black sky again and see the darkness as it was meant to be: without the buzz, and interrupted only by stars. Marina lights a cigarette and holds it up as a satellite. There are a few loose butts next to an ashtray on the window ledge, no doubt left there by Chihuahua who likes to stand alone out in the yard from time to time, to make himself seem interesting. Marina loses her appetite when she smokes, and the truth is that that's both why she started and why she quit. And now she's waiting for it to reappear, the hunger, and she hasn't mentioned to the doctors that she's smoking again. The therapist swears her appetite will come back.

'Marina, your body *knows*,' he tells her.

But what Marina thinks is that Mr. Therapist doesn't *know* shit. She suspects that he would have liked to be a surgeon but could never tell his blood cells from his blood clots. She suspects he had to throw in the towel, the kudos, and all the other more pressing issues they take care of elsewhere in the hospital. She suspects he had to resign himself to Floor 8, Psychiatry: Sudokus for the soul.

*

A few raindrops fall on the water tank. The wet black gleams: weckbleam. When she first rented Bitter last summer, it rained every afternoon, even inside the house, and she dashed around here and there catching the drips in pans and thinking to herself cheerfully, 'Wasn't Mexico City supposed to be dry? Wasn't Mexico City really, really dry?' Back then she had no more to her name than her nineteen years and some waitressing savings. The money she gets now – the fat, guilt-ridden check her father sends her – didn't exist during those first months. She stored her things in a makeshift closet built out of bricks and boards, which she painted gold in a burst of enthusiasm. (Goldasm.) She drank out of yogurt pots. She bought a mattress and a single pillow. These days she looks at the house and feels suffocated by all the stuff she's collected. She sees the money from the restaurant in everything – the restaurant and the cooks' sweat; how they'd pick their teeth with their index fingers and then, without a second thought, work the meat with their hands, blood and fat on their apron pockets. On the street the relentless Xalapan drizzle, and in the kitchen the tiled floor growing steadily more filthy as the day went on, making the soles of their shoes squeak against the accumulated footprints that marked the senselessness of it all. And that senselessness played out from one day to the next, but – she'd often felt this in the kitchen – merely repeating itself. In her growing collection of stylish pillows she sees the thousand layers of mascara on the provincial middle-class women who would flock to the restaurant desperate for a 'girls' night out', which always seemed to Marina too hysterical, too high-pitched to signal any kind of real friendship. They called each other 'girl', because youth was their holy grail. The rejuvenation cult never fails to disconcert Marina who, no matter what age she turns, always wishes she were older.

The women would call her over, 'Pst! Hey! Señorita! Miss, another pitcher of sangria.' Perfect teeth, too much perfume, never a morsel left on their plates. Some of them would shamelessly click their fingers at her, then slip her an extra tip because she knew their daughters.

'An Italian restaurant!' Marina explained to her therapist, with a floating exclamation mark. But he doesn't get the irony. He is incapable of visualizing the Italy of the Mexican provinces: Venice – its eternally vanilla sky – depicted in shoddy frescoes on the walls, and the pasta routinely, even purposely overcooked. Mr. Therapist is too worldly to even begin to imagine the stale cosmopolitanism of those who hop over the border for some retail therapy in McAllen, Texas, but don't dare venture to Mexico City. And he is far too optimistic to see how everything she owns is linked to the restaurant, to her father's temper, to the damp walls, and a social class she can despise all she wants, but which still pays her bills.

Although, in truth, this revulsion she feels toward her belongings has only developed over the last few months, since she left the hospital.

'If there are two million cushions, and a rug, and a sofa,' she asks in her session, 'how am I ever going to get out of here?'

'Where would you like to go?' Mr. Therapist asks.

But she doesn't want to go anywhere. Quite the opposite, she'd like to spend more time in her house. She wants to be home when the whomise lights up her wall. She's twenty years old, is that so much to ask? She opens the fridge. Beer, pickles, two tomatoes, mustard. A couple of yogurts, a collection of jellies and jams that Chihuahua buys and then dishes out sparingly as if they contained gold dust. There isn't any blue cheese in the fridge. There is, however, an egg. Also a set of Tupperware containers that have been there for ages and which she doesn't dare open. There's a bottle of ketchup with so much dried sauce around the hole that the top won't close, like those people who talk so much a thin layer of crust grows in the corner of their mouth. Some carrots she bought weeks ago fester in the tray at the bottom. She used one to masturbate with, then threw it away. The rest are still there. She never worked up the energy to peel them. Fuck, she'd bought them in curative mode. Linda always has a Tupperware full of crudités. Whenever Marina is over there she takes one every time she passes the fridge. Why can't she be more like Linda: seemingly laidback, but an impeccable master of juliennes?

'Popcorn. That's it. Yes,' she thinks.

It's a tiny sign, no saliva or taste-pore activation or anything, but she finds some popcorn in the sideboard and quickly pops the bag in the microwave. While it cooks, she takes the carrots out of the fridge to peel one, but instantly changes her mind. They're soggy. And that's not all. A few of them have what looks like hair on them, gray-green hair: penicillin, maybe. Disgusted, she throws them back in the vegetable tray, takes out a beer, and closes the fridge. The popcorn goes pop, pop, pop.

'You should eat, Marina love.'

I know.

She puts the popcorn in a bowl, takes it over to the sofa and turns on the TV. Chihuahua turned up the other day with a TV and now it lives on the living-room floor.

'Can I hook it up to my computer to watch movies?' Marina asked him.

But Chihuahua had other ideas: he said he'd found something in the closet that looked to him like a 'Cable cable'.

'Huh?' said Marina.

She was also going to ask, 'What were you doing rummaging around in my closet?' But Chihuahua was already dragging over the cable; a great long thing rolled up in a neurotic figure of eight which could only be his doing. They moved the TV to where the cable reached, plugged it in and NBC news blinked onto the screen. The presenter was a blond in a pantsuit, the day's dramas racing across her chest on a rotating sash, like a Miss Tragic Universe 2003.

So the cable was hooked up to cable TV. Marina couldn't believe her eyes. Chihuahua had never mentioned it. But then, so what if he had? She wouldn't have given it a second thought. She certainly wouldn't have gone out and bought a TV just to test the thing. Who could have known that all this time, lying in her closet, there was a portal to another dimension, to the day-to-day lives of the rich, of grown ups, of people who watch US TV when they get back from work to shake Mexico off, as if following a twenty-first century version of Manuel Carreño's *Manual of Urbanity and Good Manners* – 'Be sure to dismount from Mexico before entering the dining room'? Chihuahua was who. Chihuahua knew because he's a big-city boy. It was him who explained to her that the shoes hanging by their laces in the street mark drug-dealing spots; he also showed her who in the neighborhood steals the phone cables to peel them and sell the copper. What annoys Marina is that Chihuahua isn't even from the capital: he's from Ciudad Juárez. She once asked him, 'How much less provincial could your border town be than Xalapa?' To which he replied, 'Oh, Juárez is provincial, all right. But it's two countries' provinces at once.'

Chihuahua pronounces English the same way Linda does: seamlessly. Marina tries to copy him but he gets annoyed when she obsesses over his accent.

'You lot are the ones who are wrong with your litter-a-tour!' he snaps. 'It's called literature.'

For Chihuahua, 'you lot' means anyone from the green states. And that's anything south of the deserts. Marina likes arguing with him about this. It makes her feel more defined in her identity, like she belongs to something; in this case, to the South of Mexico. Chihuahua pointed out to her that all Southerners eat quesadillas without *queso* and sort of sing their sentences. She ticks both these boxes. Well, apart from the fact she wouldn't get a whole quesadilla down her these days, cheese or no cheese.

One piece of popcorn for every commercial. That's the deal she's made with her herself. And she's more or less sticking to it when the doorbell rings. Finally! She freezes on the spot. She knows Chihuahua can see her through the window, because many a night, before entering the mews, she watches the neighbors from across the street through their sheer curtains, which are just like hers. Unobserved, Marina studies the motionless figures, which look like cardboard cutouts offset by the blue light of the television, and she confirms another of her suspicions: that routine kills love.

After the doorbell, Marina eats four pieces of popcorn in a row. That makes twenty-three, or maybe twenty-five. The movie's soundtrack is the rain against the water tank: she likes watching the TV, not listening to it. Then, three bangs on the window facing out onto the street. Typical. She doesn't move. Chihuahua goes on banging. He must be soaked. Marina wants to know if he's drunk, so she stands up and opens the curtains with the most neutral face she can muster. But it's not Chihuahua. It's a woman. A stranger holding a black plastic bag above her head: a sorely ineffectual substitute for an umbrella. Her hand is resting on the window she's just pounded on for a fourth time. It's a small hand, and something about the way she rests it on the wet glass fills Marina with tenderness. It's as if she were holding it there waiting for Marina to do the same. Marina points at herself with her index finger.

'Me?'

The woman nods.

'Don't talk to strangers,' was one of the pearls of wisdom her brother gave her when she finally called home to confess she'd moved to Mexico City.

'Don't open car windows either: not to street vendors, not to the police.'

'I don't have a car,' Marina told him.

'Well, in case you happen to go in one,' he'd said. And she remembers this had pissed her off. Why didn't he say, 'Well, when you do have one'?

To open the main door to the mews Marina has to leave her house and run to the entryway. Oh, what the hell. She slips on her flip-flops, opens the door and makes a run for it. She hadn't taken into account the hail: now the floor drains are clogged and the central passageway is a river, out of which only the very tip of the bell pokes out. Marina opens the main door and the woman steps inside.

2002

Belldrop Mews is so called because, when my grandparents' house partially collapsed in the 1985 earthquake, a huge bronze bell set inside a niche on the facade fell and buried itself in what was the house's yard and is now the open passageway connecting all the houses in the mews. Almost all of us who live here have to skip over the tip of the bell (a chunk of metal protruding from the floor) to enter or exit our houses.

*

Agatha Christie dropped by with her friend, Beto's daughter, what's her name? Pina. What a god-awful name: the only thing that makes up for a name like that is that she's going to be an absolute knockout.

'Does your wife have a grave?' they asked me.

I told them she does and they gave me some flowers. Agatha Christie explained she bought them for her sister because today is the 353-day anniversary of Luz's death, and that this is a palindrome, so they went to buy her flowers from the garden center, but now there's no one to take them to the cemetery. I asked them if they learned the word palindrome in school and for some reason they burst into hysterics.

'Ana is my school,' Pina said.

Something I didn't tell them, but which comes to mind now that they've gone and I'm thinking about the flowers and the yellow sweater, is that perhaps what the Pérez-Walkers need to find solace is a machine like my Nina Simone PC: a direct line to the dead.

Noelia loved Nina Simone.

'Why did the gods make me big-bootied but not black?' she'd complain when we listened to her.

If you'd asked Noelia what she would have changed about herself, she would have answered that she'd like to be able to sing. Not that I ever asked her. There was no need. Noelia reminded you of these things, never let you forget her defects, as if to stop you from loving her too much.

'Come on, it was you who had a thing for the black girls, Alfonso.'

'That's true.'

'Did you put those flowers in water?'

'Of course, my brown sugar.'

'And count the days?'

'No chance. In my mind, you always died yesterday.'

*

'You know the type?' was something Noelia would say a lot, above all when she wanted to make sure that whoever she was talking to had understood whatever generalization she'd just come out with. For example, she might say about a nurse, 'She's one of those women who thinks she's really broken the mold, you know the type?' And about some anesthetist or another, 'That guy would bite his tongue till it bleeds, you know the type?' Or, about the owner of the garden center next door: 'He's the kind of man that crashes at the first sign of a curve, you know the type?'

I have to confess, I practically never knew the type she was on about, either because Noelia's definitions belonged to a vernacular I wasn't familiar with, or, more often than not, because she made them up off the top of her head. But after the first few years of extreme frustration (frustration for Noelia because I simply couldn't keep up with her), I ended up adopting a habit, one of many. Anything to keep the peace.

The truth is, – and I'm not saying this because I've worked out that Noelia, wherever she is, is reading what I write – I was fond of her generalizations. They were always original, or at least they seemed as much to me, someone who spent most of his life with his head in the clouds. Unlike me, my wife was in touch with the world: awake, aware of everything around her, including the mundane things that were lost on me and which it was my genuine pleasure to be made aware of. Like watching a good movie or reading a good book. At first they embarrassed me, but as time went on I came to respect the categories my wife invented. There was something almost Kantian about them: a will to develop a system. You-know-the-type was Noelia's way of organizing the people who came into our lives, and it has to be said that she was really quite good at it. She had a witch's intuition. One day an intern started working at the institute, and Noe, having only seen her one lunchtime, said to me, 'That one will climb the ladder faster than ivy, and good for her.'

Within a year, 'that one', with her measly Master's degree, had a position almost equivalent to mine, even though I, the fool that I am, hold not one but two PhDs.

The point is that I found a way to deal with you-know-the-type so that even in my social ignorance I could follow the conversation, and Noelia could build upon her catalogue of types at her leisure, convinced that I was following her to a T. I've always been proud of this excellent little solution, but in fact I ripped it off from Beto's wife.

Before her sudden disappearance from the mews, I noticed that Chela, when she didn't understand what we were talking about at the table after dinner – which was basically every time we talked about politics, which was basically every time we stayed up talking at the table after dinner – pulled a very specific face: one that made her seem interested, reflective, ever so slightly dissenting, and which masked her absolute ignorance. The face was simple: she pursed her lips. Obviously, this had a far more satisfactory effect on her, who's a peach, than on a face like mine, which has more of an overripe-papaya look about it. But I copied her anyway, adding to it from my own cache a simultaneous, slow nod. And unbelievably, it worked. So when, for example, Noelia said to me, 'Blond but with her roots grown out, you know the type?', I would purse my lips and nod slowly, and she, satisfied she'd made it perfectly clear what kind of creature we were talking about, would happily babble on without having to stop for another round of frustrating elucidations.

Deep down, I think my Noe wasn't just blunt. She had a sharper psychological instinct than those women who think they know it all, who think they're wise owls: the humanitees, Noelia called my colleagues at the institute, with a double ee. The humanitees thought – like almost all the humanities graduates, including me – that they were better than everyone else. 'Just that little bit more sensitive, that little bit more humane than the rest of humanity,' is how my wife put it. The humanitees turned their noses up at Noelia because she spoke openly about how much TV she watched in her – rare – free moments. But really they were deeply envious of her career, which was solid as a rock and way – but really way – better remunerated. They pitied her for not having children, but deep down envied her independence; the same independence they'd been so quick to boast about in their youths before trading it in for little Timmy, Tommy and Tammy, and a jealous husband. You can't ask a humanitee if she likes cooking, because she'll accuse you of protracting the phallocentric patriarchy. On the other hand, if she finds out that the man in a couple takes care of the cooking – as is, or was, the case in our house – she'll only ever see him as a hen-pecked husband.

The humanitees have very clear codes when they want to flatter one another, and are the undisputed champions of the backhanded compliment. If she doesn't think much of some-one, a humanitee will say, 'She's a real fighter.' But a woman she admires is 'the boss of herself'. Noe once whispered in my ear, 'Of course she is, because a humanitee could boss her way out of a paper bag.'

'The humanitees wear indigenous Mexican outfits, but designer, you know the type?' And yes, I knew the type, or I didn't but Noelia taught me to see them that way. She could smell the male intellectual's thinly disguised machismo a mile off, while the humanitees were blind to it. I – who was known to be happily married, am ugly, and know how to pretend I'm listening – almost always caught wind of who was all over who from the secretaries, and tried to retain the information, at least until dinner time, so I could pass it on to Noelia, because she loved that kind of thing: it was like steak to her scandalmonger's soul.

'Poor thing,' she'd say of the humanitee-lover in question, 'this is going to end in tears.'

'What makes you say that?' I'd ask, genuinely clueless.

'Oh, Alfonso, because he's clearly one of those men who buys his woman roses only to prick her with the thorns.'

And I'd nod, and purse my lips.

Was it dishonesty, all this pretending I knew the type? Of course, but of the generous, unselfish kind: the kind that makes marriages last.

'He's one of those people who nods to make it look like he's following the conversation, you know the type?'

I know it well. And, Noe, now that you're around here somewhere, let me tell you that yesterday in a bookstore café I saw a book called *Oh Lord, Won't You Make Me a Widow*, and it gave me a profound feeling of pity, the kind I haven't felt for such a long time, other than toward myself. I'd rather have my clean pain than the dirty pain of wishing for pain.

'What's it about?'

'I don't know. I didn't buy it.'

'And what's all that crap about clean pain?'

'It's something Agatha Christie told me. When you and Luz

died she decided to borrow every book on death and grief she could find in the library, then she'd come over to give me a weekly round-up of her findings. One Sunday she brought a Zen manual and explained to me that our grief, hers for her sister and mine for you, constituted clean pain. But if, for example, we'd been hurting because a boy we liked wasn't into us, well that was dirty pain, because it was no more than an invention, a pain made up in our heads, because in fact we didn't know, nor could we ever really know if the boy in question was into us or not.'

'Oh, that's so cute.'

'I know, right? And I asked her if she liked the boy in question but she went all skittish and started reading koans out loud. I might buy that book. Not the Zen manual, the one about the widow, to tell you about it.'

'Go for it, love, but don't eat in that café anymore; you know those cheap wholegrain muffins are full of trans fats.'

'You're right, I'm better off making a little soup.'

'Attaboy. And give The Girls a bath, will you? They're losing the glow in their cheeks.'

*

'There are two basic human conditions,' Noelia liked to explain during her most conflictive decade around the issue, and usually on her second tequila. 'Being a child and being a procreator.'

I'd nod. She'd go on.

'I choose to experience just one of the two conditions. Does that mean that in some way I'm choosing to be only half? It's a complicated equation, socially speaking. If you participate in both conditions, it's like you're two people: you're a daughter and a mother. I choose to be no more than one, no more than one person. There's a fair amount of coherence in that, isn't there? Well, not for other people. For other people, being no more than one person is like being less than one. Though not if you're a man, of course. No, that goes without saying. I'll put it in female terms: if you're no more than one, one woman, they assume you're fulfilling half of your human condition, or female condition, if you like. The point is – don't walk away, Alfonso –, if you're one, you're half. Now tell me where's the logic in that.'

'I didn't make the rules,' I'd say.

'But you are an anthropologist.'

'Yes, but I study pre-Hispanic diets.'

*

The sweater.

A few days ago, Linda walked into the bar carrying something yellow in her hands. When they brought her her vodka, we made a toast and she spread it out on the table. It was a small sweater. Next she pulled out a sewing kit from her bag, and from the sewing kit a needle, some scissors, and half a dozen spools of thick thread. While we sipped our drinks she embroidered diamonds, squares, circles and semicircles onto the sweater at random. At a certain point she passed it to me. I pulled back my chair and lay the sweater out on my lap. It was bigger than the clothes I usually buy for The Girls, but sat snug over my knees. It was dirty. I ran a finger over the newly sewn shapes; the taut stitching felt soft compared to the sweater itself, which was itchy. It looked like something from another era, like the knee-length socks and the micro shorts we used to wear in my day. Nobody knits itchy sweaters anymore, especially not for children. I pulled off my ring and passed it to Linda. She ran her finger around it, but didn't put it on. Then she read the inscription inside and asked, 'Umami?'

'Umami is one of the five basic flavors our taste buds can identify. The others, the ones we all know, are sweet, salty, bitter and sour. Then there's umami, more or less new to us in the West. We're talking a century or so. It's a Japanese word. It means delicious.'

I stopped to draw breath and the two of us laughed because I'd blurted all of this out in one go, like one of those machines in Italian churches you feed money to illuminate the altarpiece for a minute. Linda gave me back the ring. I gave her back the sweater, and she threaded the needle with purple cotton. Linda lives in the mews; I must have explained umami to her a hundred times, and in a far less robotic manner. In any case, ever generous, she rested the needle in the sweater and calmly asked, 'What does it taste of?'

'That's the thing,' I told her. 'Since we don't recognize the taste, the best way for me to describe it is as something to get your chops around, something satisfying. In English they say *seivori*.

'Savory?' she pronounced in perfect English.

'That's right, or sometimes they'll just say meaty.'

'I'm afraid I've never been able to get my head around it, Alf.'

'The easiest way to understand it is this: think about pasta. Imagine a portion of spaghetti. It's nothing; doesn't taste of anything. Carbohydrates, plain and simple. But if you add umami, if you throw in a bit of Parmesan or tomato or eggplant, then bingo! You've got yourself a meal.'

She nodded for a long time, and that was it. When she went (we never leave the Mustard Mug together), I was left in a state of confusion. I'd had an almost identical conversation once before; with a woman I barely knew and whom I ended up marrying.

*

For Noelia, the fact that her theories about offspringhood proved to be simplistic or naive only served to strengthen her main argument that you never fully mature if you don't move on to the second human condition; to the other side; to not being only a child, but also a progenitor (prolongation of the species, genetic dissemination, all those things). In other words, Noelia wanted her mysticology of offspringhood to be self-evident, above all in the areas relating to immaturity. For example, in a *modus noellendo noellens*:

If you're only a daughter, something in you hasn't fully matured.

As such, your arguments will necessarily be puerile.

And the more puerile your arguments, the more proof there is for the general theory that offspringhood is an irredeemably immature state.

And it wasn't like my profession made me particularly pedantic in terms of scientific proofs, which meant that, as far as I recall, I never had any issue going along with Noelia's theories, which might, say, allow us to have sorbet and tequila for breakfast some Sundays, or buy a plane ticket every now and again and set off to random destinations, just because.

*

My wife was a perfect blend of civilized and primitive. She had a pure, savage mind: Levi-Strauss would have drooled all over her. Hand in hand with her medical finesse, Noelia Vargas Vargas also had a thing for pagan rituals. Despite knowing full well that nicotine upsets the gut, for years she sustained the idea that she couldn't go to the bathroom without the helping nudge of a Raleigh. On top of that, she consulted her horoscope every day as soon as she woke up. Without a hint of irony. She checked it like most people check the weather forecast. If her horoscope revealed something negative, she would sulk; if it was positive, she'd be happy as Larry. This habit of hers irritated me during the first years of our marriage. I couldn't understand how an intelligent woman could decide the mood of her day based on something that – as she herself would admit – didn't have the least logical founding. In practice, however, her rational, sharp side, – masterfully employed in most other areas of her life – was disconnected from her moods. She used her horoscope like a guide, despite knowing perfectly well that they were no more than words written by a harried astrologer, or, as she herself suspected, by the harried astrologer's minions. It's not that Noelia believed in her stars: she believed in her horoscope. She needed it to start the day. Just like some people can't leave the house without making the sign of the cross, or without a coffee inside them. Among the many components of my wife's emotional machinery, the damn horoscope was the switch: one paragraph that determined in which mood she'd shift from sleep to wakefulness. Luckily, the effect would wear off over the course of the morning. It was a terrible ritual, but short-lived.

Right up until she died, Noelia received a weekly magazine called *Astros*, written by a certain *Madame* Elisabeta. For the last five years she had it sent to her email, but before that, for what felt like a million years, she had it delivered. And before that, when I first met her, Noelia read her horoscope in the newspaper. Every morning, she would pop out of her bachelorette apartment in her slippers to buy it. So rigorous was she in her routine that the vendor billed her weekly. I was horrified by her horoscope habit, but loved having the newspaper first thing in the morning: it was one of those wonders a relationship only knows in its early phase, like doing it in the kitchen.

Astros magazine gave you a seven-day horoscope personalized to your sign, ascendance, and even your name, which someone typed directly onto your typed copy (you could tell from how the letters of *Noelia* formed a zigzag, with those dainty typographical dances produced by typewriters). As you can imagine, it wasn't a cheap publication.

One day, Noelia welcomed into her consultation room none other than Madame Elisabeta. She turned out to be a pale, obese fifty-something with her heart in a terrible state. She was friendly and foulmouthed. The a at the end of her name, Noelia soon learned, had been her mother's idea, and wasn't just some half-baked pseudonym. At first, Noelia didn't say anything about the magazine, because in her role as a cardiologist she tended to keep her superstitions to herself. She fitted Madame's pacemaker and that was that. Except, it being December, the patient – saved in the nick of time and eternally grateful – invited us to her magazine's Christmas party. I was happy to go along, both out of anthropological curiosity and also because I was convinced that, on witnessing the commercial inner workings of Elisabeta's magazine, Noelia would finally recognize her ongoing error. But the event turned out to be nothing like what either of us expected. For starters, it was in Elisabeta's house: a big, shabby apartment where she lived with a parrot and a much younger woman who served as both lover and nurse, as well as helping out with the magazine, the cleaning, and the astral cards. Everyone referred to her as Pisces. I remember Pisces as being permanently positioned on Elisabeta's lap. There were others at the party: some astrologers, musicians, and a couple of intellectuals who could actually see beyond the shadow of their egos, which is unusual. Dinner consisted of rum (with a dash of punch), and a mountain of takeaway pizzas. As soon as we arrived, Pisces made us mark our preferred toppings on a list, and at some point she must have called to order them because not long after they turned up at the door. Fat old Elisabeta was poor as a church mouse and esoteric in the extreme, but she understood, long before Google did, the value of a seemingly personalized service.

Before I knew it, that humble soirée had washed away the bad taste in my mouth I'd had every morning on waking up to Noe and her horoscope. The fact that *Madame* existed, and that her stars were specked with parakeet feathers, cheap pepperoni, and a lustful and tender lesbian romance put me at peace with the whole issue of the horoscopes. I can't really explain why.

Everyone knows that a horoscope is like a shell: it needs to be wide and hollow enough to accommodate exactly what we need to hear. But I got tired of explaining this to Noelia, who knew it full well anyway. The change in my perception didn't occur at this superficial level (I knew that the tried-and-tested recipe – add together a planet, an illness, and a sudden windfall, whip it up into a paragraph and you've got yourself a horoscope! – still applied), but at a deeper one: as formulaic as they might be, those texts didn't appear out of nowhere. There was an author behind every one: and not some evil corporation, but a middle-aged lady who really did believe in the stars. The signs of the zodiac were Elisabeta's dearly beloved characters. She brought them to life each week with her pen, just as worse writers have done with worse characters. The open nature of *Astros* – its capacity for multiple interpretations – wasn't a failing. On the contrary, this was the characteristic – the only one, but still – it shared with all great literature: its universal ambition.

I never mentioned any of this to Noelia because I could have written her an entire essay on it (*Astrology is a Humanism*) and still she would have raised her eyebrows and told me how typically Virgo that was of me. But the point is that my rationalization of astrology as a literary art form worked wonders for me. It opened the doors to a level of tolerance I'd neither possessed nor managed to feign over the previous years, and which was the main culprit behind our early morning squabbles. From that moment on, on the days when Noelia announced over breakfast that Mercury was in retrograde, I immediately switched into consolatory mode. I would stroke her hair, compliment her, give her little pinches on her butt, and paw at her as she left for work. If, on the other hand, Noelia merrily announced something like, 'Tonight, a benevolent full moon will light my house of relationships and fall in line with Neptune,' I'd think, 'This morning she'll be strong.' And this was like a license for me to not be strong.

Marriage is nothing but a relay race, and Noelia's daily horoscopes became my handoff cues. And that's how the very thing I'd accused her of for years – having an astrological dependence – became true of me too.

*

'If all else fails,' I would say to Noelia in the periodic moments when it seemed that this time I wasn't going to finish an article, let alone get through the protracted process of revision, sending, editing, rejection, guaranteed humiliation, etc., etc. that academic life implies, 'let's go and live by the sea and I'll grow papayas.'

Growing papayas was my crowning ambition.

For Noelia, on the other hand, failure didn't factor in her professional life. Even when she was totally fed up, her reaction was never to jack it all in. Instead, she focused on the future; on 'when I retire'.

'When I retire,' she'd say, 'we'll install a jacuzzi in the yard.'

But we never did. Noelia Vargas Vargas died working. Páez would bring her printouts of ECGs which she'd read in bed. She died as she lived: among other people's heartbeats.

Systole and diastole, and that was that.

*

The finite range of rhetorical questions that plague a widower (Why? Why me? Why Noelia? Why not me?) can be deleted with the click of a button.

Are you sure you want to delete the bit about you feeling not unlike how the house looked after the 1985 quake?

As sure as eggs are eggs, Nina. Let an old widower have one tear-free space, one lucid page, however false it may read: click.

*

I'll start at the beginning.

I met Noelia in 1972 at the National School of Anthropology. She came to a seminar which I gave every year (*The Mexican Diet: Past and Present*) because she was frustrated by the weight problems killing off her patients, and determined to resolve the issue, once and for all. The idea was to attack it from a historical perspective. She wanted to educate herself. She was a doctor, she explained, and knew the many causes and consequences of carrying excess weight – her own included – like the back of her hand. (Exaggerating was her way of winning over the audience.) She used the word 'epidemic' at a time when fatness was considered to be a mere issue of will power. She hijacked ten minutes of my session, sounding off to everyone present about the cardiac conditions exacerbated by the consumption of processed food. My co-author from that time, who was both the smartest and brashest man I ever worked with, sniffed at her.

I've thanked him for this show of pedantry on numerous occasions, though never in person. His crescendo of rude little grunts during those ten minutes inevitably put me on Noelia's side. I already knew her by name, because she was one of those people who stands up and introduces herself before making a comment, you know the type?

I answered her calmly, congratulated her on her worthy mission, and talked to her about the historical role of food as celebration and the national role of food as love. I underlined the importance of eating protein and umami to promote the feeling of satiation, and for the umpteenth time I sung the praises of amaranth and its huge protein content. There were more questions afterward, probably about my main topic, because no one likes to hear that amaranth is a pseudo-cereal (it throws them into a tizzy: 'If it tastes like a cereal and smells like a cereal, then it must be a type of grain, like rice, or wheat'). And the whole thing would have ended right there if it hadn't been for Noelia coming up to me at the end of the conference to ask what this umami was, and me answering, in part because it was true, 'Ah, but you can only really explain umami in a restaurant.'

That's how it all began, and that night we had dinner and went to bed together, and then I lost the plot for a year, shacked up with Memphis, had a dream, looked for Noelia, married her – all thanks to umami – and then, as quickly as they'd come around, the seventies were over and 1982 was upon us: the country fell apart and soon afterward, one Sunday, on the outskirts of Chiconcuac, I fell off my bike.

*

I'm going to say it now, while I can't feel Noelia anywhere near: today I went to the cemetery and got lost. It took me twenty minutes to find her gravestone, even though I know exactly where it is. It was as if someone had removed my chip. That can't be normal.

*

The Mexican peso crashing in 1982 wasn't anything new, but me falling off my bike certainly was. I'd been a cyclist all my life and had never suffered more than a scratch. Then, before I knew it, I'd split my left tibia in three pieces and shattered my collarbone. My helmet saved my life, but I still had a few fractures in my skull and two hematomas that took years to be absorbed. Or maybe months, but they were some seriously long months.

It wasn't the first, nor would it be the last financial melt-down the country would see, but that didn't mean it was any less of a nightmare. The Mexdollar debacle hit us right between the balls. Practically overnight, what few savings we had were reduced to a pittance, and what was left went on the hospital bill. Thanks to Noelia I received the best medical attention imaginable. But not even that stopped me having to take time off work. I didn't leave the house for four glorious months. I drew in bed (very Frida Kahlo, but *sans* the tash, because every morning Doña Sara would bring me my shaving stuff). From that prostrate position, and from so much staring out the window, for the first time I had the feeling our great property was being wasted.

I inherited pigheadedness along with the land, and refused point black to sell up to the real-estate investment parasites. But while I convalesced in the house, all doped up and serene, it occurred to me that I too could make a profit off my plot, why not? Another important factor was that I was spending more time than ever in the company of Doña Sara, who helped us in the house and who, during that period, trotted up and down the stairs with my meals. And Doña Sara, who talked non-stop, whether there was someone there to listen or not, lived in a rented apartment. All day long she'd blather on to me about this or that neighbor, or complain about the landlord, a 'waste of space' who did nothing but 'live off his tenants' rent'. This living off your tenants' rent didn't seem too bad an idea to me in the midst of the financial crisis. And that's more or less how the seed for the mews was sown. But the truly defining factors in its construction, which didn't begin until five years later, were the sketches I produced, and the damage caused by the infamous earthquake of 1985.

*

We always said we came to the decision together, but deep down I think the choice not to have children (and later on to have them) was hers. I think I would have gone along with whatever she decided. We never put it in those exact terms, but there's no doubt that I was always more comfortable granting her wishes than imposing my own. Conceding makes you feel like a good person. Imposing your wishes makes you feel pushy. I had an extraordinarily domineering father, who I always did everything in my power to avoid resembling. And one surefire way to make sure you don't turn into a pushy father is to not become a father at all. Children scared me. Noelia was the eldest of four kids. She started changing diapers aged six. I'm an only child. I think of the diaper not as a great invention but as a deeply mystifying artifact, and I'm as much disgusted by the things themselves as by their contents.

'That,' remarks Noelia, 'is your offspringhood speaking.'

And that may be. But when later I asked Páez his thoughts on the matter he just answered, 'Diapers? Never heard of him…'

*

'Am I going senile?' is what I wish I could ask Páez.

*

Sometimes I wake up in the middle of the night and think about how much I took the name Noelia Vargas Vargas for granted. My legs fill up with a kind of black energy and I want to kick something. But the most I ever do is punch the bedspread; more like a child throwing a tantrum than a fully grown, raging man. I should have used her name so much more. I should have taken it in vain. I threw away thousands, millions of chances to savor it in my mouth. When I spoke about her I would say 'my wife'. When I called her I said 'love'. When I messaged her I wouldn't even greet her. I wrote pithily, as if we were immortal:

'You home for lunch?'

*

Noelia liked the word 'project'. It made her feel organized. She used to say that we shared a 'life project'. But, with all due respect and not even caring if she reads this, I think she never fully understood what the term entails. A project is a thing you start up, get excited about, get stuck on, lock horns with, and later, if you're proud and bold and humble and arrogant and very stubborn, you tackle all the loose ends and finish it. What usually follows is a postnatal bewildered phase, and then finally a feeling of serenity comes over you, and with that the sad realization that nothing has changed, and that in all likelihood nobody really cares about your work. Then comes a kind of peace, and after that, God knows how, the seed of curiosity for a new project sprouts in you. You set about replowing the soil and start all over again. That's how I've worked my entire life. That's how I've done everything I've ever done: the mews, the Modern *Milpa*, every single publication. Only now I can't seem to formulate a plan of attack. The plants are dying around me. I bathe The Girls grudgingly and half-heartedly. I just drink and write short paragraphs that don't really follow on from one another and that I bet not even Nina Simone is that fussed about. I'm not even a good drinker. By the third tequila I have to have a lie down, and if I sit down to write, everything comes out jumbled. And with things as they are – with no beginning, no end, no bonus points for publishing these pages – I've got neither a project nor any chance of getting over this lack-luster routine. I'll probably go on like this for the rest of my days. Linda asked me the other afternoon if we might not be turning into alcoholics. I told her we weren't, that we're C4 plants like amaranth: more efficient in our use of liquids, and capable of producing the same amount of biomass with a smaller amount of water.

'Biomass?' she asked.

'Tears,' I said.

All I'm saying with this project business is that Noelia undervalued my capacity for coming up with projects. She thought she had it in her as well. And while she had so many more talents than I did, I have to say that in this one thing I outdid her. She never had to work in that self-fueling, self-sustaining way, because she had one, ongoing assignment: a constant line of patients. And they were like the same patient repeated interminably. That's why something in me protested when she'd use the word project. A silent protest, obviously, because Noelia would talk about the 'life project' with unflagging authority, oozing self-confidence as if she were explaining the circulatory system. Even her voice changed. She might say, for example, in that firm tone of hers, 'Alfonso, you agree this whole reproduction business doesn't have any place in our life project, right?'

And what would I say? I can't even remember now. I smiled at her, I guess. Or said, 'Right.' And the truth is I did agree with her. Noelia and I always agreed. When we didn't agree on something, we got over it straight away. We would shout at each other; she had a penchant for slamming doors, and I for grabbing my jacket and walking around the block. And that would be that. We'd be over it. But it's different now. Now we really are in deadlock. Now I'd give anything for one of our fights.

Here's my final say on her misusage of the term. If what we shared had indeed been a life project, we would have wrapped it up together. I thought about it at the time, but knew that she wouldn't have any of it, just as I wouldn't have been able to go through with it. So our life together wasn't a project, then; it was the other kind of commitment: the ongoing-assignment kind. Which would also explain why the longer she's gone, the more I seem to need her.

*

The world is full of iotas, iguanas, indents, ignoramuses, indoctrinators, imposers, ifs and illusions. If you ask me, we're nothing but a bunch of idiots.

*

I'm in a rotten mood after reading an article in today's paper in which, once again, they propagate the myth that it was only corn that was grown on the manmade *chinampa* islands of Lake Xochimilco. Please! How many more studies do we have to publish before the schools will teach the truth: that they planted *huautli*, sacred amaranth, there. It was all over the place, and the Mexica ate the stem, leaves, and seeds, which they milled to make flour. The flour constituted a foodstuff of course, but it was also used for offerings. The Mexica built figurines of gods, piercing them with small thorns which they'd already stuck into their own flesh to catch a drop of blood. The Spanish were no fools banning amaranth: having one less source of energy was fine by them as long as it meant fewer local rituals to write off. They razed kilometers of plantations, and came up with severe punishments for whoever planted it. And with that, *huautli* was wiped from the face of their land and erased from memory, with the kind of decisive success that only the most heavily armed militaries can pull off. They masterminded a new history, – 'There's only ever been corn here!' – and we swallowed it. In Mexico we became obsessed with *milpas*; some of us still are, two decades and several books later. And yes, yes, *milpas* are fascinating, as are the pyramids. But there's something beyond the monumental; something just as beautiful yet much simpler, that takes place in the private lives of others: holiness on a familial scale, where food and ritual are one and the same.

But none of those little things – amaranth, or the daily miracles of faith and routine – are of any interest to pop scientists or documentary makers, who have a tendency to confuse greatness, grandeur, and grandiloquence. Either that, or they simply don't want to see it. Exactly the same as the tour guides who refuse to explain that the two windows in the famous Tulum pyramid are actually a form of lighthouse. They've done tests. People from the institute used candles to project light through the opening as the Mayans did to guide their small boats along the sole canal that spared them from having to run aground on the rocky peninsula.

The Mesoamerican reef is the second largest in the world: it starts in Yucatán and ends in Honduras. It's fascinating to see how they navigated the area, but the hoteliers on the coast don't seem to think so.

'A lighthouse!' they say. 'Boring! Better to cross that out and write in the official texts "A temple".' As if it were better to be fanatical than resourceful!

It winds me up, even now, that so many of our discoveries are systematically ignored at the hands of the *ignoramus machistus pharaonicus*. Sometimes I honestly think that we're only working in the institute for the benefit of gringo academics: we're their manufacturers of juicy details. The things we discover through our research in this country will only see the light of day years later, over there. And by there I mean, at a safe distance from the Mexican Secretariat of Public Education. It'll go like this: one day some overeducated little gringo who hasn't eaten a single crumb of amaranth in his life is going to write a book call *Amaranthus*, and in that book he'll include all the stuff I've been saying for years. Or maybe he'll use the Náhuatl word, to give it an autochthonous edge: *Huautli for Dummies*, on sale in all good retailers and airports. They'll offer the gringo tenure in Berkeley, and then the Chinese, who already plant more amaranth than anyone, will have themselves a whole new market: middle-class America (so lost in questions of diet, so lacking in tradition, so at the mercy of the latest food-group elimination fad). Tell Me What To Eat could be a description in five words of the average, educated gringo. They'll put that processed Chinese amaranth in shiny packaging, advertise it on TV and export it like plastic toys. In Mexico we'll buy it at crazy prices, and if you dare try and tell a kid it's no more than an *alegría,* those seed bars we've always eaten in Mexico, he'll knock you out with his fortified fist. I can only hope I'm dead by then.

*

Every now and then I take a trip to the little corner store, for beer or something, but Beto does my big shops, for which I'm very grateful. And I'm not just saying that in case I drop dead at my laptop. I've been thinking about this ever since Noelia died: Which of the neighbors is going to let people know if I kick the bucket? And who would they tell? The institute? And my colleagues, what would they do? Put me in a box with the institute's initials on it? Bury me among some ruins like a national heritage piece? I doubt it. Whoever finds me will have to do no more than dump me, unceremoniously, out with the trash. Maybe I'll start to smell. Me, who always scrubbed up so well! My guess is that Beto will be the first to get a whiff of me, when he brings the groceries. Hence why, even though I didn't tell him it was for this reason, I gave him a set of keys. Whenever I hear him come in I go downstairs and offer him a beer – just because; because we're alive –, and he almost always accepts. We sit out on the terrace overlooking the dead MM, where once upon a time the deep pink of the amaranth flowers swayed in the wind, and we make fruitless plans to pull up the dead plants and put in a barbecue or a small swimming pool. We chat about anything and everything until it's time for him to collect his daughter from ballet, or whatever it is. Beto talks to me and asks me questions; he's generous and takes an interest. Now that I think about it, Beto is one of very few men I've met in my life who I feel I can trust. Maybe because his wife left him. Or maybe that's why she left. Deep down, I think I'm one of those types, too. But maybe it's just my ego talking, and really I'm a person who inspires pure indifference. Better indifference than repugnance, of course, but it's not as honorable as trust. Not a callous indifference, not at all, but rather the natural product of years spent trying to go by unnoticed. Add chronic shyness to a good marriage and a series of solitary habits and you've got a perfect recipe for disappearance. You turn into a kind of Casper the Ghost: friendly but one hundred percent dispensable. As a boy, if anyone asked me which magic power I'd choose, I always went for time travel. I wanted to see without being seen. And really I think that this is what defines all anthropologists: a natural tendency to observe and a healthy dose of curiosity for all things human, but without ever reaching the levels of sensibility of the artist, the solemnity of the philosopher, or the opportunism of the lawyer. Our healthy curiosity isn't quite the systematic, slightly obsessive rigor of the spy or the scientist, and we're far from boasting the deductive inventiveness of the sociologist, or the novelist's discipline. But I guess you could say we have a little of all these things, if you're a glass-half-full kind of guy.

*

After a few days of rigorous observation I can confirm that *a*) people still dodge me on the street (they don't look at me, but they do still step out of my way, which means, physically speaking at least, I'm still perceptible), and *b*) for the first time this year I'm not thinking about dying soon, not now I can feel a project coming on (albeit one within the limits imposed by permanent grief). I have no intention of dying, not now that I've teamed up with Nina Simone, AKA Brown Sugar, and, for the first time in forty years, I'm daring to write without footnotes.

*

This is my new life on sabbatical: I don't set a morning alarm, and my eyes open automatically sometime between eight and nine. Considering the horror stories I was told as a boy, it seems I'm one of the lucky ones. Or maybe it's not that all old folk get insomnia, just that they like to exaggerate. If I had a kid to guilt-trip about how early I rise, believe me I would.

Once up, I shower, get dressed, and make myself a coffee. I've gone back to drinking it how I did when I was a pretentious student and believed that the devil was in the detail, as long as that detail was European: from an Italian stovetop espresso maker, straight. Noelia liked coffee from the machine, and since it didn't taste of anything, we consumed it in quantities wholly inappropriate for people our age.

After that I eat a banana or an egg, depending on supplies. I dress The Girls, and all three of us sit in the study, me in front of Nina Simone. Then I spend the morning writing intensively, making sure not to consult any sources other than my heart and my head. I take a break at midday to have a drink in the Mustard Mug, and raise a toast with Linda. Then I grab something to eat from one of the three stands along my block (because I've realized cooking for one is about as much fun as poking yourself in the eye with a stick). I've been plodding along like this for three weeks. I write intensively but also delete a lot because I want to do it properly: if I can't tell everything in order, I want at least to get out the important stuff.

A couple of days ago I gave the document a title page. In big letters, in the middle of the page, I wrote, *Noelia.* Then I added her surnames, and then I deleted them again. Her name isn't big enough for her. I wrote, *Umami.* It's a bit of a daft title because I've already written a book with that name, one that contains purely food-anthropological theory. But for now I think I'll leave it like that, because, at the same time, *Umami* is the perfect title. Trying to explain who my wife was is just as necessary and impossible as explaining umami: that flavor that floods your taste buds without you being able to quite put your finger on it. Complex and at the same time clean and round, just like Noelia was: as distinguishable as she was unpredictable. *Umami* is the perfect title because nobody would understand it, just as I never fully understood Noelia Vargas Vargas. Maybe that's why I never got bored of her. Maybe that's all love is. Maybe that's all writing is: an attempt to put someone in words, even when you know full well that that person is a kaleidoscope: their thousand reflections in the eye of a fly.

From time to time I read some of my passages out loud. They tend to be as rhetorical and inadequate as the one I've just written, and on the whole I delete them. You might think that if I'm reading parts out loud it's for The Girls' benefit, but I've not entirely lost the plot. Not yet. I'm quite aware that if I die it won't be The Girls who raise the alarm.

By the way, in case I do die, I'd like to leave something in writing:

> To whoever finds me and has to go to the trouble of throwing me out with the trash:
> THANKS, buddy!
> And also: I hereby hand you custody of The Girls.
> They are to be cleaned with a damp cloth.
> Do not, under any circumstances, submerge them in water.
> Cheers!

*

An anecdote came to mind when I wrote 'AKA' a few pages back. Back in the eighties, I was invited by the Complutense de Madrid (which wasn't as bad then as it is now, but worse) to give a course on pre-Hispanic diets, creole gastronomic fusion, *milpas*: all those things I can teach with my eyes closed. I slipped a selection of dry, multicolor corncobs through customs to spark the students' interest and stayed in Madrid for one complete semester, during which, for the first and last time in our lives together, Noelia and I wrote each other letters. Noelia kept all of mine, and one day last year, when she was already very ill, she asked me to read them to her. At some point I read out a passage where I'd used the word 'knockout'.

'What?' said Noelia.

'Knockout,' I said slowly, trying to improve my lousy English pronunciation.

'Yes, I heard you, but I don't know what that is. Like in boxing?'

'Exactly.'

'Let's see, bring it here.'

I pointed to the sentence in the letter, and she immediately burst into a fit of giggles; so intense that I caught them too. We laughed until we cried. We hadn't laughed like that since before we found out about her cancer, perhaps even earlier. When at last we got a hold of ourselves, I asked her what it had all been about. It turned out that throughout our entire marriage, every time I had used the acronym KO, she had read OK.

'I remember this, it was hilarious.'

'But couldn't you see it was exactly the reverse of OK?'

'I thought it was your dyslexia.'

'What dyslexia?'

'I don't know, yours. I always thought it was your own very particular brand of dyslexia.'

'You never brought it up!'

'Well, that makes us even.'

'Even how?'

'Even because you never mentioned that my miserable morning stars cheered you up!'

*

I gave Marina the Joaquín Sorolla book today. I think it would have made Noelia happy. Or maybe not, because it was her favorite, but she definitely would have agreed that if having it around depresses me, better to pass it on to the aspiring painter.

While I was teaching in Madrid, Noelia came and spent two weeks with me and became obsessed with the Sorolla Museum, mainly because it was right next to the house and had a cool yard where you could sit and read under a tree. It didn't have a café, which meant there weren't any waiters: Noelia didn't rub along with Madrid's waiters. Some afternoons we'd go together to see the Sorollas. Art wasn't her thing on the whole, but after a few glasses of wine and some tapas, boy, did she get into her painting. On the weekends, which is to say, on the days when we would head out for an aperitif, Noelia would refuse to wear her glasses; a vain habit which also meant she only saw blurry versions of Sorolla's oils. Where others would stand back and appreciate a vast landscape from afar, she'd have to get right up close, and saw nothing but brushstrokes. The clumsy chaos of oil paint smudged on canvas with a spatula; the distorted, screwball delight that were Sorolla's dabs up close convinced Noelia that she was admiring an abstract painter. Before we went back to Mexico I got her the exhibition catalog. She flicked through it with her surgical glasses on and was utterly taken aback, a little disappointed even. But later she grew fond of Sorolla, and the catalogue was always lying around somewhere in the living room.

Along with the book, I gave Marina a photo of Noelia and commissioned a portrait.

*

I've got a new, corrosive obsession: regret distilled to its purest form. For thirty years, at the end of each week, Noelia would throw her issue of *Astros* in the trash. What a damned stupid thing to do! If I had them now, I could chart my wife's morning moods over our thirty-year period of cohabitation. That would have been a real project. In my insomnia, I even considered hunting down Madame Elisabeta to ask her for the back issues. She must keep a private archive somewhere in her ramshackle apartment on Avenida Revolución, in metal filing cabinets decorated with gold star stickers. But just the thought of Elisabeta possibly also being dead – her and her parakeet – was enough to dissuade me from getting in touch. I'm scared I'll find out who took over writing *Astros*. Maybe Pisces is rehashing old issues, or publishing Google Translate versions of some obscure Polish astrology website. That's why I don't look into it, you understand. Not because I would have regretted hearing that Pisces had been left on her own. Quite the opposite. Lately, despite myself, seeing other people widowed only makes me want to say, 'Come on then, let's see how you like it.'

2001

I 'm all alone except for Cleo and the trees. But the trees
don't count because they're too tall and they don't talk
to me. Cleo is black with some brown, and she's furry, and
she's the oldest of all Emma's dogs. I scratch her belly until
her ziplings call her from somewhere and she goes racing to
them. I don't have any dogs. Not here, and not in Mexico.
Olmo and I are always asking for one, but Theo is allergic and
Ana wants a cat. Even if I don't have any dogs I still know
that dogs talk to each other, and I still know that if something is more or less the same size as you and it lives in the
same house as you, then that thing is your zipling. Cleo lives
with her ziplings and with Emma. Emma's house smells of
chimney and dog and sometimes of wet dog. She has big fat
rugs on the floor with weird drawings on them that make you
dizzy if you stare at them, and she has wooden masks on the
walls. Everything makes you feel like it's Christmas. Apart
from the masks. The masks make you feel like it's Halloween.

Cleo runs off, forgets all about me and doesn't come back.
Now I can see chestnuts everywhere and chanterelle nowhere.
The chanterelles are hiding and I am sick of looking for them.

I want to go back to the house but I don't know which way it is. I think maybe down, because we've been walking up and up and up. I follow Cleo's footprints in the mud until I reach a part that's very dry with no mushrooms and no footprints. I'm cold. I roll down the sleeves of my wooly dead pilot sweater. Where is everyone? The grove looks like an enchanted forest. I dare myself to close my eyes, but then I get scared and open them again. I try again with my back against a tree because maybe that's easier. I have to get at least to ten. And I have to count the numbers properly like how Pina showed me yesterday when we were breathing under water with the straw.

'One thousand, two thousand, three thousand, four...' I get scared and open my eyes again.

My brothers are always saying I'm a scaredy-cat, but it's not true. Only when I get scared is it a little bit true.

There are trees all around and their shadows are bigger. I feel like maybe now they might talk to me but that they won't say nice things. I get scared for real and start to walk as fast as I can without hurting my feet. I spot the house but it's so far I can cover it with my hand in front of me. The forest starts to talk and I have to run, even without shoes on, and though my feet are like a pair of mud cakes. I trip, get up again and start to cry a little, but I keep running and I keep running and crying and then suddenly there's no more shade and no more chestnuts and no more downhill. I run on the flat ground until I'm in the garden and it's sunny, and I'm almost saved, and I see everybody and I run really fast to where they are and when I get there no one pays me any attention.

They're all standing around the biggest of the new ponds. Emma is smoking one of those cigarettes she makes herself and I think she's giving a class because she's doing her teaching move, which is when she waves her hands around a lot. Ana and Pina are looking at her, ignoring me. Mama puts her hand on my head and plays it like a piano; sometimes I like it and sometimes I sit it (even though Dad says you can't sit something, no matter how much you can't stand it). I don't care if they ignore me anymore because now I want to follow the class, which is on how the new ponds work. I'm going to understand it better than Ana and explain it all to Dad when he's back from the island.

Emma says this pond is part of a system of ponds that filter all the sewage until it's clean. Mama sees my face scrunch up and explains to me that sewage is what in Mexico we call black water and white water. Black water has all the poop in it. White water has all the soap in it. Clean water doesn't have anything in it and it's just called water.

I ask Emma how the pond gets all the poop out and she says with pebbles and gravel. I really don't get this. I can feel my face scrunching up again. Sometimes I have a question but I don't know what it is and my face scrunches up like a rabbit's. Emma takes me by the hand and leads me up to where the ponds start. She has a really weird hand that feels super soft on the back but all rough on the palm. Rough like the volcanic rock outside the concert hall where I play with my ziplings while our parents rehearse. Sometimes they rehearse for so long Theo says we'll melt like lava and become part of the volcanic rock.

Emma shows me around the whole system. The system is really four ponds linked by mini waterfalls like a pond ladder. You can't see the first one because it's under the house. You can just about see the bit where the water comes out into the second one, and then between the second one and the third one there's another wall-step thing made of gravel and stones and plants. There are lilies in the third pond and carps in the fourth. They're not big carps, as carps go. Not like the ones I saw that time in a park which were like a hundred years old and had mustaches.

Emma's done teaching, she's done with her cigarette and now she wants to find a hose to clean me up because she doesn't like it when I'm brown and lie with the dogs on her fat carpets. I take off my sweater and my bathing suit and she hoses me down like I'm a plant in the garden. A brown puddle appears under me. The hard mud on my knees goes watery and dark and it runs down my legs like a dirty fruit juice, as if you could drink from me. I go back to being me-colored, and by the end I only have mud under my toenails and my fingernails, and by the very end Grandma says to me:

'That's better, now.'

But she's wrong, because without my mud I can't camu-flash at all.

2000

There are a few kids in the water. Some adults too, but they don't count. Girls sit around in bunches, like talking grapes. Pina scurries past them. She hates that Ana has gone. She walks around the pool, then walks around it again. A girl she recognizes from another weekend at the hotel waves her over.

'Maybe today we're friends,' Pina thinks.

The girl is wearing a bikini and has a braid that runs from her left ear right across her forehead like a tiara to her right ear, then flows down to her shoulders where it's tied with a white ribbon. Pina is pretty sure her mom wouldn't have the first clue how to put together something like that. She goes over, and the girl tells the others, 'This is Pina.'

Pina is just raising her hand to wave a group hello when the girl with the braid breaks into song, 'Pina the wiener, she's a Filipina! Pina the wiener, not even Latina!'

The shrieks from the three girls remind Pina of her alarm clock on school mornings. Wrapping her arms around herself, she walks away from the swimming pool, burning her feet on the hot flagstones. Pina grits her teeth; she will not cry.

Her grandma wouldn't like it if she did. And anyway, her grandma's not even from the Philippines.

'Don't go,' shouts one of the girls.

But Pina has already snuck behind a bungalow. In another one just like it, her parents are having one of their fights.

She makes her way to the end of the hotel, walking behind the rooms, sidestepping stones, ants and cigarette butts. Behind each bungalow there's a clothesline stretching between the iron bars on the windows and the parking-lot railing. She slips underneath them. Most of the clotheslines are empty, but when they do have things on them, Pina walks without ducking and the fabrics brush over her face, and for a second it's like she's Isadora Duncan, who's always wrapped up in fabrics, at least in the photos Pina's mom has on a wall at home.

Close to the parking-lot entrance, Pina comes across a few bushes pruned into different shapes: one is shaped like a chicken and the rest like spheres, or perhaps eggs. Some of the eggs are bigger than the chicken. Behind the bushes there's a cast-iron bench. She sits down. It's scorching hot but she wills herself not to move. The bench has a parking-lot view. There's nobody there but the cars. Nobody's cars. She counts them so she doesn't have to think about the bench burning her legs. There are fourteen. Heat waves rise off the tarmac under the car tires, and if she stares without blinking, it looks like the parking lot is slow dancing.

Pina realizes she's still holding the banana her dad gave her before hustling her out of the room so she didn't see the fight. She'd forgotten all about it and now it's brown where she's been squeezing it. She sees a security hut close by with one of those windows that looks like a mirror and wonders if there's anyone inside. Slowly, she peels her banana. She must do everything slowly today, so that the sun goes away, then the moon, and then they go back to the mews and she can tell Ana all about the braid girl and the fight. Days without Ana are like the TV on mute.

The other day, Víctor, Ana's dad, told them that it's not true that the mute button changes the sound to a frequency that only mutants can hear. But when he left the room, Theo went on insisting it was true and that Víctor would never admit as much because then he'd be left with a bunch of freaked-out kids wetting the bed each night. Theo also explained to them that this year, the year 2000, is called The Year Zero Zero, and we'll count the next years like this: Zero One, Zero Two, Zero Three. They're not going to put the twenty at the start anymore, because it just takes up space.

'It's gonna be like when Mexico took three zeros off the peso, and one million became one thousand and they called them new pesos. But you don't remember because you girls were just babies then.'

'And you weren't even born!' said Ana.

'Exactly. I'm part of the new-pesos generation and so, unlike you, birdbrain, I know how to count the new years.'

'And when we get to ten,' ask Pina, 'will it be Zero Ten?'

'Excellent question, Pi!' said Theo, turning his back on Ana. 'It'll go like this: Ten, Eleven, Twelve, just like that, without the zero. I'll turn twenty in the Year Thirteen, which is good luck.'

Pina wasn't altogether convinced. And then Ana swore to her that Theo had made the whole thing up and the years were going to be called Twothousand, Twothousandandone, Twothousandandtwo, Twothousandandthree, like you count the seconds, but obviously not so fast. She might be right. But Pina does believe the other thing, the mutant thing, or at least she kind of believes it, because when you press mute on the TV, it doesn't go totally quiet, not like when you turn it off properly. There's a sound that isn't exactly a sound but isn't silence either. Maybe it's true that the TV's transmitting something for someone far away.

Pina is nibbling on her brown banana with her front teeth, like a rabbit in slow motion, when she sees the bushes move. Two girls and a boy emerge from behind them. Since they weren't expecting to find her there, they're not sure whether to sit down or not. The boy ignores her, but one of the girls shoos her with her hand, like you shoo a dog. Pina shuffles down a bit toward the edge of the bench. She concentrates on her banana, to show she's minding her own business. She examines the imprint her two front teeth have made on the fruit's flesh, and the space left intact between them.

'Alright,' says the boy. 'Who's first?'

The girls let out nervous laughs and one of them points to the other. The pointed-at girl shakes her head and sits down next to Pina.

'You first,' she says to the other girl. 'It was your idea.'

The girl on her feet says, 'All right,' and gives her right hand to the boy. Pina is waiting for something gross, like him kissing it.

'Girls' names first, boys' after,' says the boy.

'No,' the girl says, 'the other way.'

'It's easier the other way.'

'Exactly.'

'Fine, whatever.'

'OK, OK, fine, girls' names first. Will it hurt?'

'Girls first?'

'Yeah.'

'Get on with it already!' says the girl next to Pina. She pulls her feet up onto the bench and hugs her knees to protect her legs from the heat. She's wearing sparkly plastic sandals. Pina's mom would never buy her anything like that. Her mom likes leather shoes; she likes Pina to go barefoot: she says it's natural. Without letting go of the girl, the boy lifts his right index finger so that everyone can see the nail, which is longer than the others. Víctor and Pina's dad also have one nail longer than the rest, on their thumbs; they use them to play the guitar. But it seems this boy uses his nail for other things, because after showing it off he places it on the back of the other girl's hand and starts to move his finger: he's scratching her.

'A,' he says, still scratching.

'Almond,' says the girl.

The boy stops scratching.

'Almond isn't a name,' he says.

'Uh-huh, I know, sorry. I just got nervous.'

'Only names, got it? That's the last time I stop before the second z, OK?'

'OK,' the girls say together.

Pina says it too, with a nod, but luckily no one notices. The boy starts to scratch again.

'A,' he says.

'Alma,' she says.

'B,' he says.

'Berta,' she says.

'C,' he says.

'Claudia,' she says.

The boy goes into a trance, scratching the same spot, at the same speed, and reciting the letters of the alphabet. The girl, by contrast, becomes more and more fidgety. She squirms, but without moving her hand, which the boy is holding onto. She reminds Pina of those butterflies fixed to the bottom of frames with a single pin. When they get to m, the girl raises her voice ('Monica!'), but doesn't take her hand away. She hesitates at p and Pina wants to whisper her own name to her but she doesn't dare. Whenever she tells people her name they look at her funny.

'Paula!' the girl says, and the game goes on.

'Q.'

'Queta!'

'R.'

'Rocío.'

'S.'

'Savior'

The girl's friend wrinkles her nose and asks Pina under her breath, 'Savior?'

Pina shrugs. The boy goes on reciting the alphabet and scratching, doing his best to hold the girl's hand still. She's started to do little jumps. Pina and the friend get up and move in closer to see how the hand is doing: it looks pretty red under the boys nail. Not blood red, but definitely hives red.

They move on to boys' names. Armando, Bernando, Claudio, Damián, Efraín, Fernando. The girl starts to cry. Her friend puts her hand on her shoulder.

'Get out of here!' the girl says to Pina.

Pina goes back to the bench. Of all the words the girl has said, 'Get out of here' are the only ones that aren't a name, and the fact that they were directed at Pina makes her feel important. She realizes she still has the banana in her hand, all sticky between her fingers. She flings it into the bushes. Nobody notices.

By the time they reach Humberto, the girl has her neck cocked to one side with her eyes closed. Then the boy says i and her head pops up.

'Idiot!' and she pulls her hand from the boy's clasp.

The friend sniggers but immediately shuts up again. The girl holds her right hand with her left and looks at it as if it doesn't belong to her, as if she can't understand where it came from. The boy still has his finger out, in position, but there's nothing to scratch anymore.

'Are you OK?' asks the friend.

The girl wipes away some snot with her forearm.

'You were almost there!' says the boy, picking the blood out of his nail with the corner of his swimming shorts.

*

The swallows gather in the afternoons. Pina sits down on a lounger to watch them. At this time of day it smells less of chlorine and more of the flowers that hang from the trees like little open hands: purple and yellow. Pina imagines herself all grown up with flowers like that in her hair. She imagines admirers hot on her heels: the boys, now men, fighting over her. Fighting over who would get to take her flowers. It's

Sunday, and there's hardly anyone left in the pool. Her dad is in the bungalow and her mom went out for a walk. Flights of swallows swoop down into the old chimneys on the main building's domed roof. Pina is counting them, and if she gets to more than a hundred her parents will stay together; if she counts less than a hundred, they'll split up.

A boy gets out of the water and walks toward her. Pina thinks he might start calling her names like the braid girl. She looks up at the sky, but even then she can tell the boy is approaching.

'Hey,' he says, and Pina immediately recognizes his voice. He's making her lose count and she doesn't want to.

'Wait,' she tells him, and starts counting aloud so he gets it.

'Eighty-four, eighty-five…'

The boy turns around so he's facing the swallows too. His swimming trunks drip onto the flagstones, and in the pool's reflection the birds multiply.

*

'Ana, Berta, Carmen, Diana, Esther, Fernanda, Gema, H…, H…, Helena, Irma, Julieta, Karla, Luz, María, Natalia, Omara, Pina, Quintana… yes it *is* a name!, Raquel, Sonia, Tania, Úrsula, Vicky, Wanda, Ximena, Yolanda, Zamuela… I don't care, Armando, Bernardo, Carlos, Domingo, Eduardo, Félix, Gerardo, Horacio, Ilario, Jacobo, Kiko, Luis, Mariano, N…, N…, N…, Núñez, ouch! Nothing, Nobody, Nepal. Norberto? I give up! Octavio, Pedro, Quetzalcóatl, Raúl, Saúl, Tito, Uva… Uber… Under, I give up!'

The boy cleans his nail and Pina thanks him. They sit on the bench. He grabs her other hand and she immediately snatches it away. She doesn't want to play again. The boy says he only wanted to take her hand, that's all. But she knows you can't trust anyone around here.

'Do you know how babies are made?' she asks him.

The boy gets up, disappears into the bushes and never comes back.

Pina hasn't told a single lie all day, so why does she feel like a liar?

III

2004

Luz turns three years dead today. Mom fixes herself up a bit (she lets her hair down) but is in a terrible mood. She burns the toast. I spill juice on the floor and she says, 'Perfecto.'

When she goes to brush her teeth she complains that dad, who's just shaved, has left hairs in the sink. Dad and I mutter to each other, 'Patience,' and when Mom finally announces, furious, that she's not coming with us, I think we're both relieved. Dad tries to convince her anyway, but she's unswayable.

'This year I have a stand-in,' she says to him. And to me: 'Pull up any weeds you spot, will you?'

Then she hugs me way too tight, as if she could pass on whatever it is I need to be her surrogate by osmosis.

'Come on,' I say from inside my headlock. 'Let's go say hi to Luz.'

But the name has an electric effect on her. In a flash, Mom lets go of me and walks off to her room, wrapping her hair back up in her rag. Today it's the black silk one. It's embroidered with silver flowers and in another lifetime it was her very special concert shawl. But tragedies take the shine out of objects. Ever since Luz died no one around here seems to care about clothes or furniture anymore. Not even the instruments seem to matter much. Utilitarian things: the cello, the piano, the timpani. Nothing but buoys.

*

I never knew my parents did this while we were away at camp.

'Every year?' I ask.

'Every year,' says Dad. 'And we always stop by that flower stall there.'

He parks, gives me some money and I go by myself. In fact they've only come twice, which isn't all that much. But the new life already feels old. We have new customs. The first time we went home without Luz I thought I'd never be able to walk into our room without expecting to find her there, playing with Bedtime Bear.

But now her bed is my chaise longue and Bedtime Bear is in a box someplace and I don't ever expect to see her when I come home. If I think about her it's to imagine what she'd be like now: she'd be eight. Pretty soon she'd be wearing a training bra and I'd have to explain to her what to do if she gets her first period in school. I'd show her how to tie her sweater around her waist just in case, and tell her not to panic if she spots a dark stain in her knickers, to keep cool and to come looking for me in my classroom. We would be in the same school by now.

'And Luz,' I would say to her, 'don't you listen to those girls who say using tampons is like having sex, because they're eleven and they're liars.'

I swear some girls in my class talk about having learned to use a tampon like it was sailing across the Atlantic. All that's missing is the slideshow, like the one Emma gave us when she came back from Niagara Falls.

The flower arrangements at the stall are for old ladies. For dead old ladies or for old ladies who think their dead were really cheesy. I take three sunflowers, pay for them and, getting back into the car, remember something basic: Luz isn't buried where we're going.

'Next year,' I say to Dad, putting on my safety belt, 'we'll bring flowers from our yard.'

Dad starts the car and corrects me:

'Our *milpa*.'

Then, smiling, he uses the name, maybe to make up for Mom's reaction earlier:

'Luz would have loved your *milpa*.'

*

The grave is small and made of cement, not too different from my planters, only with a lid. The lid says: *Luz Pérez-Walker, 1995–2001*. And underneath: *Beloved daughter and sister*. Be-loved. Like an order. I'd fantasized about this moment, about what I'd say to Luz. But in my fantasies it was raining and Luz was somehow able to listen to me. Now the sun is beating down and there's not a patch of shade in the whole cemetery. She's dead, and I have nothing to say to her. Was she beloved? She was my sister. 'Bina', she used to call Pina. 'Sana', she used to called me (a mix between sister and Ana, although she didn't come up with it: Olmo and Theo used it before her). One time, Bina and I changed her outfit twenty times and put makeup on her: she'd let us do anything. Yes, I guess she was beloved. Her death certificate was made in Michigan. *DECEASED*, it says in capital letters. I hate this word. It sounds like diseased. But you can be cured from a disease. And, anyway, Luz wasn't sick. She even knew how to swim. She must have got caught up in something, that's what we think. Luz's body is in ashes in the lake. At the time it seemed logical, to cremate her and put her to rest with Granddad. But now I can't understand it: why would we leave her there? I wonder if my brothers think about her while they're out fishing. I wonder if they have anything to say to her.

I brought Alf's big shears with me, but I don't spot a single weed. I use them to cut the stems of the three sunflowers then I arrange them on the grave until Dad and I agree on a nice composition. But almost straight away I mess them up again. If there was one thing Luz wasn't, it was tidy. Dad agrees.

'When she was really little,' I remind him, 'she used to get baby food everywhere.'

He laughs.

'One day,' he adds, 'I had to clean mush from the ceiling. The first time that ever happened out of all four of you kids. That girl had arms like a baseball player.'

A blow to the chest, there, a few tears that come to my eyes but don't fall. 'That girl.' That's exactly what we no longer have for Luz. What is it? Irreverence? Nerve.

'You little shits,' Dad calls my brothers sometimes.

'Scaredy-cat!' he says to me when I refuse to eat chili.

Being dead means this, too: nobody dares insult you anymore, not even out of love.

I feel good when we leave. Sad but interesting. And clean. The only thing missing is the soundtrack. I ask Dad to sing something and who knows why but he breaks into '*La donna è mobile qual piuma al vento, muta d'accento e di pensiero*', a family classic. Mom used to sing it in the mornings.

'Now I feel like a pizza,' I tell him, and he passes me his phone.

I call Mom and she asks for a bacon-and-onion pizza, even though normally she refuses to eat anything from a box. Dad cries at the wheel on the way to the pizzeria. Discreetly. No heaving chest, no little sobs, just tears running down his cheeks, like in the pictures the guy in the park near our house used to make: he would kneel down on the floor, and with a spray can and a spatula paint the same scenes over and over, in a matter of seconds. His favorite subject was a clown with a single tear rolling down his cheek. Now I realize I should've given him some credit: it turns out that there are actually people out there who cry like that, in my own home even. Isn't this called a revelation? Some people might call it that.

When we get home, Mom's not angry anymore. She's sad and gentle: she eats some pizza and says it's good. Afterward, we flop on the sofa together and she strokes my head.

'It shouldn't be called an anniversary,' I say.

'That's what your dad always says,' she replies.

'I invented a word.'

'What is it?'

'Graycholy.'

'One of Marina's.'

'Yeah, I borrowed it. By the way, are you going to make it up with her?'

'If Chela and Pina made it up, why not, eh?'

'What's that got to do with anything?'

'Did you pull up the weeds?'

'There weren't any.'

'Hm. It must be because there's no body there.'

'What's that got to do with anything?'

'Could you bring me a blanket?'

*

Dad comes with us on our second trip to the garden center, to oversee his investment. But he's his own budget's worst enemy. Pina and I watch as he falls prey, over and again, to the shop assistant, but we don't say anything. I'm glad Pina's back and that she seems as psyched about the plants as I am. It's another assistant today: not the pervert, but a young guy with dreadlocks. He makes me feel awkward. I chew the inside of my cheek, then force myself to talk to him.

'I'm regenerating the oxygen in my mews,' I tell him.

'Nice,' he says, his eyes on Pina.

We leave the garden center so overloaded with goodies that Dad decides to go get the car. While we wait for him at the entrance, a lady comes up to us.

'How much for this?' she asks, pointing to our newly acquired cherry-tomato plant.

Pina butts in before I have time to answer.

'Two hundred pesos, *señora*. Go ahead, try one.'

The lady tries a tomato and buys the plant off us. I'm so impressed I'm lost for words. By the time Dad parks up and opens the trunk, Pina is already back, a replacement cherry tomato plant and eighty pesos change safely tucked away in her pocket. She got back yesterday, but she still hasn't told me anything about her mom. She says to wait till she develops the photos. She took her old film camera, but now 'Chela has a digital one.' It makes me sad that she calls her mom by the same nickname we all use for her. I must have pulled a face because next thing she says, 'She asked me to call her that and I like it.'

'OK,' I say, 'OK, sorry.'

In total we have: two aloes, a lemon tree, a lavender plant, and various unidentified succulents. After today's trip we can add the cherry tomatoes and two specimens of a tall plant called *Monstera deliciosa*, but which for some reason has the nickname 'skeleton'. It has huge, dark green leaves with roundish holes in them. I guess that's where the name comes from: the holes being the eye sockets in a skull. Or maybe it's subtler than that: the holes the dead leave behind, something you can't say. We also got a few other pretty plants: one of them looks like a red cabbage; the others are all green. I'm going to put those ones together in the planter nearest the house, because according to the dreads guy they like the shade. I already have the soil for the *milpa* corner (the *milpa* has been 'downsized' and now occupies just one corner), and next week we'll go buy the turf. I'm pretty excited about that as well. As I understand it, you just lay it out like a rug.

As soon as Dad leaves us alone in the yard, Pina lies face down on the picnic table. She's wearing a pair of hot pants so short you can see the smile of her butt cheek poking out on one side. It reminds me of last summer: we were sitting on a bench outside a shopping mall when a girl walked by and Emma said, 'She'll kill herself if she falls off that skirt.'

'Look!' shouts Pina, pointing to the basil I planted two weeks ago.

Some little flowers have blossomed on it. I call Mom and she opens the sliding door. She'd been practicing in the living room and has red eyes and a vague smile, like she does when she tells us she's sorry.

'You need to pull them off,' she says, pointing to the basil with her cello bow.

'Why?'

'If you leave them on the leaves fall off, and the leaves are the bit you eat.'

'Why?'

'Just listen to me, will you?' she says, and slides the door shut. One by one, Pina and I pull off the little flowers. It occurs to me that if I'd known, I could have taken them to the cemetery. It's a silly idea: they're tiny. But Luz was too. Tiny, I mean. She used to sit on my lap, hug her legs, then curl into a little ball so that I'd hold her.

'Squeeze!' she'd say.

Sometimes I was scared I'd hurt her or break something, and I always let go sooner than she wanted me to. We all did. My brothers held on a bit longer, but not much. Luz always wanted to be squeezed more.

'Squeeze, squeeze, squeeze!' she begged Dad, and he would squeeze her with a single arm.

I don't want to, but I can't help imagining her in her box, in the cemetery. But that's another silly idea because there's not even anything in that box. It was too expensive and complicated to bring the body back to Mexico.

'What?' I ask Pina, who's staring at me.

'Are you crying?' she says.

'Are you stupid?' I say, and she goes off in a sulk.

2003

The woman is absurdly beautiful. That's how Marina sees her: with an adverb. She shouts to be heard above the racket of the hail against the tile roof:

'You'll go to heaven for this, missy!'

'Thanks,' Marina says, because she can't think of anything else to say. But what she's really thinking is, 'An evangelist!' and 'I am such an idiot!' And then, this time in her brother's voice, 'You have opened the door to an unknown, soaking wet, and possibly dangerous evangelist.' But she can't stop staring at her.

'I'm a friend of Beto and Pina,' the woman yells, pointing to the house on her left. 'Do you know Pina? Does she still live there?'

Relief. Marina knows Pina. She's Linda's kids' little friend, and yes, she lives with her dad in Sour House.

'They're not in?' Marina shouts.

'Do you think I could come in for a second?' the woman shouts back.

Marina thinks, 'No,' but says, 'Of course.'

They run to her house. Marina opens and closes the door

with a yank and a shove. You can't even hear the door slam for the storm. Her feet are soaked. The damn drains in the mews become blocked at the first drop of hail. She kicks off her flip-flops and dries her feet, rubbing each one against the opposite thigh.

The woman emerges from under the black trash bag and, after studying it for a second like she's making sure she hasn't left anything valuable in there, she reopens the door and tosses the bag out into the passageway. This surprises Marina, maybe it even annoys her a little, she can't decide. Is the woman going to take the bag with her when she goes, or leave it there as a memento? Will the bag get caught up among her plant pots or will it float off toward the bell, or even to her landlord's doorstep? The woman shuts the door again and Marina thinks to herself how, even on the balmiest, rain-free day she wouldn't have heard it closing, so gracefully and soundlessly the woman carries herself. What's more, whereas before she seemed stooped under her bag, now Marina can appreciate how upright she is. She feels another wave of fear, but this time it's quieter, perhaps offset by her curiosity: it sounds less like one of her brother's reproaches and more like the muted hum of a neighbor's radio. 'She's no evangelist,' says the radio host. 'But a hardened criminal, maybe? A member of an elite kidnapping gang?'

The woman rubs her arms and shakes out her thick black hair. Then she takes a moment to stretch, and in one long breath regains her natural shape and size. Short, but seemingly taller with her plumb, proud posture, the woman fills the space she occupies. She's also dripping wet. She points to a broken chair next to the door and Marina says, 'Be my guest, ma'am.' But the woman doesn't sit down; she hangs her jacket on the back. It's an oversized denim jacket.

'This is really so cool of you,' says the woman as she unties her scarf: a flimsy, tie-dyed thing, so youthful it ages her.

'Come in, ma'am,' Marina says.

'Bah, let's drop the formalities,' says the woman, drying her hair with the scarf.

'Come in,' Marina says, pointing her to the living room. 'I'll get you a towel.'

The last time Marina spoke to her dad on the phone, he said, totally out of the blue, 'You're not a little girl anymore, Dulce Marina.' And she felt robbed, because that's what she'd been telling him since she was about twelve! And now he was trying to take the credit for discovering the fact, not only robbing it from her but also slyly sugarcoating it in her full and sickly name (Sweet Marina, ugh), which no one apart from him and the Federal Electoral Institute ever used. She'd felt like the victim of a postal crime; like he'd stolen a letter she was expecting. It had been deeply infuriating, but all she had managed to say to him was, 'I know, Dad.'

And he'd gone on:

'At your age your mom had already had her first child.'

'I know that too.'

After they'd hung up, Marina welcomed a kind of pure, clean rage: a healthy development. But now, the taste of that rage comes back to her as she looks around the bathroom for the least dirty towel. She really did not like the tone of the woman's 'let's drop the formalities', as if she were the host and Marina the intruder. Marina inspects herself in the mirror for a few seconds, no longer than that, but long enough for her to feel embarrassed about how long she's taking, because she is, after all, the host. She grabs the green towel, the one she uses least, and heads back.

She finds the woman sitting on the yellow sofa. Not leaning back into it; just perched on the edge, very erect, but not tense. Quite the opposite in fact: she looks perfectly at ease. (Mellow-yellow.) And Marina feels irritated again. How can this woman seem so comfortable here in her home, as if they'd had a prearranged appointment, as if she were a social worker sent to check if Marina is sticking to her recommended daily intake of calories? Marina doesn't know how to hold her back straight without stiffening all over, and as a general rule she resents people with good posture.

The woman points to the wall opposite the whozac wall.

'What is Doctor Vargas doing up there?'

Marina flinches. It takes her a moment to take in the fact that this woman knows her neighbors.

'Her husband commissioned me to paint her portrait,' she answers. 'But in the end he didn't want to hang it in his house. He paid me and everything, it's just he gave it back.'

'Maybe he didn't like it.'

'Maybe.'

'I'm not saying it's ugly.'

'He asked me to paint it like that. In the style of Joaquín Sorolla.'

'They always were a little pretentious.'

'Can I get you a coffee?'

'Do you have tea?'

'Chamomile.'

'I'll take that.'

Ugh, thinks Marina as she puts the kettle on. She really didn't like that response at all; like it was a concession on the woman's part. Nor does she like her turning the TV off without asking. Or the fact that she wasn't even the slightest bit surprised to learn that Marina is a painter and that people actually commission her to paint portraits. When Linda first saw the portrait she'd cried, 'Bravo!'

Marina's not scared anymore. She's pissed, and getting more so by the minute. Pissed at herself, or at the woman, or at the completely absurd fact that it took her twenty years to feel the slightest anger toward her father, and two minutes with this stranger. Everything's the wrong way around.

'I'm getting her out of here the moment she's finished her tea,' thinks Marina, but at the same time she tunes the radio to a jazz station, as if preparing the house for a long, lazy night with friends. She doesn't wait for the water to boil. As soon as it starts simmering, she pours it into two mugs, adds a couple teabags from the ones Linda leaves when she comes for class, and goes back to the living room. She sits next to the woman and hands her one of the mugs.

'You collect cushions?' asks the woman. 'They're rad.'

'Thanks,' Marina says, looking down at her tea and blowing into it. Then, realizing her error, she adds, 'It's not chamomile.'

'Yerba mate,' the woman says, reading the label on the teabag. 'Far out,' she says, 'I haven't drunk one of these since I was in Patagonia.'

'Ah,' Marina says, and she takes little sips on hers while looking at the woman's feet. She's wearing heeled brogues with laces, and the tips are ever so slightly pointed, ever so slightly witchy. They can't be from here. Or maybe they are, but not from this decade.

'Are you Mexican?' Marina asks.

'Born and bred,' the woman answers. And then, 'My name's Isabel, but call me Chela.'

*

They begin in Patagonia, then move onto the marihuana Chela happens to have on her and which she offers to Marina as a thank-you for entertaining her while she waits for her friends. She hands it over with a little curtsy, and Marina accepts it, shrugging her shoulders.

'Obligreenation,' she thinks. Green out of obligation.

But once she's smoked the weed, it opens up Marina's sternum and launches her into a rolling monologue about everything that's wrong with art at the service of the market and moreover with the very design degree she's pursuing; about everything that's wrong with Chihuahua, and in Chihuahua, poor, poor Chihuahua: indoctrinated by the border. Chela listens, and every now and then she says, 'The border you saved yourself from. The fat bullet you dodged, my friend.'

Marina thinks that's taking it a little too far, but thanks Chela anyway. She hasn't spoken like this in years; with real freedom and creative license, with someone who listens without charging by the hour, and who tells her she's right (right on!), just because. Maybe this unexpected visitor will turn out to be more effective than all the pills, the therapy, and the Lord's Prayer put together. Marina imagines passing the joint to Mr. Therapist: he accepts it, takes a toke, and holds the smoke in his lungs as he says, 'Weed, Marina, knows what the body doesn't.'

Back in the real world, Chela is telling her about a fling she'd been having these last months, with a Swedish dude who never came because he was into Tantra. It doesn't seem such a bad policy to Marina.

'All men come too fast,' she says.

'I know,' Chela says, 'But it's no good if they hold it in. They get frustrated. It's like all the semen Patrik won't let out turns into bile.'

Marina isn't sure what to say to this.

'Want a beer?' she asks.

'Why not?' Chela says.

They go together to the kitchen, but Chela freezes on the spot the moment she steps foot inside. She puts her hand to her mouth, looks at the screen door and wells up. Marina doesn't understand.

'What?' she asks.

'Nothing,' answers Chela, rearranging her expression so quickly that Marina convinces herself it's the weed making her see things. Chela goes around freely opening drawers until she finds the bottle opener, but the ease with which she moves about the house no longer annoys Marina. Now, Marina notes, she's started to admire her. Oh, to be someone like that! Someone who turns up any old place and settles right in.

Back in the living room, Chela opens a large bottle of beer, pours it into two disposable cups – tilting them to control the head –, hands one to Marina and together they make the anticlimactic, silent toast of plastic on plastic. Chela puts hers on the floor, raises her arms and says, 'Confession.'

'I've already told you so much!' Marina says.

'No, I have a confession,' Chela says.

'Oh.'

'I told you a lie. I'm not a friend of theirs. I used to live in Sour House. We had a kitchen just like yours.'

Marina raises her eyebrows. That's all. She can feel how, after a few hours spent together, her body is naturally starting to mimic Chela's movements. Or, perhaps it's not at all natural? She doubts herself, then asks Chela, 'I'm sorry?'

'I'm Pina's mom, and I didn't dare knock on the door.'

'Why?'

'Because I haven't seen her in three years.'

'You mean, they're in?' Marina asks, lowering her voice as if they might hear her from the other side of the passageway.

'They might be.'

'Isabel! Why don't you go over right now?'

'Right now I'm stoned. And please, call me Chela. My mom was Isabel.'

'Why didn't you knock?'

Chela gets up, takes a few steps, sits on the floor and opens her legs. They're short and strong-looking. She rests her elbows on the triangle that has formed between her thighs, lowers her forearms and pushes her open palms against the floor, her fingers stretched wide, bits of carpet poking out between them.

'I don't know,' she says. 'I chickened out.'

Marina wants to interrogate her. Is she scared of Beto? Does he have custody? Is her being here illegal? But she'd rather just raise her eyebrows. She'd rather go on talking about Chihuahua. Chela took her shoes off a while ago and now Marina studies her bony feet, perhaps the only imperfect part of her anatomy. She'd still be up for seeing them without the socks, though: to see if they're as brown as her arms, to see if she paints her toenails or not.

'What's with all the little boxes?' Chela asks.

'Light bulbs.'

'Why so many?'

'Because I changed them all today.'

'Why?'

'It's a long story.'

Chela drops it. She takes both her big toes with each hand and lowers her chest to the floor. Her legs are just as wide open as before, but now her whole torso is level with the rug. She turns her head to the side and rests her cheek on the floor. Is she going to fall asleep like that? Marina looks at the boxes scattered around on the floor. She looks at the whozac on the wall and remembers all her good intentions. She looks at the time on her cell; it's not raining anymore and she considers telling her guest that it's getting late, that she needs to go because it just so happens that tomorrow is the beginning of Marina's new life: a healthy routine, a life devoted to her art and wellbeing, and so she really must get an early start. But on the other hand, she doesn't want her guest to leave. Now that she has her cell in her hands, Marina knows that the moment Chela goes she'll call Chihuahua; she doesn't want to go to bed alone. Better if Chela doesn't leave. It's his turn to call.

'You're so flexible. Do you do yoga?' she asks.

'I teach Pilates at my beach, al fresco.'

Marina sits thinking for a moment, then asks, 'Do you know about the Iconoclastic Controversy?'

Chela, her cheek still resting against the rug, purses her lips, as if weighing up the question.

'The what controversy?' she asks eventually.

'Iconoclastic.' Marina explains, 'The iconodules were in favor of having images in churches, while the iconoclasts were against it. There was a big fight. In the end the iconodules won, obviously. That's why there are so many crucifixes all over the place. Anyway, my point is that the other day I saw a Pilates video and an idea came to me: if you know what your Pilates teacher means when she asks for "praying hands", that's thanks to the iconodules.'

'I don't ask my students to do that.'

'Oh.'

'But it's interesting. Where did you learn that?'

'College. I take Art History. It's the only subject I like.'

Chela raises her torso to a forty-five degree angle, puts her elbows back on the rug and rests her chin in her hands. Then she covers her face with her hands and says, 'I never finished high school.' Next she opens her mouth wide and slides her fingers down her face, pushing hard to drag her cheeks down like in Munch's *The Scream*. Marina laughs.

Chela asks, 'Won't you teach an uneducated girl more of that neat stuff?'

'Symeon the Stylite, ever heard of him?'

'Never.'

'He was a fifth-century Assyrian monk who only ate once a day and spent twenty hours on his feet, genuflecting on top of an eighteen-meter-high stone pillar.'

'What for?' asks Chela, sitting up.

'According to my teacher, this guy's the true father of performance.'

'I have a friend who does performance. She's really famous because after 9/11 she spent days at a metro station in New York whispering through a megaphone: *Please do not despair*.'

'I'm taking English classes, did I say?'

Chela gets up. She wraps one knee around the other and puts her hands together as if in prayer. She does three squats on one leg. Marina laughs. Chela hobbles toward her in the same position until she reaches the sofa and crashes onto it.

'I'm hungry,' she says.

The Symeon story makes Marina think that her own problems with food – her sick tendency to waste it – is not such a big deal after all. But she doesn't say this to Chela, or what she's thinking: 'And you, Marina? Are you hungry? No idea. What have I eaten today? Oats–Yakult–twenty-five–pieces–of–popcorn–beer.'

Chela picks up the popcorn bowl. She polished off the last pieces hours ago with her tea. She picks out the remaining husks and gnaws them one by one, like a poised mouse. Her back still perfectly straight, she collects the husks in the palm of her other hand.

'Do you have any other children?' Marina asks.

Chela says no and drops the husks (clink, clink, clink, they cascade into the bowl).

'Did you eat dinner already, before I showed up?' she asks.

'You don't look like Pina,' Marina says.

Chela lets out a huff.

'Pina looks Asian,' Marina goes on.

'It's from Beto. Isn't that kinda obvious?'

'Yeah, they both look Asian. Why?'

'Beto's mom was Japanese. That's essentially why he's so square. Can we eat something, please, please, please? I'll make it. I'm an amazing cook.'

'I don't have anything in.'

'Impossible.'

They go to the kitchen in their socks. Chela roots through the store cupboard and fridge and then announces she's going to make some crepes.

'You, sit,' she says, and Marina sits at the breakfast bar where she tends to slump while Chihuahua cooks up fights. Well, he cooks meals that end up as a fight when Marina can't manage to eat them.

Marina feels like she's sitting in front of a movie, the way she likes them: with the sound off. She watches Chela braid her hair, rub her hands together and make herself at home in the space, getting out sugar, flour, and milk (all those raw materials Marina buys then leaves untouched, like someone who collects perfumes for the bottles). Then, out of nowhere, she brings up the question she's been meaning to ask: does Chela know Linda?

'Of course,' Chela says. 'Linda and her husband knew my husband before we all moved here, from the orchestra.'

This surprises Marina.

'Is he a musician too?'

Chela frowns.

'No, Beto's a bureaucrat.'

Marina doesn't say as much, but that's exactly what she'd imagined. Nor does she mention she finds Beto rather attractive, with that particular appeal of sad men.

'Cultural bureaucrat,' Chela continues, 'there's a whole breed of them in this country. You'll hear him playing guitar in his free time, but he's got a banker's soul. He's a good dad; I'll give him that. But he was a tyrannical husband. Not violent. Quite the opposite: a complete walkover. I'm the only woman I know who got a divorce because of a crisis of boredom. In fact, we never did get a divorce. At least not as far as I know. Do you know anything about that?'

Marina laughs.

'Why didn't you knock on Linda's door?' she asks.

Chela looks at her as if she hasn't heard, which isn't physically possible. Marina makes a mental note to try this in the future: when someone asks her something she doesn't want to answer, she'll just stare at them, as if waiting for them to talk.

Chela passes the flour through a sieve, making a mound in the salad bowl, and with her finger she carves a crater at the peak. She breaks the egg over the mini volcano then throws in some sugar. With a fork, she whisks it all together. Next, she puts some butter to melt in the microwave, announcing, in the process, that by French standards this would be 'cheating'. She whisks and whisks and then covers the mixture in the bowl with a dish towel.

'You have to let it rest a couple of minutes,' Chela says, opening the fridge. Without the slightest fuss, and in one swift move, she takes the moldy carrots from the tray and throws them in the trash. She refills the plastic cups and stands by the screen door looking out onto the water tank. Marina is still at the breakfast bar.

'I couldn't bare to. I think Linda might hate me. Víctor won't. But she might. She's so opinionated, so spirited. Plus, she copes with four children when I couldn't even handle one. I don't think she'd even let me in the mews, actually.'

Chela looks at Marina through the reflection in the door, raises her glass and says, 'Thanks for letting me in.'

Then she turns around and lights the stove.

Now Marina thinks about it, Pina is also absurdly beautiful. A kind of oneiric beauty, with those Buddha-like almond eyes and that perfect, slim nose. It's a wonder she can even breathe. She shouldn't think like this, she tells herself, when it wasn't all that long ago that that little girl drowned. Marina is never pleased when Pina turns up unannounced, because the Pérez-Walkers pay per hour, not per kid. Plus, her presence changes the order of things, so that Ana and Theo, who on the whole leave each other in peace, are suddenly overcome with a feverish urge to rip each other apart in front of their guest. When Linda hired Marina, she told her she was the first nanny the kids had had in their lives. With four kids! Marina doesn't get how she can look after them all and play the flute, or the cello, or whatever it is she plays, the one-woman band. Suddenly, the pedestal she's put Linda on seems out of reach. Obsolete. Would Linda really not open the door to Chela? Marina thinks she would, then that she wouldn't: she doesn't know what to think. Would Linda be pissed if she knew that Marina had let her in? She takes a certain pleasure in the idea of going against the woman she so obsessively compares herself to. In their next class she'll tell Linda that she got stoned with her old friend Chela. Let's see how she likes that.

'The first one always turns out badly,' say Chela, as she rolls a perfect circle of whitish batter around the pan.

'How come you know how to make crepes?'

'I picked it up in a hotel in Belize. Crazy life, eh? That's what people around here must say about me, right? Lost, irresponsible, a terrible mother.'

Marina wants to tell her the truth – that they've never once brought her up – but she doesn't know how to break it to her so that it sounds less offensive. She gets to her feet and opens the door to the yard. The smell of butter is making her feel woozy. Linda spreads the mixture with a silicon spatula that Marina bought on offer and has never used. Marina watches, trying not to show her utter fascination. She cups her beer with two hands as if it were hot chocolate, and takes comparative notes. Could she be like this woman? A lover of men and food and freedom? Will she ever feel at ease cooking? Or fucking?

'A wholesome woman. A whole lotta woman. The whole shebang,' Marina thinks.

And Chela, as if intuiting some of what's passing through Marina's head, says, 'I turn forty this year.'

What's that supposed to mean? Is forty old? Marina does the math. This woman, so much more of a woman than she is, is closer to her mom's age than to her own.

'How old is Pina?'

'She turns twelve tomorrow,' Chela says. 'That's why...'

She doesn't finish her sentence and Marina doesn't probe any further. Tiny volcanoes erupt on the surface of the crepe.

Chela flips it. There's something planetary about the side now facing up: a pattern of concentric circles that vary in color where one part took a millisecond more or less to cook. Marina decides to change the tone of the conversation; the last thing she needs is to take on Chela's drama.

'It looks like the growth rings on a tree,' she says.

'I haven't seen her since she was nine,' Chela says, and she slides the crepe onto a plate. The side facing up now is whitish like a pasty baby, and doesn't have growth rings or indeed anything that speaks of the universe on it, apart from some disconcerting craters where the volcanoes erupted. Chela starts a new crepe.

'Pina?' Marina asks, stupidly.

Chela nods, keeping her eyes on the pan. Every time the edge of the batter mixture goes solid, she presses it down with the spatula and the liquid rushes in to replace it, until it too sets. She didn't apply this level of neurotic vigilance to the previous one.

'Do you know why I called her that?' Chela asks. 'After Pina Bausch. Do you know who Pina Bausch is? She's a seriously important choreographer, a genius, a…'

Her sentence deflates. Chela focuses on her spatula like a child in front of a videogame; her eyes detect setting edges in an instant, and without blinking, so the tears that start to fall from them don't seem to have any relation to her, or to what she's saying. Marina once went to a water park in the port of Veracruz with a wave machine where jets of water would shoot out. That's what Chela's face reminds her of. She flips the crepe and it's ruined, its rings disturbed too soon by the spatula.

'I haven't seen my dad for a year and a half,' Marina says.

She's not sure why she said it, maybe to distract Chela, or maybe because she'd like to be able to talk like her: to cry without making a big song and dance about it; to say through tears and laughter, 'My dad could make you a perfect club sandwich, blow gigantic soap bubbles, and then drink too much and answer everyone with his fists. Well, everyone except me. Not every night, but like the club sandwich: from time to time. And sometimes he'd break things: my mother's teeth, my brother's ribs.' And Marina would like to add, 'And I, like an idiot, could never get mad at him.' But all she says is, 'A ballet choreographer?'

'Bausch? Contempo. Contemporary dance, you know what that is?'

'More or less. You're a dancer too, right?'

'Not anymore.'

'What, one day you just said enough is enough?'

'No. I couldn't find any contempo in Mazunte.'

2002

B ack in 1982, while I recovered from the bike accident, Noelia took up the habit of calling me as soon as she got to work. Since we had nothing to say to each other, having only just eaten breakfast together, she would give me a report of the traffic she'd encountered on the way from our house to the hospital, putting on a voice that she thought made her sound like a sports commentator, but in fact only made her seem like a tattletale.

'He overtook me on the right!' she'd say. Or, 'I saw a man hit by a car right outside a church. There are no morals anymore!'

When, almost twenty years later, she began chemo, I took it upon myself to give her a report of the traffic I saw from the bus window on my way back and forth from the institute or the market. But it was invariably so lame, so half-hearted and obviously half made-up that Noe eventually ruled that I didn't have a driver's sensibility and was better off telling her about my fellow passengers on the bus. That was much more fun. I like to think that never learning to drive saved me a lot of ball ache. I would have let everyone overtake me, left, right, and center. Boy, it would have driven my wife nuts, me calmly waving on my aggressor.

Back to 1982. Once Noe had finished her traffic update, we would hang up and I would draw in bed. The rest-and-recuperation instruction manual they'd given me in the hospital was too boring to actually read, so I'd asked my night nurse, AKA my wife, and she gave me the gist of it: *Forbidden to work*. And that is how I came to spend my recovery period drawing, a hobby I'd loved as a child, and something I'd spent almost my entire adult life putting off. I soon realized that every time I had a pencil in my hand I'd draw houses. Design them, if you like. All those months spent cooped up in the house of my childhood, adolescence, and adult life (more or less on the spot where I'm writing this now) convinced me I should have been an architect. Architects have the sensibility of an artist, a pinch of philosophical coherence, a healthy dose of opportunism and even their share of scientific rigor on a basic, structural level (the level that stops houses falling down on top of them). But more than all this – and in radical contrast to anthropologists – the work of architects actually serves a purpose.

*

Umami starts in the mouth, in the middle of the tongue, activating salivation. Your molars wake up and feel the urge to bite, beg to move. Not that different in fact, albeit less powerful, from the instinct that drives your hips to move almost of their own accord during sex. In that moment, you only know how to obey your body. The body knows what needs to be done.

Chomping is a pleasure, and umami is so darn chompable. Chompable isn't a word, but I don't like chewable. Chewable is what they call those vitamin C tablets. Chompable seems more ad hoc to me, more of a treat, more sinful. Or, as Agatha Christie would say, 'delish'.

In cookbooks they use the word 'rich' to describe umami. I like 'rich' but it doesn't translate well into Spanish, because in English it connotes something complex, filling, satisfying, while *rico* just means tasty.

If we delve back to the beginning, perhaps umami doesn't start in the mouth at all, but rather as a craving, at first sight.

*

I dug out a letter I wrote to Noelia from Madrid on July 21 1983.

All I can say, my love, is: Bravo to me! I've made a friend! He's a philosopher. He was leaving the library the other day at the same time as me. Next thing I knew he'd crossed to my side of the street, and we went on like that for twenty minutes, until we reached the same block, both of us suspecting the other of following him. Later we laughed about it, of course: it turns out we're neighbors. He's Spanish and he's called Juan (aren't they all?). Best part is he's just as lonesome as I am because he recently came back from a long exile in Mexico. We've got into the habit of going for a drink – or four – when the city heats up. Yesterday I asked him where I should go to buy some bathing trunks, because I'm thinking of making the

*most of the dead hours (so many hours without you!) to
learn how to swim. That would be nice, wouldn't it? If
I do learn, when I get back, we'll go to Acapulco. We'll
go even if I don't learn. I'm craving the sea like never
before. It's Madrid's heat (dry as dry can be). It leaves me
KO. Anyway, the point is, my Noe, that Juan answered
my bathing-trunk query like this: 'In Madrid they've hit
upon the ultimate ontological proof, and it goes like this:
"If it exists, you'll find it in the Corte Inglés."'*

*

I was always grateful to Noelia for not filling our house with
archetypal cardiology paraphernalia. In some egocentric ety-
mological retracing of the Latin word *cura*, Mexico's 'curers'
seem to think their role also includes 'curating'. Nine out of
ten of the doctors we knew regurgitated, ad infinitum, exactly
the same exhibition in their offices: 'Mexican Paperweights –
a retrospective'.

Handing out paperweights is an elegant way to take the
register at conferences, and they come in all shapes and
sizes: glass paperweights (usually pyramid-shaped); copper
paperweights (boasting Bajío-style motifs); hard plastic paperweights (in the shape of a pill); rubber foam paperweights
(always anatomically graphic: the heart and all its nooks and
crannies, with the name of some drug written in florescent type
under the alveoli); rock paperweights, brass paperweights,
aluminum paperweights. Paperweights that have nothing
to weigh down, because even doctors have had to get with
the times and start using computers. And scattered around

these gallery pieces we find the accompanying explanatory exhibition texts in the form of diplomas, photos of dogs and children, odes to the Beatles, Mexican flags, gifts from patients who, having faced the light at the end of the tunnel and then been brought back, become remarkably magnanimous (metal knights, little painted plaster saints). One recently recovered patient gave Noelia a gold charm in the shape of heart. She had it melted down and turned into earrings. Truth be told, we weren't entirely innocent of the curating crime ourselves: we too collected our fair share of superstitious figurines, although that was during the Year of Reproduction.

The reason I'm thinking about this – about the aesthetics of doctors' consulting rooms – is because I've spent the whole week seeing doctors. What can I say? Going to hospital isn't what it used to be. To start with, it's no longer my friends who look after me, but rather their putative children. They respect me because they knew who my wife was, but I can't find it in me to respect them, because none of them seem old enough to shave, let alone treat me. It's not what it used to be because back in the day a trip to the hospital meant time away from the institute: a day off. It's not what it used to be because back in the day I would walk out of there with my ego well and truly boosted (the doctors would compare me to the most virile flora and fauna: an oak! A bull!). Nowadays I leave bewildered, afraid I've been hoodwinked; the same feeling you get after talking to a plumber. None of that flora or fauna stuff: I'm just told in the most mechanical of terms that this or that pipework is blocked.

It's not what it used to be because before, after my appointment, I would go up to Cardiology and sit in my wife's little waiting room: to make her uncomfortable, for a laugh, of course, but also to marvel at that other personality of hers, that other person Noelia was at work. So mine, and yet – it was clearer there, with her in her medic's coat, than in any other place – so irrefutably only hers, so beyond me, so much something other than what we were together. In flora-and-fauna terms, an autotroph.

*

Anchovies, tomatoes, and Parmesan cheese all contain glutamate. That is, they are umami-y. The same with chicken and beef, Worcestershire sauce, kombu seaweed, some hellish spread called Marmite which we tried in England (I hated it, Noelia loved it), mushrooms, and – though only on the inside – our wedding rings (both my ring, which I wear on my finger, and Noelia's, which is tied around my neck with a piece of embroidery thread Linda gave me from her sewing kit the other day at the Mug). Now I wear it like Linda does: like a necklace. On the inside of the rings – which are both gold, because deep down we were traditionalists – it says: *Umami, 5-5-1974.*

We got married in Morelia, with my tiny family and the whole army of Vargas cousins. They gave us dishware, vases, and a German Shepherd which we passed off to the first nephew who said 'I'll take it!' They also took a ton of pictures, which we keep in a box. They're color slides. On our tenth or maybe twentieth anniversary we projected them onto a wall while our friends drifted around the house sipping martinis.

On our wedding day, Noelia wore white flowers in her hair but a pink dress, which not one of her aunts failed to comment on. Preempting their disapproval, I wore a white suit to compensate. They didn't appreciate that either. It had bellbottoms. My mustache was bushy enough for a bird to nest in. What bad taste we had in the seventies, and how shamelessly we wore it. I'm sure if I got out those slides now I'd be scandalized myself by those aunts' outfits.

Another option we considered for our rings was to engrave them with the word *Bonito,* then the date. The idea came to us because it was in the scales of the bonito fish that they first identified monosodium glutamate, which is the salt umami is made from. What's more, the word perfectly summed up our relationship: *bonito*, meaning lovely, meaning beautiful. But in the end we threw that option out the window and opted for the 'less pretentious' umami. Go figure.

*

Noelia liked the color pink and not only wore it on her wedding day, but pretty much every day (The Girls, too, when they came along). Pink shoes, pink skirts, even a bag in a hideous Barbie pink; the kind the humanitees can't abide. They've outgrown it. If the humanitees ever wear pink, it has to be Mexican pink. The humanitees, at least in springtime, wear a strict Luis Barragánesque palette: yellow, white, Mexican pink. The rest of the year they wear dark clothes in shiny materials that completely outshine them. Nothing, on the other hand, could ever dull Noelia's natural sparkle. If this were one of those pretentious academic articles, like the ones I used to be an expert in, I'd say, 'Nothing diminished her intrinsic luminescence.'

*

My first article on umami came out in September 1985 and was, of course, spectacularly ignored. The earthquake probably played some part in this, but it's also true that there's barely a soul on the planet who reads the institute's journal. In fact, judging by the amount of typos, I'm not even convinced the editors read it. They take years to publish something, and when the time finally comes their presentation is mind-blowingly bad.

'Love, I think bad tends to mean good these days.'

'And how would you know?'

'There are a lot of kids in the hereafter, Alfonso, if only you could see.'

'Suicides?'

'Car accidents, mostly.'

*

Since tipping – that most healthy of customs – doesn't exist in the academic world, we settle for citations. As an academic, you can assume, more or less with good reason, that if you did a good job someone will eventually quote you. Personally, I'd rather get tips. Although, having said that, one of the best things that ever happened to me was thanks to a citation. I was quoted by Doctor Nakahara, a student of Doctor Kikunae. Kikunae was the first man to isolate monosodium glutamate, at the beginning of the century in the University of Tokyo. That is, the first man to discover and name umami. Well, Nakahara was one of his most faithful disciples and he quoted me, not in an academic paper, but in a biographical article he wrote to pay reverence to his teacher and to demonstrate that he was famous even in the Third World, all the way over there in Mexico. And thanks to that quote we struck up a pen-friendship so solid only the invention of the email could finish it off. In one of our correspondences, Nakahara sent me this clipping:

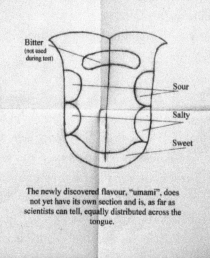

Map of the Tongue

Bitter
(not used
during test)

Sour

Salty

Sweet

The newly discovered flavour, "umami", does not yet have its own section and is, as far as scientists can tell, equally distributed across the tongue.

When the house half collapsed in 1985 and we ended up having to write off the whole building, move to Morelia for a year, and come up with a new 'life project', it occurred to me to dig out the sketches I'd made during my period of convalescence and convince my wife that we should throw ourselves into converting what was left of the house into something else entirely: a set of houses we could rent. And that's when we discovered that the inordinate quantities of painkillers I'd consumed during my recovery had led me to somewhat overestimate my artistic ability. But Noelia, who spent the whole of eighty-six in a private clinic we'd set up in her cousin's house, seeing patients who were all, in one way or another, relations of hers, said, 'Do what you like, love, just get cracking so we can go back to Mexico City.'

'Not true! I also always thought your drawings were good.'

'By which you mean bad.'

'It doesn't work both ways, smarty pants.'

*

I feel it is my duty to point out, in case I die and someone finds this, that Harvard has publicly repudiated the little map of the tongue Nakahara sent me. Now, if you think about it, anyone with two brain cells and a drop of lemon on the tip of the tongue (supposedly the area that only distinguishes sweetness) could have exposed it sooner, but this didn't occur to those of us who took the map as a given (basically because it came from Harvard; we smarty pants are suckers for the smartest smarty pants). Anyway, it turned out to be a load of baloney. But it was a good map; at least, it served us well as a foundation for our plans for the mews, with an added dose of artistic license.

*

The houses in Belldrop Mews are arranged as follows:

● BELL	▓ UMAMI
X YARDS	88 SWEET
▯ PASSAGEWAY	≡ SOUR
	‖‖‖ BITTER
	⁖ SALTY

And they're occupied as follows:

Bitter House: Marina. A young painter who doesn't eat or indeed paint much, but invents colors. For example: fusciaranth is the color of amaranth; she did that one for me. Cloggray the color of dirty water, and a pointed reminder that the gutters in the entry hall don't drain properly. Rainbowrket, that's my personal favorite: it's the multicolored light you find under the street-market awnings.

Sour House: Pina and her dad, Beto. Her mom, Chela, walked out in 2000, and left behind a letter which Beto hid and Pina spends her life trying to find. Agatha Christie told me as much.

Salty House: Linda Walker and Víctor Pérez. Musicians in the National Symphony Orchestra and owners of the school thanks to which my life is set to an interminable, unbearable fluty tune. Their kids: Ana, AKA Agatha Christie, Theo and Olmo. And Luz, in loving memory.

Sweet House: The Pérez-Walker Academy of Music. The little sign next to the bell reads 'PW'. That's all, because I don't have planning permission for my tenants to go around setting up schools. But in any case I turn a blind eye, because there are worse things than trying to spread a little bit of sol-fa in the world. And because otherwise they wouldn't make rent.

Umami House: Alfonso Semitiel, AKA me, and The Girls. The Girls are two reborn dolls who belonged to their exquisitely beautiful mother, Noelia Vargas Vargas, God rest her soul, and who I now dress and groom on an almost daily basis. One of them breathes.

*

The other day, out of nowhere in the Mustard Mug, Linda told me why she isn't playing the cello at the moment. She says she can't trust her arms. She says that sometimes she's in full flow and her arms just turn to jello.

'Did you carry her?' I asked.

She said she did, and then I understood. Or at least I think I did. Because sometimes, in the middle of the night, my arms wake me up too. Mine don't turn to jello. They go stiff; stiff at the memory of Noelia when I carried her dead. I'd carried her countless times before, especially during the last months, but she'd never weighed so much. And it wasn't just my sorrow, I'm sure of it. She really, physically weighed much more.

'Why?' Linda asked me.

'Why do the dead weigh more than the living?'

'Uh-huh.'

'I guess it has to do with the lack of muscular tension,' I told her. 'When you carry someone living, no matter how weak they are, they still carry themselves a little as well.'

'Maybe that's what dying is, don't you think?'

'Weighing more?'

'The moment you stop carrying your own weight.'

*

What I like about writing is seeing the letters fill up the screen. It's something so seemingly simple, so perfectly alchemic: black on white. To plant worlds and tend them as they grow. If you're missing a comma, you add it, and now there's nothing missing. Everything this text needs is here.

And white on black, too. The pauses, the spaces, or as my friend Juan the philosopher would say: the ineffable. Everything missing from this text, its absences and silences, is here too.

I don't know if it's my age, or the sabbatical or what, but writing this I've started to realize just how fragile the system of referencing – to which I always adhered – is. Now, the academic etiquette that regulated my writing for years seems as much of a mask as those fake star-spangled nails young ladies these days wear. Bibliographical citations were invented as masks for men incapable of holding a conversation, let alone keeping eye-contact with their interlocutor. Men as dull as dishwater and deep down as insecure as the next person, but with a thin layer of intellectual pretension coating them. Timid men with delusions of grandeur. In other words, men just like me.

*

Noelia was competitive as hell. The idea of missing a convention or conference or any opportunity to come first in something horrified her. Whenever she received a prize or award she turned into a visionary, declaring that to be the first woman to achieve 'x' opened the doors to the next generation. She knew that women were on the back foot, and never missed a chance to say as much in public, but saw this more as a challenge than a handicap. It was her, by the way, who used the word handicap in questions of gender. I once heard her tell a female junior doctor who called her up crying because a doctor had put his hands on her leg, that women in medicine certainly could get to the top in Mexico, but that the trick was to keep Paralympic runners in mind.

'Do you know how professional handicapped athletes get ahead?' I heard her ask, still in her inspirational voice.

'No,' the junior must have answered.

'With twice the effort and half the visibility,' Doctor Vargas explained.

*

It was during our stay in Morelia after the earthquake that Noelia began to regret not having had children. Perhaps it was a byproduct of the survivor's aftershock that ran through us all. Or maybe too much exposure to the family: her brother's heart attack, her quitting smoking, and the overdose of Sundays spent with cute nieces and nephews. She couldn't sleep. She would switch on the light at three in the morning and ask, deadly serious, 'Aren't we missing out on something?'

I would tell her that, yes, one always, irredeemably misses out on something, and that if we'd had children we'd also be missing out on something: something else. But she only ever heard me up to 'yes'.

And that's how all of a sudden the decade we'd invested in defending our decision to not try for children threatened to repeat itself. Now we'd have a child and spend the next decade defending our decision to be mature parents. I was already well into my forties.

'Your wish is my command,' I told her.

And we did try, hard, but not with doctors and needles and little cups. We decided – or rather, Noelia did, in a typical snub against her own profession (ah, those people who criticize their own profession, eh?!) – that she didn't want anything to do with assisted conception. If we were going to have a child, it would be Fate who gave it to us. So, quite simply, she stopped taking her pill, and we began going at it like rabbits in a race against the menopause.

The Year of Reproduction – which was how we later came to refer to the period in which we returned to Mexico City, and which was really more like three years – coincided with the construction of the mews. We were investing so that our imaginary future ward would never want for anything. They were exhausting, superstitious and anxious times, but they never got the better of us. The truth is that we both showed ourselves to be skeptics, as much with regard to the builders as the pregnancy. And this brought us closer than ever. We suspected everything and everyone: in particular the pair of doctors we consulted, but also the construction foreman.

Saturdays went like this: we'd pay the builders their weekly wage, wait for them to leave, then make love. Apart from Saturdays and the odd siesta, we had an ovulation calendar stuck to the bathroom wall. I never really understood it, but in practical terms it worked like this: Noelia said, 'Now!', and her wish was my command.

We kept clay figures at home. Imitation pre-Hispanic pieces. The kinds of knickknacks educated Mexicans buy. Apart from this educated Mexican: I got them free. Every year the institute gives its researchers a bonus coupon packet to be spent in its own stores. I never cared much for their folkloric CDs or gimmicky T-shirts, but during the Year of Reproduction, the coupons found their use: we stocked up on figurines. In fact, we took collecting pretty seriously. On a chest in the living room we arranged a selection of little fertility goddesses from different cultures. A couple of them were made from amaranth, which I was already investigating by then. Our friends even donated their mythical figures to our cause (although both Noelia and I suspected that they blew out the candles they lit for us the moment we left their houses).

One day during all this, I arrived home to find all the little statues with their heads covered with strips of cloth. When I asked Noelia what it was all about, she answered, '*a*) How have you not noticed they've been like that for three days?, and *b*) it's a plan I came up with, to wake them up with a bang.'

'How do you figure that?' I asked.

'I cover their heads with a cloth, right? Then I leave them like that a few days, and around midday on Sunday, when the sun's at its brightest, I whip off the cloth and pow!'

'Pow?'

'They wake up with a bang.'

'And why do we want them to wake up with a bang?'

'So they get a move on, Alfonso. So they grant us our little miracle.'

Our little miracle, of course, was the child we never had. The child we never asked for. Or rather the child we asked for, but without sufficient faith to make the gods get a move on. It didn't work. In 1991, Chela and Linda, our tenants with whom Noelia had been spending all her free time (supposedly to get some pregnancy training in), each gave birth to a baby girl. They were ten years younger than her, and by the end of the first month helping them in their new lives as mothers, Noelia decided that the whole thing was way too much at our age and decided to have her tubes tied, just in case Fate came to bite us in the ass.

Of course, it wasn't as easy as all that. We cried the tears we had to cry. The statuettes remained covered up. I was fifty. She had just turned forty-two. We decided we'd be grandparents to the little neighbors, if they'd have us, and we let go.

*

When something was a bit insipid, a bit lacking in meatiness or flavor, Noelia and I declared it 'Umami No'. It sounded Japanese.

*

Feeding is another area of arrested development if you suffer from the condition of offspringhood. That's how Noelia justified her weight-gains and -losses, which began when she quit smoking.

'I don't have anyone other than myself to feed.'

'What am I, chopped liver?'

'You're not growing, Alfonso. And you don't count: *a*) because you're skinny, and *b*) because it's you that feeds me.'

There was one period when I was less skinny: during that fateful year in Morelia I put on six kilos (me, who's always been a beanpole), I guess because the army of aunts would feed us at the slightest encouragement. Noelia put on fourteen kilos, and that on a diet. But in Morelia a light dessert is when they substitute sugar for condensed milk.

I think I'm putting on weight now, actually. It must be all the take-outs and tequila. Maybe I should head to the supermarket, resume old habits, make myself that soup. I used to make chicken stock every Sunday and use it to make all kinds of soups during the week, plus whatever you could whip up with the shredded chicken: sandwiches, tacos, salads. Sometimes I fantasize about investing in a battery-operated mechanism that makes The Girls eat. And since I know that no such thing exists, the rest of the time I fantasize about inventing it. Why did I become an anthropologist when I could have been an engineer, an inventor, a carpenter?

Yesterday the postman delivered an invitation from the institute to a seminar so rhetorically and pompously titled I wanted to scream. The academy is the place where the middle classes puff themselves up with their Sunday-best words and endorse the myth that knowledge is power. Load of boloney! Knowledge debilitates. Knowledge inflates the ego and starves ingenuity. To know is to use the body less and less; to live a sedentary existence. Knowledge makes you fat! Thank God I'm not advising any doctoral students at the moment, because that'd be my aphorism of choice to rip apart their empty theories about the latest trendy sacred pseudo-cereal (no doubt quinoa, which, by the way, was never eaten in Mexico). The new kids on the block can argue with me till they're blue in the face. Go and scrape the potsherd, for Christ's sakes! Use your brain and your microscope and don't go making up crap when the truth is ten times more interesting than the drivel your tiny minds come up with!

Knowledge pisses you off.

*

A list off the top of my head of the things Noelia would buy in the supermarket without stopping to think:

Flip-flops, especially the kind with patterns on them. I must have given away a thousand pairs, but every time I clean out a closet, there's another one.

Tin foil.

Canned tuna. This was an old tic of hers: before she met me, since she practically lived at the hospital, she ate the same salad, over and over, which she'd picked up when she did her junior residence. It consisted of one can of tuna, another of corn, and a few tablespoons of Hellmann's mayonnaise. (Noelia made a point of stressing the mayonnaise brand whenever she passed on the recipe to some malnourished resident: in her day, only the nurses used McCormick; residents ate Hellmann's.)

Sugar-free gum (at the cash register). She only ever chewed gum when she drove alone, because she was paranoid she'd fall asleep at the wheel.

Paracetamol.

PAM: 1-cal cooking spray.

*

Noelia once said to me, 'Being only a daughter is so Umami No.'

*

PAM cooking spray – that piteous substitute for oil which I refuse point-blank to use – came into our lives kicking and screaming. Lulú brought it for us. Lulú is Noelia's cousin from Boston, and was the undisputed chief promoter of my wife's esoteric side. Every time she came to stay she'd bring a new tarot-card game, or a year's worth of Chinese horoscopes, or a book on her latest diet. The pair of them were hooked on Weight Watchers for about a hundred years, during which time Lulú sent boxes and boxes of points-based, readymade food without ever giving a thought to how deeply it offended me.

In exchange, whenever Noelia went to the States for a conference, she would take Lulú a box full of handmade tortillas and Mexican bits, because her cousin was one of those émigrés who spends their life idolizing their homeland. When it got easier to get hold of Mexican products over there, Lulú became more and more picky. She only wanted Noelia to bring her things from the market; nothing prepackaged. One time they stopped us at customs and we had to hand over all seven kilos of the Oaxaca cheese we'd attempted to sneak through. Try as Noelia might to play up her credentials for the customs officers, nobody would believe her that that stringy, by then ever-so-slightly-tangy cheese was pasteurized.

Lulú lived outside of the country and, to some extent, outside of time. As far as I recall, she was the only one of our friends and family who never stopped making hypothetical comments about our hypothetical children. She never gave up telling us about how gringas were having babies later and later, about fertility clinics, about how she was going to take our kids to see God knows what team over there, because she was a baseball nut. She probably still is. I mean, in all likelihood she's still alive, it's just I haven't seen her since Noelia's funeral. I remember she took care of the flowers.

Lulú didn't have children either, or a partner. In her own words, she didn't even have 'a dog to whine at her'. The day she turned up with a tub of Cool Whip, she presented it to us with the words, 'Not even God, who invented the penis, could have come up with something this good and this low in calories.' But that was the only reference to a man I ever heard her make. I know she had several, because she was a fine-looking woman and because, once Lulú had taken herself off to the guest room, Noelia would fill me in, jumping into bed possessed by a kind of gossip hyper-frenzy, which only sleep, generally mine, could snap her out of. It was during one of these sessions that Noelia let on how the idea of the reborn dolls had come from Lulú.

'What are they?' I asked. 'It sounds esoteric.'

'They're dolls that have been reborn,' Noelia explained.

'Reborn how?'

'Like, they're not dolls anymore. When they're reborn, they become babies. Sort of to console those people who don't have children, you know the type?'

2001

My job is to take all the dirt off the death trumpets with a toothbrush. It's really hard because the dirt is the same color as the trumpet so you can't tell when to stop. When I think I can't get any more off I put the trumpet in a salad bowl full of warm water and Grandma rubs it with her fingers to make sure. Her hands look like mine when I've spent ages in the lake. Now I have clothes on again and it feels all toasty. When the trumpets are as clean as clean can be, we give them to my mom and she puts them in with the garlic and tomatoes that are sizzling in the pan. Sizzling is what you call the sound of loads and loads of snakes talking at once.

'What do you paint your hands with?' I ask Grandma.

'My nails?'

'Yup.'

'With varnish.'

'Would you like Emma to paint your nails?' my mom asks me.

I shake my head from side to side. Of course I don't. I know what varnish is and how much it pongs.

*

We eat at a table on the terrace, which Grandma calls the porch. I'm hungry. Everything smells of oil and garlic. Pina doesn't like garlic because she's dumb. Ana likes garlic as much as I do, especially the burnt bits. My mom takes two pieces from the pan, gives us one each, and we chew on them happily. Pina pulls a face at us like she's disgusted. She says to me, 'Jeez, Luchi Luchi, who would have known?'

'Known what?'

'That you're not a vampire.'

Emma gives us cotton serviettes instead of paper ones and I sit all elegant, like the elegant ladies on the planes who wear neckties and little hats and give out peanuts.

'I can't be a vampire because I'm a peanut, right?' I ask, and everyone says, 'Right,' apart from Ana, who rolls her eyes and stays looking at the sky like when she wishes we weren't sisters at all.

Emma serves the pasta from the pan and some wine that her friends on the other coast make. She serves us girls a little bit too, but it tastes gross. Only Pina likes it, but then she says that her mom also likes wine and her chin trembles like she's going to cry, but then she asks Grandma for some Coca-Cola. Ana and I laugh, because we know Grandma hates Coca-Cola. But then Emma explains to Pina something she's never explained to us.

'Coca-Cola is the sewage of the empire,' she says.

Ew, no wonder my mom never let us touch the stuff.

'Is Michigan an empire?' I ask, while trying to wrap my spaghetti around my fork like my mom wants us to.

Pina says it is and that the emperor is called Michelin.

'That's not true,' Ana says. 'The emperor is called Umami.'

'And is he a baddie?'

'A really bad baddie,' Pina says. 'He eats little girls for breakfast.'

'Nuh-uh, no he isn't,' interrupts Ana. And then she says to Pina, 'Don't tell tales to my sister!' And to me she says, 'Umami is the best emperor in the world; if a little girl goes visit him in his castle, Umami will grant her a wish.'

I want to ask more but Mama and Grandma put us to work in the kitchen. They give me a special spoon, like the teeny-weeny baby of the one you use to scoop ice cream, and I have to use it to make melon balls. First you dig it in the fruit, then you turn. I'm the queen of the melon balls. I have to put them then in glass dishes where Ana then serves a scoop of ice cream and Pina adds a spoon.

Grandma makes tea. She puts a white cloth, two mugs and a jar of honey on a tray.

'Why are there bugs in the honey?' I ask her.

'They're not bugs,' she says, 'they're special mushrooms for adults. But I've got something special for you kiddos too,' she says, and she pulls out a tin of long cookies with a chocolate middle. She asks me how many I want and I say, 'Lots.' She puts one cookie in each ice-cream cup and hands me the ones left over. Ana gets all jealous. She hates it when I get presents and she doesn't.

'I'll give them to you if you tell me where the emperor's castle is,' I say to her.

'Done.'

I give them to her and she whispers in my ear, 'You'll

never reach it, because it's at the bottom of the lake.' Then she sticks her tongue out at me and walks off with my cookie tin. Pina sticks her tongue out at me too, just because.

When we go out with the dessert, Emma gives us a round of applause and my mom sings a song she really likes about a donna, which is Spanish for doughnut. Except it's not in Spanish.

'What language is that?' asks Pina.

Mom says it's Italian and then we all teach Pina the song. Turns out it's not about a doughnut as I always thought, but about a woman. My mom keeps on explaining all the words but I'm not paying any attention to her because I'm thinking about something else. I'm thinking of how my ziplings and I are always hiding to drink a drink that is actually made of poop.

*

Ana and Pina go watch their TV series in one of the bedrooms. They bought it yesterday in Penny Saver and it has a zillion new episodes and it's all they ever talk about. I don't want to watch it because, even though they say it isn't scary, I've seen vampires on the cover, so it's scary.

Grandma asks me if I like hammocks. I tell her I do and she takes me to the front terrace, where her old truck lives. Our rented car lives there too, but not today, because the boys took it with them. And the little path that connects the house to the highway is there too. Plus some muddy shoes, some chairs, umbrellas, and a giant ball of threads hanging from the roof. Emma unravels it and it turns out the ball is the hammock. She ties it between the two posts of the terrace.

'Porch,' Emma corrects me.

'I thought the porch was at the back.'

'That too. You've got your front porch and your back porch.'

'And your middle porch,' I say, but she doesn't laugh.

I climb into the hammock and she says, 'Lift your head,' and when I do she slips a cushion behind it.

'I never used a pillow on a hammock before,' I tell her.

'It's the civilized version,' she says.

'I'm not sleepy.'

'I know. It's to make you more comfy.'

'Will you rock me a little?'

Grandma rocks me for way too little before she stops and says it's going to rain.

'How do you know?'

'Because the dragonflies are out.'

She goes into the house and comes out with some paper and a can of pencils. Then she kisses me, and when she's gone I take my foot off the hammock and push myself on the edge of the table until I'm really, really rocking. Every now and then I have to take my foot off and do the pushing again so it's not so boring. I liked Grandma before, but I don't like her anymore because I feel like she brought me here to get rid of me. I bet she wants to talk about adult things with my mom. She doesn't know that at home I always hear everything anyway and nothing bad ever happens. I try to reach the can of pencils with my toes so they make an avalanche but she left them too far away. I think I want to go back to the front porch, or the back porch. I don't know which is which anymore. Then I think I'll go when the sun stops shining on my feet, because it's really yummy. The sun that passes through the threads of the hammock draws shadows on my legs. The shadows are like eyes, and they can see everything I'm doing and everything I'm thinking.

I guess I do fall asleep a little bit in the end because when I wake up the eyes are gone and I'm cold and it's raining. I want my mom, but when I go inside the house I see Cleo on the sofa, and maybe it's better if I lie down there because there's a blanket and because Grandma will find me here and feel bad for leaving me outside with so little on. But I can hear them laughing outside and I fall asleep again before anyone comes and finds me.

When I wake up again it's almost nighttime. Cleo and two of her brothers are asleep on the rug next to my sofa. I can't hear the adults, so I make myself into a caterpillar with the blanket and go out onto the porch to find the grown-up girls. Just like I found the trumpets. The table is covered in dirty plates, but there's no one there. I hear voices and run toward them. It's not raining anymore but the grass is wet. I find Emma sitting by the biggest pond. The ledge is made of bricks but she's stroking it like a dog.

'Who are you talking to, Grandma?'

'To her.'

I look around.

'Her who?'

'Emma.'

'You're Emma.'

'You too.'

I laugh, but I don't really feel like laughing. I ask her where my mom is. She leans her head to the right, pats the side of the pond and says, 'I made it.'

'I know,' I tell her. 'You told us this afternoon already, and yesterday, and the day before that.'

'What a pretty wig. Purple really is your color,' she says.

She's speaking like she was asleep. Maybe she's sleepwalking. She has her hand over the water, palms facing down, and she's moving them slowly, as if she was waving.

'And Mama?' I ask her again.

Emma points to an orange carp and says, 'There she is!'

'In the pond?'

'Yes! Your mom turned into a fish.'

I don't believe her. Plus, she's laughing.

'It's true, honey; ever since she was a little girl, once a month your mom turns into a fish.'

She nods her head saying, 'It's true, it's true', which makes me doubt her.

'Which one?' I ask, to try to prove her wrong, and she points to an orange carp, but I can't tell if it's the same one as before. It swims off and hides among the lilies.

'How can you tell?'

'Because her eyes shine differently,' she explains, 'like a mammal's.'

I can feel my lips start to quiver.

'Don't you worry now, she always comes back.'

'Don't be a liar,' I tell her, but my voice is very small like a flea so I run off.

'Come back,' says Emma, but I don't turn around and she doesn't follow me. I want to get lost in the trees, and I want a wolf to come and bite me so that when Grandma finds me she feels really, really bad about lying to me. But I'm too scared to go into the grove. It's dark between the trees. Scaredy-cat!

You spent the whole morning in there! I run back into the house from the side with the terrace and the hammock, and go straight to my sister's room. Ana and Pina are sitting in the dark in front of the TV. There's a girl on the screen who's half green and her head is spinning around and around like a carrousel.

'Is this your series?' I ask them. But Ana screams, 'Get out! It's not for kids!'

I don't like it when she shouts at me. I throw my blanket at them and go to Mama's room. It was her room when she was a little girl. There's a patchwork quilt and instead of a door it has a woven curtain in different colors which Mama washes when we come. She washes all the curtains in the house every time we come because Grandma doesn't really care about the dust. Sometimes it makes Mama nuts that Grandma lives camuflashed between the trees and the dust. I pick Bedtime Bear off the floor and we climb onto her bed. It's made of iron and my mom says it's a princess's bed, but I don't think princesses' beds squeak this much. Ana and I always used to sleep here but this summer she sleeps with Pina in the TV room. A bunch of airplanes hang over me and Bear: wooden planes Mama made with her dad when she was a little girl, before they moved to the lake, and before her dad shacked up with Emma.

Mama's first cello lives in one corner of the room. It's basically the size of me. I feel like pushing the cello over and breaking it a bit because my mom isn't here, because I don't know where she is, but I don't want to get down from the bed because the green girl really scared me.

Someone opens the curtain to the room and I scream, but it's only Grandma. I thought we were mad at each other, but she smiles at me so I guess we are friends again. I think she's here to say something nice to me, like how I'm a sugared peanut, but all she says is, 'Look who came back.'

Grandma draws the curtain more so I can see. On the other side of it there's Mama, soaking wet. Her clothes and hair are dripping on the living-room rug and the rag in her hair has gone dark it's so soaked. There's a water lily stuck between her boobies. Mama was in that pond! I feel my mouth fall open like they do in cartoons.

'You see?' Grandma says.

My mom inflates and deflates her cheeks. Cleo and her brothers run in barking at her. Dogs really, really don't like fishes.

2000

P ina hears the camper rumbling outside. Chela went to start the engine because it has to heat up a while before they can take it on the highway. On all fours and still half-asleep, Pina feels a sudden urge to run out and stop her. But she doesn't. It's a steady rumble; Chela won't leave without them. She searches carefully under the bed, her heart still beating fast. Beto is checking the closets in the bungalow. Pina hears them opening and closing. When she comes out of the bedroom, her dad is in the kitchenette, tapping his fingers against the worktop tiles.

'Nothing there,' Pina says.

'Let's get out of here then,' he says.

They switch off the lights and leave together.

Beto is wearing a suit but no tie. At this time of day, his eyes look like two slits behind his round glasses. The shoulder pads on his gray jacket are creeping up his neck, crumpled by the weight of the load he's carrying: a backpack, a suitcase, the coolbox, a basket. Pina sings softly, 'Little donkey, little donkey, on the dusty road,' and he joins in, 'Got to keep on plodding onwards, with your precious load.'

It's not yet dawn. The bungalows have their eyes closed. The trees, the grand domed roof, and the two long chimneys where the swallows live are all reflected in the pool. The surface is perfectly still, and Pina can't tell if the blue is the water, the sky, or a mixture of the two. She regrets not having swum once all weekend.

They reach the security hut and open the gate. It creaks, but given the racket the camper is making it makes little difference. Pina feels bad for the people sleeping; for the people who have Golfs and Nissans and brothers and sisters. But she's also pretty happy, because she's wanted to leave this place since the second they arrived.

'What happened to you?' her father asks her.

Pina realizes she's fiddling with the sore on her hand.

'I fell,' she says, 'and scraped it.'

Beto crouches down, still loaded up with everything, and says, 'Can you move your wrist?'

'Yes.'

Pina shows him, moving it slowly and pulling a pained face so he believes her. She walks over to the camper and Beto opens the sliding door. She gets in, and he loads their stuff.

'Bonjour, mademoiselle,' Chela says, but Pina doesn't answer. Her dad doesn't like it when Chela speaks French because she learned it with a French boyfriend. When Dad isn't around, her mom tells Pina all about her old flames who always came from far-off places like the princes in fairytales.

It's weird to see her mom up and dressed and at the wheel so early. She's wearing a flowery dress and a black cardigan. Normally when Chela takes Pina to school she's dressed for dance class. She often stays like that all day. One time a boy in her class asked Pina why her mom came to pick her up in pajamas.

'Leotard and leg warmers,' Pina had corrected him. 'Contemporary dance.'

But the boy just gawked at her as if she too were wearing a nighty. And that's generally how it is at school: nobody knows who Pina Bausch is. Everyone assumes Pina's name is Asian. Apart from Ana, of course. Ana knows who Pina Bausch is because Pina told her when they were like six, with a VHS cassette which they still play from time to time, even though they're nine now and they have to take the VHS player out of the closet every time they want to watch it. In the video there's one piece where Pina Bausch dances around a room full of tables and chairs without ever opening her eyes. Sometimes Pina and Ana still try to walk like that, but they always end up bumping into something or each other. One time they made Luz and Olmo try it in the yard and Olmo split his head open on one of the concrete planters.

The camper drives into and then out of a small, sleepy city. From the window, Pina sees three children walking alone along the side of the road. They're wearing uniforms and carrying big backpacks. Pina would like to propose they give them a ride – there's enough space in the camper – but she worries that one of her parents will say yes and the other no, sparking off another row. They take the highway. Beto sings, 'Little donkey, little donkey, had a heavy day,' but nobody joins in. His tie is in the food basket, rolled up like a big, smooth snail.

Last night, in the bathroom, Pina picked at her scab and then watched as it changed color under the stream of tap water. It went from the dark red of dry blood to a light, almost pretty pink. It's only the size of the edge of a nail and it almost doesn't hurt. But it does hurt a little. Enough to make up for the fact that she only counted ninety-seven swallows.

*

Pina likes roads, but not when they come to an end. It bugs her when someone says, 'Nearly there.' She gets antsy and starts to hope they never get there; that they get a flat. Or maybe not a flat, because that would slow them to a stop, and what Pina wants is to keep on moving forever and ever. What she wants is for whoever's driving to miss the turn and keep on going. Pina likes the going, not the getting there. Right now, for example, they're just going. No one's saying 'nearly there', because they've only just set off, and Pina feels at peace; her heart isn't racing; nobody is going anywhere without the others. Her mom is at the wheel. She has her hair in a bun and you can see her dancer's neck, which Pina likes so much. Her dad is looking the other way, out the passenger window. The headlights on the camper illuminate the road ahead.

They used to have a normal car. Pina liked lying underneath the rear windshield on top of the trunk cover. That's what she remembers most of all about the car: how she'd watch the clouds and trees rush by, and lie under the rain without ever getting wet. She also remembers how her dad didn't want her to travel like that, but her mom did, and that one day, to prevent them from fighting, she said she didn't even like traveling under there like that anymore, which was a lie.

Then, one day, while she and her dad were doing her homework in the living room, they heard a loud, persistent honking coming from outside. Eventually, Beto drew back the curtain. Pina watched from the sofa how his faced transfigured, and then how he dissolved into laughter. She ran to the window and there was her mom in the street, doing pirouettes and *jetés* around a red Volkswagen camper to introduce her new toy. She'd left that morning in the regular car and come back in this carriage, which has been getting them around ever since. Dad's reaction that day had been contagious. Pina strokes the memory like a cat, and like a cat, the memory purrs, giving off the precise feeling of that afternoon: him and her doubled up in the living room, and her mom outside, dancing on her own, but for them.

*

Chela puts on some music. It's Tracy Chapman. Pina likes the song 'Fast Car' because that's exactly how the camper goes. Sometimes, if the journey is really long, her dad says, 'OK, enough, right?' and changes to his Mozart CD, which has a dinosaur sticker on the case. Pina put it there because it's old-fogey music.

'Mozart is just baroque oom-pah-pah,' Pina once said, and her parents had fallen about laughing. She knew that what she said was funny because she'd heard someone say it during one of Aunt Linda's rehearsals, and everyone had fallen about laughing then too. The truth was, she didn't know what it meant.

'Don't mess with my man Amadeus,' her dad had said.

Now Pina wants to ask if he remembers, but she can't be bothered to raise her voice over the roaring camper. Sometimes, even without the roaring, Pina can't be bothered to speak. She doesn't like breaking the silence. Like a bubble she can choose when to burst, or like the highway ending, she prefers to put it off. Sometimes it's not possible, because the air is heavy after a row and it falls to her to come up with something else to add to the air to clean it, even if she doesn't want to. Sometimes she knows even before she tells a joke that her parents aren't going to laugh, but she tells it anyway. Because when there's a dirty silence in the car or at home, it doesn't matter if the joke is any good or not: her parents just won't be in the mood. But she has to tell it anyway, like covering a stain with a doily. Just as people on the news go on hunger strikes, her parents go on long laughter strikes. And Pina often goes on talking strikes. She'll only talk a lot with Ana, and occasionally with her dad, who asks her lots of questions. With her mom she won't talk so much because whenever she tells her anything it's as if Chela knew it already.

From her position stretched out on the backseat, Pina turns to face forward. The buckle on her safety belt digs into her but she tells herself to put up with it. She wraps a blanket around her and feels better, but now she doesn't see the landscape as it whooshes by so the road is pretty dull. She changes position again, now in a grump. Then she raises her feet and presses her toenails to the window. It's cold. When she takes them away the mark is left on the condensation. It's like leaving footprints without having to go anywhere. When they disappear, you just put your foot back. When it gets too cold, you put your foot back under the blanket.

It's like her mom, who comes and goes, and then, just when Pina thinks she's not going to remember her anymore, comes back. She spent a lot of time this weekend thinking about that. Because of the fight, of course, but also because of the floor all around the pool. It was made of clay paving stones. When the soaking-wet kids ran past they left their footprints there, and then, gradually, the footprints disappeared and it was as if they'd never been there. Pina thinks that the boy who scratched her hand the night before isn't as bad as the other boys. The other boys from Planet Earth.

She sleeps for a while, and when she wakes up the sun is coming up. They're parked up by the side of a tollgate. Pina sits up and looks out the window. Her mom is buying a cup of coffee and her dad must be in the bathroom because she can't see him. She puts her mouth up against the window the way her mom hates. When she sees her, Chela points to her polystyrene cup, which is her sign for, 'You want one?' Pina shakes her head. Chela shrugs her shoulders twice, which is her sign for, 'Your loss'. Pina counts the things around her. There are five people at the food stand: two of them are vendors and they're wearing aprons and puffy, layered skirts. There are four cars at the tollgate: one of them is a truck and another has bicycles tied to the roof. There are three dogs loitering around the stand. There is one dad coming out of the bathroom. Chela points at her cup, now facing Beto, and he shakes his head. Chela gives another two shrugs. Pina thinks, 'Coffee strike.' There is one dad, one girl, and one camper waiting for one mom who's chatting with the two vendors.

*

They set off again. It's light now and they're getting close to the dip in the road that Pina always dreads, but at the same time craves to see; from up there you can see the layer of scum you're heading into. Mexico City sits waiting under the scum. Mexico City lives under the scum. Sometimes a few towers or roofs might poke out from beneath it, but in general, in the first hours of the morning, the scum is sealed: like something you could bounce up and down on. But it does let you in. The scum swallows you and makes sure you forget all about it. This is its chief characteristic: as soon as you enter the scum, you stop seeing it. Pina knows this, and yet she struggles to believe it every time she's there on that slope, looking down on it; at how thick, how gray, and blue, and brown it is, and semi-solid, like a dirty meringue. She just can't believe she'll forget about it. And she tries to keep it in sight for as long as possible, but the scum always disappears eventually. Only once or twice, around mid-morning in the schoolyard, has she thought she could make it out above her, high, high above the school, blurring the outlines of the taller buildings. Pina greets it quietly: 'Hello, scum.' According to Theo, Mexico City kids have that scum in their lungs, and they pollute the places they visit just by exhaling.

About halfway down the slope, the camper pierces through the scum. It disappears in an instant. Pina is doing everything she can to keep the scum in sight – 'see it, see it, see it' – when her mom lets out a scream. The camper lurches, then carries on as if nothing had happened.

'What the fuck?' her dad says.

'A bathtub! There was a bathtub!' her mom answers, pointing to a spot that's impossible to make out among the trees and going at that speed. At the first chance she gets, Chela comes off the highway and starts driving up and down side streets. Beto asks her to get back onto the highway. The sudden change of direction has riled him: he wants to make it to the office on time. Chela ignores him. Pina pinches herself. It starts to rain. Theo would say, 'That's the scum peeing on us.'

*

They spend a long time swerving puddles and stones, none of them saying a word, and with the music off. Despite herself, Pina starts to think her dad is right and that her mom just imagined the bathtub. But she doesn't say anything because she's on opinion strike. Her mom says she didn't imagine it, that they should leave her alone, that she's going to find it. And she does. They turn a corner and there it is, clear as day. All the houses in the street have either gas tanks or water tanks or plants on their roofs. Except for one, which has a bathtub on it: it's filthy and old, and has gold feet.

'It's got lion feet!' Chela says, as if this made up for the horrible hour they've just spent looking for it. And for a second Pina expects a burst of laughter; silently, she tries willing her dad to laugh like he did when Chela bought the camper, so that the three of them can all burst into an infectious, unifying fit of hysterics. But her dad just says, totally dry, 'De-lux.'

Chela parks up behind a driverless taxi and gets out of the camper like she knows where she's going, protecting herself from the rain with her flimsy cardigan. She looks a bit weird with her flowery dress in this place were the taxis live. Pina gives herself permission to talk again.

'Why are the houses gray here?' she asks.

'They're stained by the smog,' answers her dad.

'Is this where the scum lives?'

Beto says, 'Yes.' Then straight away, 'No.'

Pina explains that she already knows what the smog is. Her school closed one time because of it and she was allowed to stay in her pajamas all day long for days on end.

'You're not going to make it to school today,' her dad says.

'That's alright,' Pina says, and she passes Beto his tie.

'Thanks,' he says, but doesn't put it on.

The metal door her mom has just knocked on opens, and a fat man appears in the doorway. He's not wearing a T-shirt, and he only lays his eyes on Chela for a second before closing the door again. Chela shrugs and Beto raises his eyebrows, which is the sign for, 'I told you.' But then the man comes out again, now wearing a T-shirt. A little girl peeps out from behind him, staring at Chela.

'Maybe she has no mom,' Pina thinks. 'Maybe she wants mine.'

Chela talks to the man, points to the rooftop, puts her hands together, and eventually it looks like the man says something back to her. She walks back to the camper. Beto leans in toward the driver's door and winds down the window.

'How much have you got on you?' she asks.

Beto opens his wallet.

'Five hundred pesos.'

She takes all the cash, leans half her body through the window, rifles through her bottomless handbag, takes another couple of bills and, as a parting gesture, grabs the coins sitting in the camper ashtray. Beto is still holding his empty wallet, which is now gaping at the middle like a black fish freshly gutted by the monger. Chela is radiant with all that money in her hands and her hair sticking to her face in the rain. She blows Beto a kiss. Pina takes her money from her backpack and offers it to her: it's a ten-peso coin, but Chela doesn't accept it.

'Save it for the bubbles,' she says, and she blows another kiss, this time to Pina.

'What bubbles?' asks Pina, but Chela has already turned around. It's her dad who answers.

'She means bubble bath. To put in that thing.'

They watch as Chela hands the man the money, and he hands it back to her. She gives it to him again. He gives it back to her. This happens three or four times until at last the man pockets the money and lets Pina's mom into the house. She closes the door behind her. This is when Beto, who up until then had been sitting with his head leaned back against his chair, sits up. He moves his nose in toward the windshield. Not long after, they see Chela appear on the rooftop accompanied by a lanky boy. Pina's chest is beating so hard and fast that her admiration feels like fear.

'That's my mom!' she wants to say.

Her mom is shouting something to her dad. They can't hear her, but get the gist of what she's saying from how she's moving her hands. Beto lets out a sigh.

'Don't get out of the car,' he tells Pina as he opens his door. Before he's even closed it again he's landed his feet in a puddle, soaking his socks. He slams the door, damning this and fucking that, and runs to the house, trying but failing to protect himself from the rain with his hands. His white shirt goes see-through. Before he's even knocked, the same girl opens the door. She looks at Pina for a second, then closes the door behind Beto. 'That's it,' thinks Pina. 'The little girl has won: she's going to keep my parents and I'll end with the fat, shirtless man for a father.' She shakes the thought from her head by turning her attention to her mom on the roof. Chela has broken into dance.

The lanky boy watches her, laughing nervously until Beto emerges onto the rooftop. The lanky boy leaves them to it. Pina tenses up, then climbs onto the front seat to watch her parents argue in the rain. Her mom's happy and her dad's furious, that much she can tell from the camper. Between them, they manage to pick up the bathtub. It's heavy. They put it down. He shouts. She gesticulates. They pick it up again and inch their way towards the edge of the rooftop. In one single motion, they tip the tub over. Brown water pours out. And that is the last image Pina has of her parents together: they're standing on the roof of a house in the middle of the scum, tipping filthy water onto an already flooded street.

IV

2004

I planted the corn. The rest is just watering, tending, and jotting down any observations in the margins of my books. One of them is *The Urban* Milpa *Manual*, published by our very own Alf in 1974. On the front there's a photo of the mews before it was the mews. In the background you can see the huge house that was here originally and the rest of the plot, which is fully planted, with a group of hippies working 'the field'. Among them I can pick out Alf, just as skinny but with lots more hair: dark, frizzy and long. And on the house's facade I spot the bell, which would fall eleven years later and bury itself in the passageway forevermore, like the sword in the stone.

The plan is to plant the beans once the corn stalks reach a half-meter. The beans will give back all the nitrogen the corn has taken from the soil. Apparently this is important. I have to plant two or three bean shoots for every corn stalk and guide them so they climb. The nitrogen trick will make the new soil last for lots of cycles. This is what they call crop rotation and it will ensure we made a sound investment: my dad with his money, and me with my summer.

Once the bean shoots reach the third of the height of the corn stalks, I'll have to plant the squash seeds. We'll see how the whole thing pans out if I have to survive high school at the same time. For now, the yard looks breathtaking, if I do say so myself. Apart from the *milpa* area at the back, the rest is now a lawn and the planters are full. I just have one empty planter, for the tomatoes I'll plant when my brothers are back. We put the old picnic table back where it was, but now it sits on grass. The turf cost the most out of everything, but Dad's happy; he comes out barefoot in the afternoons after the rains. We dry the benches with a flannel and sit out there. I read and he plays his new toy: these exotic Indian drums called tabla. The name tabla makes it sound like it's just one drum, but in fact there are two of them: a big one and a little one. Before you can play it you have to learn how to talk tabla. Dad goes to class once a week and each night he rehearses little sounds which he then tries to reproduce with his hands. I've got the basics down already: Right hand: *Taa, Tin, Tete, Tu.* Left hand: *Ga, Ka.* Just don't ask me to reproduce them on the drums. Dad plays until his tendons start to ache.

'You don't last very long,' I tell him.

'Oh yeah? Well, your buddies' parents get wrist-ache just pushing a mouse around. How sad is that?'

Dad thinks he's so special because he doesn't own a laptop or have an email address. When he turned forty he promised himself he'd learn a new instrument every two years. But since Luz died he hadn't taken up anything. Then, a few weeks ago he came home with the tabla. Mom hasn't commented on it, which means she approves.

Yesterday a letter arrived from my brothers. It doesn't matter how many email chains she forwards us, Emma also keeps her faith in snail mail alive. The letter is written in English, as custom dictates, but it's a shop-bought card instead of the artsy handmade ones she used to sit us down to make once a week at camp. I was crazy about writing letters, but my favorite part was sealing the envelopes with colored wax, which you had to melt and press with the copper stamp Emma had with her initials on. We keep one of the letters framed in the living room. Our four hands are printed onto it, each a different color, and even though it's started to fade, Luz's tiny print there means no one dares touch it. Maybe it'll disappear entirely. Acrylic, I think it is. Or maybe gouache. I'm going to ask Marina how to restore it.

If you ask me, my brothers have it easy. Men in general have it easy: they spend pretty much their whole lives gawking at girls' chests without even having to wait for their own chests to grow something worth gawking at, or for their hair to grow only to then spend their lives shaving it off. Pina pulled me up on this last point, though.

'And what about facial hair, then?'

She might have a point. As soon as she forgives me for what happened the other day I'll tell her as much. This happens sometimes with us: we stop talking for an afternoon, or even a couple of days. One time we didn't talk for almost an hour in the same room because she made fun of me for using the word 'bygone'. She doesn't get it. 'Bygone' is an awesome bygone word.

The letter doesn't say anything they haven't already told us by email, but it makes me happy anyway; happy not to be there with them. And because in it they repeat the one really important thing: that they got my seeds. I've done my research, you see. It seems knobby tomatoes don't just grow from a single plant that you can plant. So now I've got myself an 'heirloom tomato-seed kit' which I bought online. I paid with Mom's credit card and my brothers are going to smuggle it back in their suitcase. I have no idea how to say 'heirloom tomato' in Spanish. To me it sounds like a shady character: the Heir of the Looming Tomatoes. Or like some kind of macho saying: 'You must stay home and weave, chosen heir of the loom.' But when I told Pina this she just said, 'Get over yourself, Elizabeth.'

Every three months, since I was about eight, Emma sends me a box of books. She buys them by the kilo whenever someone in her county dies, and then sends them on to me. For two whole years I got nothing but Agatha Christie novels. Whoever Emma's neighbor was (RIP) he was a major fan. During those two years everything around me was a clue, and Pina would respond to anything I said with a 'Cool it, Christie.' Alf never stopped calling me that, but he also never tells me to calm down or get over myself.

I thought that Emma wouldn't send me any books this year seeing as I boycotted camp, but a couple of weeks ago a box arrived full of Elizabethan classics written in an elegant and long-winded English. That's where Pina got Elizabeth from. What's in a name? My nicknames are determined by the reading preferences of dead folk from Michigan. Maybe now – because of all the Elizabethan and because I skipped the US trip this summer – my spoken English will disappear altogether. If they ask me my name, I'll answer, '*Taa tin tete*

tu,' and I'll have to communicate with Emma solely in writing. I only ever practiced speaking English at summer camp.
Emma would say to me, 'You're so pretty, kiddo.' And I'd
answer in my best Miss Marple accent, 'Why, thank you, my
dear!' Which doesn't mean I believed her.

'You're so pretty,' I say to my yard.

*

I take Pina a few cherry tomatoes from my plant and she
forgives me for calling her stupid for no reason the other day.
She comes over with her new hula-hoop and is gobsmacked
by how it all looks now it's planted. Mom made lemonade and
I take sips from my glass while Pina tries to make the hoop
hula around her waist.

'I think Daniel has a lover,' I tell her out of nowhere.

'The neighbor?'

'Uh-huh.'

'No way!'

'Yes way.'

'How do you know?'

'The other day I went and knocked and he was there but
he didn't open the door.'

'And?'

'And I peeked a look under the door and saw some shoes.'

'So what?'

'There was a pair with high heels too, just sort of lying
there. And Daniela doesn't wear heels.'

'Men are scum.'

'Where did that come from?'

'It's what Chela says.'

'Shall I tell you something else? When Emma went to the University of Michigan in the seventies, the women weren't allowed to go in through the main door.'

'Seriously?'

'Uh-huh. There was a little door to the side with "Ladies' Entrance" written on it.'

'That's awful! And it wasn't even that long ago. But, shall I tell you something? If Theo isn't careful, he's gonna turn into a *macho*.'

'Theo? But he plays the piano!'

'Uh-huh, but he never takes that T-shirt off. The one with the naked girl on it.'

'She's a pin-up girl.'

'It's deprading.'

'Degrading?'

'Whatever! It's wrong.'

Pi lets the hoop fall to the ground and she sits down at the table. I pour her some lemonade. I feel strong and tan. I pass her the glass and illuminate her, Marina-style, 'It isn't wrong, darling: it's *vintage*.'

'What really is wrong is Chela giving me a hula-hoop.'

'Wrong how?'

'Like she thinks I'm still nine.'

Mom opens the sliding door and says, 'Look who came over!'

Marina emerges from the kitchen, as if summoned by my impression of her. The second she sees Pina, though, her eyes drop to the floor. Marina always avoids Pi. It's one of those things that goes on in the mews and which we all know about but nobody understands. The same with Alf, who every evening takes The Girls around the block in their stroller. Pina doesn't care. I think she might even like it: it amuses her. She says hey to Marina and offers her a go on her hula-hoop. Marina tries it while I tell them all about the Iroquois, a tribe of American Indians who had their own constitution and shared out all the powers equally: only the women could be chiefs of the clan, and only the men could be chiefs of the military, but the chief of the clan was the one who chose the chief of the military.

'And were there less wars?' Marina asks.

'No idea. What I do know is that they planted a kind of *milpa*. I'm using their technique actually, it's called the Three Sisters. The three sisters are corn, bean, and squash.'

Marina and Pina look over at the plants in the planters.

'No,' I tell them, and point to the part where it looks like there's nothing but soil.

They nod, unconvinced.

'It'll take a few months to get going,' I say.

The window opens and Mom whistles for me to go over. I'm convinced she's going to tell me to get rid of Marina, and that by some secret Protestant mafia law she's not welcome in this house. But instead she passes me a clean glass. It has movie characters on it and a straw built into the side. Theo got it in a fast-food promotion. Mom says, 'It's the only plastic one we have.'

Marina blows her a kiss, but Mom doesn't react: she's staring at something else. I think she's about to notice that I planted the corn. She might be able to tell from the notches I made in the planters where I'm going to tie thread to mark out the plot (I don't want anyone stepping on my three sisters thinking there's only soil there). But her eyes are on something else.

'Pina, where did you get that?' she barks, all weird and aggressive. My mom never calls her Pina.

I look at my friend. She's holding the cuddly dog I found the other day. Marina looks at it too and shouts, 'Patricio!'

'Did your mom have it?' my mom asks.

'What?' Pina asks.

'That was Luz's dog!' she says.

'It was mine!' I tell her.

'I remember that, Ana. When I first met you, you wouldn't let it out of your sight,' Marina adds.

Pina is still looking at my mom, clearly feeling hard done by. Mom studies my face carefully and then raises her arms.

'You might be right,' she says, before disappearing from the window. For a minute we think she might reappear at the screen door, but we can only see our reflection, which shimmers on the glass in the sun. When you look at all of us three together in the glass, we don't look that different. No more than corn does to bean, or bean to squash.

Marina lights a cigarette and every now and again, without saying anything, passes it to Pina, who takes strategic drags facing away from my house. Smoking is a dumbass thing to do. But a dumbass thing that right now makes me feel pretty jealous. I don't want those two to be friends. I can't believe they're sharing the cigarette and the hula-hoop and they haven't even insisted that I try, all because I said it was a dumbass thing to do. Although it also bugs me the way Marina is so awkward every time she sees Pina. Something went on there that no one will tell me. One day everything was fine, then Marina did something and my mom ran her out the house, and suddenly there were no more English classes, and no more babysitting. Every time Pina and I ask my mom what happened she just raises her eyes and starts singing, which is her way of summoning her powers of discretion.

Before leaving, Marina says to me, 'I made you a color.' Then she whispers in my ear, 'Gleenery.'

'Shall we go grab an *horchata*?' Pi asks.

'I'm on a diet.'

'Quit it, will you? You're not fat.'

'OK, but you're buying.'

'OK,' she says. 'I'll see you at the bell in an hour.'

God knows what she's going to do all that time. Probably her hair. Since she came back, Pina spends her life grooming herself. She walks off and I stay outside reading *Euphues and His Anatomie of Wit*. But 'reading' is a manner of speaking really: it's more like deciphering a code. *But thou Euphues, doſt rather reſemble the Swallow which in the Summer creepeth vnder the eues of euery houſe, and in the Winter leaueth nothing but durt behinde hir: or the humble Bee, which hauing fucked hunny out of the fayre flower, doth leaue it and loath it: or the Spider which in the fineſt web doth hang the fayreſt Fly.* For a millisecond, I wish my brothers were here. If I were reading out loud to them with a British accent, Olmo would be chuckling and Theo would be composing a song for our non-existent band, The Honey-Fucking Bees.

When the sun gets too much for me, I go in. It feels cool, almost cold, and unlike outside, it's dark. I can't see two centimeters in front of me when I go through the door, and I trip over something. It's Mom. She's on the floor. I yelp. She laughs.

'What are you doing there?' I ask.

'Oh, just my jujitsu,' she says.

'Doesn't jujitsu involve some movement?'

'Not this kind, no.'

*

We're all eating dinner when Pina brings up the launch party.

'It'll be open to the public and pay-on-the-door,' she adds.

'Are you kidding me, Pi?' Mom says.

Dad pours Beto some wine, then some for Mom, and he says to her, 'You used to sell lemonade.'

'Different times,' Mom says. 'Different country.'

'You and I sold crickets, do you remember?' Pi asks me. 'You'd trap them and I made little holes in the containers so they could breathe.'

I stare at Mom and, without knowing what exactly I'm referring to, say to her, 'I've earned it.'

'Totally,' adds Pina. 'The girl's been slogging away. Look at her arms, she's bionic!'

I flex my right bicep. Dad feels it and pretends to be impressed.

'Beto and I bought your crickets off you then let them go in Alf's *milpa* once you were asleep.'

Beto whistles and says, 'I'd forgotten all about that.'

'Can we have an inauguration?' I ask.

Mom is wearing a blue rag. She smiles at me, does Protestant hand, but in the end says, 'Fine.'

'But only once your brothers are back,' Dad adds.

'Duh,' Pina says, almost offended, as if we'd already taken that into consideration.

'And by invitation only,' Mom says. 'And free entry.'

'Voluntary donation?' Dad pitches in. 'Hey, if people want to help, why stop them?'

Mom takes one slow, deep breath, which I know means 'OK'. Dad holds out his hand to me, then to Pina.

'Deal,' we say, and shake on it. But on the inside, I say something else. On the inside I say, 'Squeeze!'

*

Pina and I go over to hers. The adults stay in my living room. Dad said we had to celebrate Pina and Chela's reconciliation, hence tonight's dinner, but only Pi, my parents and I know that. We told Beto it was in honor of us starting high school next week.

Pina passes me an envelope with some photos she developed. It's pretty weird seeing her mom again. Was she always so good-looking? I tell Pina that the beach looks great and how jealous I am that she got to see hatching turtles. Then I let her braid my hair because she swears on her life she knows how. She doesn't of course, but this is a necessary experiment. Daniela gave us elastic bands from her brackets. (She looks terrible, pregnant with brackets.) She told us that if we sleep with our hair in braids then take them out in the morning we'll have 'created volume'. We need volume for the yard inauguration. Pina braids and braids and tells me all about the beach at Mazunte and the people there and the turtles. Eventually she tells me that the weirdest thing is that the same thing happens as when she was little: when she's with Chela, she doesn't dare speak. Like she wants to say the right thing, but she thinks about it so much that in the end she doesn't say anything. She says that this doesn't happen with anyone else; apart from boys she likes. She says she bucked up the courage to ask her mom what the notorious letter said, and Chela told her that she didn't remember.

'Did she say sorry for leaving?' I ask her.

Pi shakes her head, looking at me in her dressing-table mirror.

'Did you get a boyfriend?' I ask.

'No,' she says. 'Men our age are all useless, Elizabeth, Liz, Lizzie; from now on I'm going to call you Lizzie.'

'Men our age aren't men yet, Pizzie.'

'What are they?'

'They're youths.'

'They're what?'

'They're fayre flies with fucketh for brains.'

*

Pi has been asleep for hours. I can't sleep because my braids are itchy and because the things she told me are crushing down on my chest. I don't know if I could see Chela again; if I could manage not to hate her till the end of time. Or maybe I can hate her so my friend doesn't have to. I could be a hate surrogate and Pina could let it all go and just forgive her. Maybe she has already. Not only for leaving, but also for what Chela confessed to Pina and Pina just told me now, before falling asleep: that last year, for her birthday, Chela came all the way here but didn't get farther than the doorway. She was here and just left without a word. That makes me angrier than anything. That, and what the letter said.

It's easy to hate Chela, but I can't sleep at the same time as I do that; I keep waking up and it's all still there, all jumbled up inside me and it's like when Luz died: like I want to go back in time, open the door to the mews and catch Chela hesitating in front of the entry buzzer and make her ring the damn thing. At some point I notice the window is no longer black. I get up to look at the stereo: it's five thirty in the morning. I get dressed, go downstairs and cross the larynx barefoot, stopping to touch the bell with my toes. It's much colder than the floor. I stay like that for a while, like a charactress from a movie: standing alone, the dawn sky spelling sadness over me.

The other thing Pina told me was this: when she came back from her mom's beach, Beto finally agreed to show her the letter. It's just one sentence; one that none of us could have ever imagined. I think that's actually what's brought on the insomnia, because how many years have we spent wondering if it was a suicide note, or if Chela was really a spy and had been forced to leave on a mission? Basically, wondering if she wrote something that shed the light on her disappearance. But what's breaking my heart is that the letter doesn't say anything. The letter says: *Pina, I only ask that you finish high school.*

*

At home, the screen door to the yard is open. At first I'm worried, but then I walk closer and see my mom out in the middle of the lawn with a cup of coffee in her hands. She looks lost there, still in her white nightgown and with a woolen shawl wrapped around her half-heartedly, staring at it all as if she were deciding whether my plants are fact or fiction.

'What are you doing here?' I ask gently, taking her hand.

She's barefoot too, and her wheat-colored hair is loose. Her wedding ring hangs between her collarbones. She never liked wearing it on her finger. Dad says she put it on a chain three weeks after their wedding. I realize then that it's been ages since I saw this part of her body: it moves when she breathes, up and down, and the ring catches in the light of a streetlamp. Her shoulders look like two tennis balls implanted under her skin, the same as my brothers': I didn't remember that. Has Mom been hiding her body, too? I run a finger along the furrows between my braids and the itching starts up again. We look down at our feet. Mom holds on to my arm and shows me how, if you go in to touch the grass from the side, the droplets land on your toes. We have the same feet, too wide for pretty shoes. And now we have this too: dew, silence, green things.

Mom clenches her toes and pulls out a few blades of grass. She regrets it immediately and looks at me like a little girl who's just done something naughty. I shrug my shoulders.

'It doesn't matter. We've got more. More of all of this.'

Then Mom blinks at me slowly, which I know means 'thank you'.

2003

They've only just sat down when Chela says, 'Now we're going to talk about happy things.'

The crepes, the cutlery, two plates and a selection from Chihuahua's jelly collection are laid out on the table. They've also decanted some water from the twenty-liter bottle in the kitchen into a pitcher. Marina, who never sits at the table, feels like she's taking part in a simulacrum.

'You start,' Chela says.

'I invent colors,' is the only happy thing Marina can think of.

'With paint?'

'With words.'

'How do you mean?'

'Like... this one I thought of earlier. I'm still not sure if it works: "blacktric".'

'An electric black?'

'Exactly.'

'Nice. You got anymore?'

'Scink is the pale pink you find after you pull off a scab. You know the one?'

'Totally!'

'Dirtow is the dirty yellow on the edges of sidewalks where you're not meant to park. Cantalight is that melony orange you only see at twilight. Briefoamite is the ephemeral white of sea foam.'

Chela has her mouth full so she says yes with her index finger. 'Go on,' she gestures.

'Green-trip is the color of ecological guilt-trips.'

'Amazing!'

'Suddenlue is when you're fine one minute and sad the next.'

'Amazing!'

'Hospitachio is the pistachio green color of hospitals. Burgunlip is the color of your mouth after a few glasses of red wine. Insomnlack is for the dark rings under sleepless eyes. Rainboil is that complex blend of petrol colors you see on the tarmac at filling stations. You know the one?'

'You've got a talent, missy,' Chela concludes. 'And remember: talent doesn't grow on trees. My happy thing is my hotel.'

It's not actually hers, but that's what she calls it: 'my hotel'. Entitlement never goes unnoticed by Marina. Chela recaps her three years on Mazunte beach: she started out waiting tables, and slowly climbed the ladder to become manager. She talks about the turtles and their little eggs, about the police bribes, and the insufferably ignorant tourists; she talks about a Colombian, an Irishman, the best sex of her life, the best weed of her life, high levels of THC. Or did she say OCD? Marina can't concentrate with the food there in front of her. And because she doesn't like how Chela interrupted her: she had more colors, tens of colors to tell her.

'How old are you?' she asks.

'Thirty-nine. I told you in the kitchen.'

'Right.'

Marina pushes pieces of crepe around her plate. She ate almost half of it with relative ease, when it was still hot. But now that it's gone cold and sticky she can't face another morsel. And right there and then, as she tries to think up a way to clear the table without offending Chela, she decides whose side she's on. Even if there are no sides here, she doesn't care. She's on Pina's side. She's on Linda's side. She's with Belldrop Mews. She stands with the people who face city life head on; who take the rough with the smooth. What is this beach-creature – this siren, this goldfish – doing in her house anyway?

Chela is showing her photos of the hotel on her phone, but this only disenchants Marina further. From somewhere inside of her, her brother demands, 'Is-this-what-you-left-your-daughter-for? For a tan and a nametag? For a joint and a hammock?' As much as Marina wouldn't mind having a go at all those sunny, jaunty, multicultural experiences herself, they just don't seem appropriate for Chela. Not at her age! Her nametag reads *Isabelle*. Please! Marina is presented with the clearest picture of Chela's particular brand of confusion – the kind that smells of Indian Sandalwood but is barely distinguishable from the scent of church incense –, and she feels nothing but disgust for it. At the same time, and quite unexpectedly, Marina welcomes a new, spontaneous admiration for her mother, who is very submissive, it's true, but at least isn't confused. Señora Mendoza distrusts all kinds of smoke. She never bought into either the hippies or the puritans, and she boils cloves and orange peel at the first whiff of a cigarette in the house.

Right there and then, Marina knows what she has to do, and not just as an excuse to get away from the food on the table, but because what she's about to say has to be said. She's known since the kitchen and has just been putting it off. So now she gets up and carries her plate to the sink, and when she comes back she puts one foot up on a chair, props herself against her knee, lights a cigarette and says, 'I have to tell you something, OK?'

She's doing it all wrong. She knows she's doing it all wrong, but the hospital jargon has taken the reins.

'Empowerment,' she hears in her head. Power is a bucking bronco. You have to mount it. It's a rabid bronco and you have to take a single running jump to get on. At least that's what goes on in Marina's head every time someone mentions empowerment.

Chela has her eyebrows raised, amused but also attentive, open. She puts her phone down.

'Luz. Linda and Víctor's little girl?'

'Yes...'

Marina sits down. The bronco has bolted. She looks at the table, suddenly ashamed. She doesn't want to be the one to say it. It's not a happy thing, for starters, and moreover it has nothing to do with her. There's a spot of caramel on the plastic tablecloth. Marina rubs it off with a serviette and the serviette gets all clogged up in the caramel, breaks apart and makes tiny paper tacos.

'What about her?' asks Chela.

'She died. Two years ago.'

All the air leaves Chela's body. You can hear it – one long breath – and in its wake, a feeble whimper. She also raises her knuckles to her mouth, frowns, and bites her hand. A moment of transparent emotion which reminds Marina of their age gap, because she doesn't remember ever having reacted to anything like that: with an exhalation of empathetic pain.

A moment later, Chela gets up and goes to the sofa. She rolls a joint, and the whole time her eyes weep in that same disconnected way, as if they were simply raining. Under her breath, over and over again she says, 'Fucking hell.' Marina joins her on the sofa and they smoke in silence, each of them perched on one end, separated by a small lake of yellow vinyl and an ashtray with the words 'The Mustard Mug' on it. Neither woman's feet touch the ground: Marina is hugging her knees and Chela has her legs crossed in lotus. On the radio, Nina Simone melts the words 'daddy', 'sugar', 'bowl'.

'I miss him,' Marina thinks. 'How sick am I?'

She misses her daddy like one misses the light of a house where you no longer live. A subtle but unremitting absence: his sullenness, a phantom limb. Or not his sullenness, but certainly the tension he planted in the air. And the other thing: the subsequent release. The exhaustion the family collapsed into after he'd walked off slamming the door, like a kind of post-coital bliss, only post-violence. A silence so passive it felt like peace.

Chela lets out a snotty giggle.

'One time,' she says, pointing with her chin to the portrait of Doctor Vargas, 'Beto went to wake up Noelia in the middle of the night because I had a terrible pain. She came round in her nightgown, checked me over and diagnosed me with trapped wind. That's what she said to me: "Don't worry, Chelita, this is what we call 'trapped wind', and it'll pass in no time." She gave me a few Pepto-Bismols or something like it and sent me to bed. But the next day I went to the hospital and it turned out I had peritonitis.'

'One time,' Marina says, 'my dad put on a show with soap bubbles just for me.'

Someone had hired out the restaurant for a birthday party and Marina was in the kitchen when a clown went in to ask for a tray with some water. Up until that moment, she hadn't minded being the girl in the kitchen. In fact, she liked it, because she felt superior to all the other kids who didn't work. But the clown thing she did mind, Marina explained, because they weren't allowed out of the kitchen, and she and her brother had to watch the show through the round windows in the swing doors, Marina propped on an upturned bucket which she had to move each time a waiter went in or out. But later that same night, among the remaining balloons and the chairs already turned upside down, her dad rehashed the show for her in a modest private function. He made her sit down at the table in the middle of the restaurant, then served her a Coca-Cola in a wine glass and all of the leftover cake – half the birthday girl's name still legible in the icing. Whereas the clown had used two sticks and a rope to make his bubbles, her father filled a soup bowl with warm water and washing-up liquid. He wet his hand in the mixture and then slid the tip of his thumb outwards against his index fingertip, forming, once the two fingertips were touching, a small, thin film. He took a drag of his cigarette and exhaled into the film between his fingers, which inflated into a bubble filled with smoke. She wanted the bubbles to last longer. That's what she remembers most clearly: that they lasted a very short time, less than normal bubbles, because they never really managed to float. She asked her dad to stop doing it with the smoke, but he wanted to do them like that. It was one of the clown's tricks. The bubbles came out a kind of green-gray, and when they popped a waft of smoke hung in the air for a moment before disappearing. Back then Marina didn't have a smoker's mentality, and wasn't able to appreciate what she now points out to Chela:

'What an ingenious guy, no? Great way to justify his ciggie in the middle of a kids' party. You'd never get away with it today.' And then, without a pause, Marina adds, 'I wish my dad had walked out on us.'

'You don't mean that.'

'I do. He was a dad to remember, not to keep; he still is.'

'What are you trying to say to me?'

'Nothing.'

Marina wants to talk about the shoes. About the witchy, leather shoes.

'Where did you get those shoes?'

But Chela ignores her. She crosses her arms, clutching a hand with each armpit, and leans forward. 'Do you think,' she asks very attentively, a lot like Marina's therapist, 'I should go knock for Pina tomorrow? For her, I mean, would it do her any good if I did?'

But Mr. Therapist never asks her truly difficult things like this. Marina would rather go back to talking about herself than answer this, even if it means conjuring the unfamiliar first person: she'd rather be analyzed than handed the threads that tie other people to their children. She'd rather Chela ask her anything else: even about her weight.

Marina blinks in an attempt to look confused; she wants to do a Chela and ignore the question, move onto something else. Weren't they talking about her? Yes, about her and her dad, or about Doctora Vargas, but not about Chela, and certainly not about Pina. At the same time it flatters her in some way that Chela asks for her opinion. But it also – she realizes finally, and not without some surprise – makes her mad.

It makes her mad. Really pisses her off. They drive her fucking crazy, these irresponsible parents, and she can feel the carbs pulsing in her legs: the rage and the energy. The crepes start to ferment in her bile, and the real intentions behind dessert become clear to her: *a posteriori* comfort: that goddamn fixation of parents with alleviating their guilt with sugary treats. Of making everything better by having kids. Procreation as a palliative. She too, by the way, has considered it: stopping her pill to see if at last Chihuahua will agree to move in with her, to share the bills: 'Bat for the same team,' she says. 'As if putting up with you were a game!' he says. The last time they fought, Marina asked him to 'contain her'. Later on, with a helping nudge from Mr. Therapist of course, she saw the connection: she wants someone to contain her, and that's why she flirts with the idea of becoming a container herself, of fabricating a living remedy in her tummy, something to entertain them, something that'll renew them. (The game is: Russian Dolls.) And then? If it doesn't work out you pack up and move to the tropics. Marina instantly throws the idea out again. She wants to take her pill right now in case Chihuahua calls, but Chela is still there in front of her, waiting attentively, doglike. Marina spots the bronco, takes a running jump and straddles it.

'Truthfully?' The nape of her neck shudders.

Chela says yes, smiling to encourage her to go on. She has some wrinkles on her cheeks that Marina hadn't noticed until now; two semicircles, which don't make her any less beautiful, but simply exist there as evidence that life doesn't turn out how you plan it.

'Truthfully, I don't think it'd do her any good,' Marina says.

She knows she's doing it all wrong, but it feels right to do it wrong. She even moves her hands like her therapist does when he's explaining things.

'She must have grieved very hard for you. And if she's already processed that, if she's already gone through the different stages, you're only going to come and whip the rug from under her feet. Some damage is irreversible, in my view.'

Chela doesn't stop nodding her head, very slowly, soaking in the wisdom that Marina – at least at this moment – really does believe she possesses. In the second before she continues her monologue, Marina asks herself what Linda will have to say about all this: will she see that Marina is doing Pina a favor because Chela is a mom to remember, not to keep? Or will she disapprove of Marina's impromptu project? Anyway, it's too late to go back now. Marina can feel a small vortex winding its way up her sternum; her jargon bulb lights up; she defines every one of the grieving stages; pontificates briefly on the Electra complex; she comes up with absurd artistic references for the loss of a mother: the *Pietà*, 'but the other way round'. And all the while one part of her is saying, 'keep-your-nose-out-little-girl', and the other part sticks two fingers up at her inner brother and leads her on in her blundering revenge (for all the damaged kids out there!) while she takes Chela's hands and tells her, 'Don't fuck her up any more than you already have, Chela.'

And that's when, very slowly, Chela stops nodding her head, unfolds her legs and bends over like a folding chair to do up her witch shoes. And she does all of this so slowly Marina can't tell if she's leaving or just feeling chilly. But then she gets up, goes toward the door, and by the time Marina understands that Chela is indeed listening to what she's said, that Chela is leaving the mews without having knocked on her daughter's door, her daughter who she hasn't seen in three years, Marina understands the price of that invisible bronco, she understands that she's spoken her last words; her final, malignant, and satisfying words. And before Chela has even opened the door, Marina is awash with a feeling of remorse, or perhaps just of abandonment. Everything is tinged with that Sunday feeling: the end of a play date (the game was: Afternoon Tea). Marina then makes what she deems to be an aesthetic effort to concentrate, appreciate, and mentally record these last Neptunian moments, as the beautiful, defeated beach-creature wraps her flimsy scarf around her neck, takes her old-fashioned jacket from the back of the chair and puts it on. Chela then opens the door, picks up the soaking trash bag, and wraps it around her head like a cape, or a hood, the most pathetic of armors. Chela is leaving, and Marina didn't tell her – isn't ever going to get the chance to tell her – that her first name is Dulce. And yet, before closing the door behind her, as if she somehow did know, and from inside the two parentheses that cup her mouth when she smiles, Chela promises her, 'You'll go to heaven, sweet Marina.'

2002

Reborn dolls are handmade. The people who make them are known as reborners. Once Noelia had made up her mind to buy herself a little doll, she did some research on the sketchy, dial-up nineties Internet and chose a reborner who lived in Stratford-upon-Avon: so that's where we went. For the first time, tiny size-0 garments – all strictly folkloric – found their way into our cases. Noelia bought the clothes as a gift for the reborner, but we both knew that they were actually for Maria (as she'd already decided to name her doll).

'Noelia,' I said, 'calling a doll dressed up in traditional Mexican outfits Maria is as ludicrous as calling a dog Pup, or a pub The Tavern, or a wine bar Bar à Vin.'

To which she replied that Maria was going to be neither a pet animal nor a drinking establishment, and that she wasn't best pleased about me calling her a doll, even though that's precisely what she was, and even though Chris had told us that it was very important that we never forget that that's precisely what she was. The way Noelia saw it, given that we didn't have a snowball's chance in hell of forgetting she was a doll, it was hardly necessary to keep reminding ourselves every five minutes, and so wasn't it just better if we didn't refer to the doll as a doll, because she didn't like it, period. I was about to protest but she held up her index finger and said, categorically and when we were already on our flight to Heathrow, 'Promise me you're not going to call her that again, at least not between us.'

I promised, but I also told her that 'baby' made me very uncomfortable. And so we agreed to call her 'the girl'. The girl seemed more neutral to me. No, if I'm honest, it seemed more ironic. It gave me the hope (the false hope, as my wife would make sure) that I was going to be able to keep my distance from the whole thing. For me the girl was a thing. Then they became two things. And then, inevitably, they became The Girls. But that came later.

Chris was an American lady Noelia exchanged emails with before she decided to adopt a reborn in Stratford-upon-Avon. Noelia read me out her emails, which recounted Chris's deadly-boring life in microscopic detail. I can't say I thought much of Chris, and then she started sending me separate emails urging me to understand my wife's needs, after which I positively loathed her. Chris was a consummate collector, not to say sick in the head. Her fifty-plus collection of reborns had their own outhouse in the garden, and on top of names and surnames, they'd each been assigned their own hypothetical future.

'So-and-so is going to be a doctor like you,' she told Noelia when she went to meet Chris in person, taking advantage of a cardiology conference in the States.

My wife returned from that trip explaining to me that *a*) Chris is a psycho killer with frills, you know the type? and *b*) she was going to buy herself a reborn, whether I liked it or not. Chris was also a reborner, but a lousy one. A large part of the decision to go to England was to avoid offending Chris who, according to Noelia, 'would've sniffed us out the very second we ordered from *any* other reborner in the States.' I'd never been to England, so I didn't argue with the casual paranoid presenting herself to me.

We spent three days in London and then drove all the way to Stratford on the wrong side of the road. To say *we* drove is a manner of speaking, of course, because I don't even drive on the right-hand side, let alone the wrong one. I map-read. We settled into our hotel, then went to meet the reborner and put in our order. More than anything we wanted to make sure that there was a dark-skinned model in the reborner's catalogue, and that she wasn't going to lumber us with some totally inappropriate little blond dolly. Without having told me, Noelia had packed a bag with photos of us from childhood so that the reborner (what was her name? Marissa? Melissa? I don't know, but I'm sure it had a double s in there because that was my prompt to be doubly condescending) could take inspiration from our younger faces. I spent the whole visit swinging between the giggles and pure disgust. I was pretty unbearable really. Noelia sent me to the car and ended up ordering Maria alone.

I remember lots of painted wood and a little yard at the back of the hotel in Stratford where we lived while we waited for Maria's rebirth. Hidden among the flower pots was a life-sized stone statue of a pig. I remember the stairs with their Persian carpets, and how they perplexed me. I still can't figure it out. Are they made to measure, or are they existing carpets molded and nailed down to each step? But my clearest memories are of the breakfasts. Served on porcelain dishes with domed metal covers, the whole thing was incredibly imperial, and totally unbefitting a modest, four-bedroomed guesthouse. Each night, on a little list, you had to mark a series of crosses against whichever food you wanted to appear on your porcelain dish the following day. Noelia and I ticked the same boxes every night: sausages, roasted tomatoes, and baked beans (with bucket loads of added sugar), which gave rise to a fleeting but intense obsession. I remember that when we got back to Mexico I tried to make them with black Cuban beans and brown sugar: an all round disaster. That's one thing I've learned about food through pure empirical research: food is a patriot. Under no circumstances will it be replicated outside of its mother country.

One morning during that week, Noelia announced that she could contain her curiosity no longer, and called the reborner to ask permission to come and see Maria-in-the-making. It was a big mistake. Seeing her in the oven was far from pleasant. She was deformed.

'She's not deformed,' Noelia corrected me. 'She's just still in parts.' Noelia, who was never politically correct, suddenly got all high and mighty, precisely when we were in the company of a woman who couldn't understand our Spanish anyway. Melissa, or Marissa, didn't speak anything other than incomprehensible English. But she was a smiley, strapping woman who laughed so heartily it was infectious: even I – amid my waves of serious grumpiness throughout the trip – cracked up when she got going. I put my moods down to the fact that I was constantly questioning my wife's sanity, and with it my own, because, as I've explained to Nina Simone a thousand times, we were two people and one person at once. We were a compendium. A compilation. An unequivocal unified compartment. Something like that.

That thing about us not understanding a word the reborner said is pretty much true. For example, she pronounced 'breather' 'brida', and had to write it down before either of us understood what in God's name she was on about. The brida, as we called it from then on, is a simple mechanism you insert inside the doll's ribcage and which, once activated, makes her chest rise and fall rhythmically. In other words, it sort of makes her breathe. Battery-operated breathing. At first we said we didn't need it, but later, when we were sitting alone together by a pub fire, Noelia admitted she was drawn to the idea.

'Why not? If we're already spending a fortune on this girl, why not have the most high-tech, ultra-snazzy, extra-plus model possible?'

She was so enthused that I even called the reborner myself, from the pub's telephone. With some scotch in me for courage, I told her that we did want the brida after all: we wanted the girl to 'breathe'. The only problem being that you can't do scare quotes over the phone, and perhaps that's when my irony started to fade.

We didn't go back to see Marissa Melissa until adoption day. In the meantime, we visited gardens and castles, and saw a ton of very green grass and two Shakespeare plays. They call it adoption in the reborn world; the moment you first come face to face with your new baby. Isn't it more like the moment of birth, that first meeting between parents and child? Why do they call it rebirth? As far as I've understood it, the idea is that the doll is born in the moment of assemblage, when the adoptive parents aren't present, just the creator. The reborner. Melissa. Or Marissa. And then it's *re*born (it's reborn as a baby is the idea, like when Pinocchio becomes a boy) in the moment of adoption.

Noelia and I were in the local pub when Maria was born. In the pub, downing pint after pint of beer so heavy it was like drinking umami, and laughing at ourselves to the point of tears. But on the day of the adoption we were serious. I was overcome with that feeling of liberation you only feel when you're miles from home, and decided I was going to be understanding and try to enjoy it all, if only to make Noelia happy. Melissa Marissa presented us with Maria in a box with a clear plastic lid.

No amount of Shakespeare or art galleries really prepares you for such hyperrealism. That's why some people hate hyperrealism and don't consider it art at all: to them it's a righteous, full-of-itself style that constantly puts your sanity and senses to the test. We could have referred to her as the girl, or doll, or whatever we'd wanted, but Maria looks as much like a newborn baby as I look like a withered old man. We opened the box, oohing and aahing, then cracked open the bottle of lukewarm champagne we'd brought for the reborner, and took turns carrying Maria. We learned how to dress her, how to wash her, and how to change her batteries.

Once back in our hotel room with the girl, we opened the stroller we'd bought a few days earlier in London and discovered it didn't fit in the room, so we tried to ask for a bigger one. We never got to the bottom of exactly what happened, but it was clear that the owners weren't in the least amused by Maria because they ran us out of there without the slightest hint of that famous English gentility. Not really knowing what to do, we drove back to Melissa Marissa's house to ask where we could find another hotel. At first she burst out laughing, then she cried a bit (on seeing Maria, who she thought she'd said goodbye to forever), then she insisted we stay the night in her house.

It was the most god-awful night of my life. The reborner inflated a blow-up bed on the floor of her studio. The mattress and bed linen were comfortable enough, but whichever way you turned there were bits of baby. The really terrible parts are the limbs and the heads, because the torsos and pelvises on reborns are made of an agreeable enough material, and look a bit more like a pincushion or a ragdoll, so aren't so horrifying. In the room though there were arms and legs in pristine vinyl, not yet coated in the layers and layers of paint they give them. Others were already painted in complex tones, and I don't know which were worse: the ghostly white ones, or the ones that looked like real skin. Not to mention the half-made dolls, which still hadn't been assembled but looked totally lifelike. In order to sleep without feeling watched I had to lay a T-shirt incredibly carefully over a little table with three finished heads, which Marissa Melissa was clearly in the process of stitching, pore by pore, with fine baby hair.

Noelia and Marissa Melissa stayed up until the early hours of the morning drinking tea and nightcaps and playing with the dolls. God knows how much they must have drunk. All I know is that when I woke up *a*) there were various reborns dressed in traditional Mexican attire and *b*) Noelia had bought a second doll. I was too intent on getting out of there to argue, and the money was all hers, so I kept my mouth shut.

This was a girl, they explained to me tenderly, who somebody had adopted and then returned! Like a pair of shoes! Noelia called her Clara, at least at first, because she was blond and pale. If you looked closely, around her eyes some veins showed. For the life of me, I couldn't shake the feeling that those veins – which I knew had been painted on – were in fact showing through her pale baby skin. In short, Clara was just as gut-wrenchingly disturbing to look at as Maria. You could stop breathing waiting for them to. But Clara didn't have a *brida*, so you'd sit there expectantly and she wouldn't move a muscle. It's the same even today. Some days, the stillness of The Girls is the only thing that'll convince me they aren't alive.

*

Like all the other doctors I know, Noelia didn't go to the doctor. It's a specific bullheadedness of specialists who think that the smattering of general medicine they learned thirty years ago will keep them safe from all ills. Noelia self-assessed, self-diagnosed, self-medicated, and, at a glance, would assess, diagnose, and medicate me too. Her non-cardiological diagnoses often fell short of the mark. Of course, her own misdiagnosis proved to be much worse, but at least once she messed up pretty badly with me. It must have been around 1987. I remember we were in the middle of the construction work on the mews and The Girls weren't around yet. One Friday I started to feel really, really unwell and Noelia had me on paracetamol and tea right up until the following Monday. By the time I woke up on Tuesday my eyes were yellow. I had a severe case of hepatitis, and only survived it because we ran that second to the hospital where they hooked me up and pumped me full of all sorts of drugs. She herself took far too long to go and check out her pains, which I'd guessed were her body's way of protesting against her incurable addiction to work. But by the time she did have some tests, the cancer was already terminal.

*

Carefully placing Maria and Clara in their boxes first, we folded up the stroller, waved Marissa Melissa farewell, and drove to the airport. On the way there we listened to the album that had become a kind of soundtrack to the trip, because someone had left it in the rental car. Noelia loved that album, which was sickeningly schmaltzy. Or perhaps she just wanted The Girls to preserve some link to their past, because driving along she suddenly declared that they were no longer going to be called Maria and Clara, but rather Kenny and G. I asked if she understood that Kenny was the name of a boy, and she laughed.

'Seriously,' I told her, and when we stopped for gas I showed her the CD.

Noelia, who never wore her glasses on vacation, had seen the long hair and guessed that Kenny G was a female saxophonist. She moved the album right up close to her nose to make absolutely sure she wasn't right, and then, after thinking about it for a second said, 'Makes no difference, the names are staying.'

Once on the plane we flipped a coin to decide who was going to take which name. Kenny is Clara, the one who can't breathe. G is the one with the brida. I change her batteries every three weeks, but ever since Agatha Christie branded me a polluter, they've been rechargeable, and during the time it takes for the light on the charger to go from yellow to green, G doesn't breathe. But I sit her right up next to Kenny, who's used to living like that, and she teaches her. I don't expect anyone to believe this, but they've been good sisters to each other.

*

Noelia decided to have chemotherapy. Not because she thought it would work, but because she refused to sit around twiddling her thumbs. Luckily, she also agreed to take huge doses of antidepressants, which helped her live out her last months more or less in peace. They put me on the same ones. I still take them. When I'm about to run out I write a prescription on one of the pads still left in the study with her ID and details on. And I fake her signature, which is something I've known how to do since we got married and I was a junior researcher with no rental income to rely on, so all our groceries went on her credit card.

Lately I've doubled my dose, telling myself I take it for the both of us.

*

Like all daughters who are only a daughter, Noelia had an incomprehensible relationship with her mother. She always felt the urge to call her at the slightest problem, but whenever she was around, the mere tone of her voice, the rhythm of her breathing, or the volume of her chewing was enough to drive Noelia insane. I didn't sit through a single meal with them in which they weren't both putting the other down. Only in her rare lucid moments – generally led by a mixture of alcohol and guilt for some rude reaction on her part – would Noelia admit that the things that most irritated her about her mother were also behaviors she repeated without noticing. Like, for example, only ever buying cheap shoes that gave her blisters.

The one time I thought I'd point out how similar they were, my wife answered, 'You can be a real iguana sometimes, Alfonso, you know that?'

*

I didn't like the hepatitis story. And I especially disliked Noelia telling it in public. It showed me up as unmanly and impressionable. I thought it was proof of how she did whatever she liked with me and I just rolled over and let her, limp and compliant. I didn't and still don't negate my hen-pecked condition, which I've always acknowledged publicly and with my head held high. But I felt that the details of these sacrifices should stay between us. The story of my hepatitis seemed especially intimate to me, and I always felt affronted when I had to listen to it at a dinner party, as if Noelia were telling everyone the story of how, when we first met, I couldn't sleep spooning but now I can't sleep any other way. I also converted to the religion of hugs, sweatpants on Sundays, even frozen fish (despite knowing it's drying up lake Victoria). She even convinced me to watch romantic comedies with her every now and then. Nowadays, to get to sleep I have to prop two pillows behind me. But the pillows don't hug me or warm me up when I come back from the bathroom. Before going to bed I sing to Kenny and G, and tuck them in like Noelia did every night since the day we brought them to Mexico.

One thing Noelia never spoke about at dinner parties was The Girls. And I was grateful to her for that, but now I regret it. Or rather, I don't regret it, but I've changed since then. Before, if Noelia took The Girls out on the street, I was so uncomfortable I'd run around in circles making sure the neighbors didn't see us passing by with the stroller. Now I couldn't care less. I don't care if I'm the crazy old man on the block. Some months ago now, I started to show them off around the mews and explain to anyone interested that they are indeed dolls, but special dolls. Turns out the real girls adore my girls. In the evenings I put them in the stroller and take them for a turn, whistling. I still don't dare take them beyond the mews and onto the street, but I'm contemplating it.

'You'd look hot walking them! Like a sexy granddad.'

'What a generous liar you are, love, thanks.'

'Take them out, it'll do you good.'

'I'll give it a go.'

*

About her friends with children, which was all of them, Noelia would say, 'Their lives shrink.' But when it came to other women like her, the only-a-daughters, she would scoff, 'Career women!' from the very height of her own hypocrisy.

'Well, that's the pot calling the kettle black! If there's anyone who's devoted their life to their career it's you,' I'd point out.

'I don't consider cardiology a career.'

'Oh no? What would you call it then?'

'A vocation,' she'd say, and then, a second later, roar with laughter.

Her friends assured her that it wasn't true; quite the contrary: when kids fell into the mix, life proliferated, grew big, enormous even. You lived for two, three, six. It wasn't true that you never got to go to the theater anymore, and in any case watching the person you gave birth to grow up was better than any damn play, how could she think of comparing the two things!

'Oh, the arrogance!' Noelia said to me. 'How dare she compare her little brat with the arts?' But she took it back in an instant, 'I'm sorry, it's a classic only-a-daughter symptom to confuse maternal love with arrogance.'

But the truth is Noelia didn't fully understand those mothers. It wasn't within her powers to, just like it wasn't within mine to understand her relationship with The Girls. I became agitated every time she invited me into the pink room. Nothing in that space went right for me, and you could tell I was an intruder, like one of those people who visit Saudi Arabia and dress up in local garb to sneak into the mosques, but get found out because everything about their demeanor screams tourist. Oh, wait, that's me too.

Our childless life was neither big nor small. I don't know exactly what size you'd call it: regular. And having The Girls opened up a space that we hadn't had before. The bedroom is full of saccharine knickknacks that my normal self would detest, but the truth is that lately I feel good in there among all the frills and lace. Sort of understood. Or maybe just seen. Only Noelia Vargas Vargas knew how to see me in this life. And now I have no way of knowing how much of me existed only by virtue of her gaze.

*

It took Noelia's cancer for me to stop seeing the dolls as mere dolls and to start seeing them as The Girls. I supported Noelia in her whims for years, but inside I always kept my distance; a kind of protective irony. When Noelia wanted the room upstairs for them, I accepted. When she wanted to line the walls with imported pale-pink and bone-white striped wallpaper, I asked myself who was I to put up a fight if she was footing the bill? When she bought the booster seats and started to take The Girls with us in the back of the car, I told myself that what doesn't kill you makes you stronger. And, looking back, the emotional rollercoaster that The Girls brought with them acted like a shot of youthfulness in a marriage where we took most things for granted. Sometimes I was embarrassed by Noelia, and at other times proud of her. Some days her little game seemed funny, and others it broke my heart to see her there in the house carting around a baby who wasn't a baby. And who wasn't mine.

One time, a police officer smashed in one of our car windows because Noelia had left The Girls in the backseat while she popped into the bank. The police officer thought he'd played the hero, and afterward, Noelia had to slip him a bribe to mitigate his resentment at having 'saved the lives' of two inanimate beings. I always understood my wonderful wife's care as one of her little eccentricities. Or a hormonal process, maybe. A secondary symptom of the uniquely named pain she felt in her uterus. Because, of course, Doctor Vargas Vargas coined an illness – half-Italian, half-Latin – to explain the pain that an only-a-daughter felt when mothers and their children went past: *uterus mancanza.*

It was all very weird, but also harmless. When people gave us funny looks I would become defensive, sort of animalistic, sort of ready to go for the jugular of normal people and things. Did I think the whole reborn thing odd? Of course I did. But it didn't hurt anyone, and it made her feel better. The way I saw it from my privileged view in the royal box, the symptoms of *uterus mancanza* had hit Noelia too late in life; just a pity, perhaps. But it knocked her for six, and the fact that she found ways to alleviate the distress she felt, well, that's the opposite of odd, isn't it? That's garden-variety maternal impulses: by taking care of The Girls she was looking after herself. She took the reins, identified what it was that hurt her and found the best palliative out there. Isn't that taking responsibility for yourself? Moving beyond your childless condition to a state of maturity (that supposedly unachievable state for people who are only a child)? And yet, if I ever tried to congratulate her on any of these things, Noelia would answer, 'Doctors, eh? Only ever treating the symptom!'

*

I'm writing with news: today I took The Girls to the Mustard Mug. It was a real palaver. First of all they didn't want to let me in with my 'granddaughters'. I explained that they were dolls and they didn't believe me. The entire kitchen staff (of two) had to come out and confirm that they weren't babies before the barman would believe me. And then he became all aggro thinking I was there to sell them. In the end I had to resort to emotional blackmail, reminding him of my extremely loyal custom to the Mug. Between taunts and apologies, eventually they let me in, and the adrenaline only stopped pumping through me when I was back at my usual table. My bones ached. I was hot and bothered and red in the face. I drank too quickly, with each sip seeing more and more clearly what the others had spotted the moment I walked in with the stroller: that I am a ridiculous old man.

But then Linda showed up, and, as if it were the most natural thing in the world, I picked up one girl and she picked up the other. We held them in our arms as we spoke. And then I was seized by a new, let's say triumphant, happiness.

'It's my right,' I wanted to say. 'It's my right as an old widower to have something to love. Something that isn't a someone. Something that can't die on me.'

But now the happiness and the triumphant feeling have passed. Now I'm hungover in my study at four o'clock in the afternoon. The sun is too bright; it's showing up all the dust on the furniture. I go around in obsessive circles thinking *a*) it's time to grab the mop and get on with my house chores, time to seek the semi-peace they afford me; and *b*) that I didn't get to choose a damn thing.

I would have liked to have children. Lots. Tons of them. Or at least a few. At least one. Half. A piece.

It's not the first time I've thought this, but it is the first time I don't want to delete it.

*

Amaranth, the plant I lost my head over, has a bland flavor. Not only is it Umami No, it's also Tasty No. There's no doubting the tremendous power of self-deception. I've always had a fine palate. How can I have only just seen what was right under my nose? Maybe you have to get to my age to see the wood for the trees; to spot the little ironies in the things that preoccupied you and into which you poured all your energies. And then you have to measure it all up: length by width by depths of absurdity. But in the end you have to laugh. You have to laugh at everything in this life.

'That's my chicken, god damn it!'

'Noelia, I'm so glad you came. I was missing you. There's something important I want to tell you.'

'I'm all ears.'

'The Girls and I are going to do some work in the yard today. Since the whole *milpa* went to pot, and it turns out amaranth doesn't taste of anything anyway, and the climate's all wrong for papayas, I'm going to put in the jacuzzi you always wanted.'

'Ooh, Alfonso, you have no idea how jealous I am!'

'Don't you have jacuzzis in the hereafter?'

'We don't. But you'll be pleased to hear we all go around butt naked.'

2001

'Do you turn into a fish, too?' I ask Grandma as she helps me into my pajamas.

'No, that's a gene from Granddad. I don't have it.'

'Is that why you threw his ashes in the lake?'

'Yes.'

'Does Ana know?'

'No,' Grandma says. 'Nor do your brothers. Just you.'

She lets me stroke the soft side of one of her hands. With the other she wraps my curls around her fingers, then lets go, because she likes seeing how they spring back. She explains everything in English but I understand her anyway. She says when Mama was a little girl and used to turn into a fish in the middle of the week she would let her off school. Now my mom walks into the room with her nighty on. She's dry again, apart from her hair, which is two different colors when it's wet: yellow where there are knots, brown where it's straight. Mama points at my pajamas.

'Mushroom!' she says.

It's one of Theo's T-shirts, from when he couldn't think about anything other than Mario Brothers.

'Why aren't there any like that in your backyard?' I ask Grandma.

'*Amanita muscaria*,' she tells me. 'Pretty, but lethal.'

'And they speak through their noses!' Mama says.

'They don't speak through their noses,' Grandma says, and she gets up from the bed and pushes my mom out of the room. They blow me air kisses and I catch them, though not all of them: some fall on the quilt. Before drawing the curtain door, Grandma asks if I want the light on and I say no.

'What a brave little girl you're going to be,' she says, and turns off the light. They walk away and I hear them giggling until I can't hear them anymore.

I lie there wondering, 'When?' then sing myself a song to be brave right now.

'Amanita,' it goes, 'Amanito musico, amanita Mario mani-tomario...' But it doesn't work. Maybe I'll be brave when I last a hundred long seconds under the water with the straw. Either I'm going to get brave, or turn into a fish. Or both: I'll be a brave fish and I'll swim down to the bottom of the lake to where the Emperor Umami lives. I wonder if his castle is pretty like the ones in books.

*

I don't know when Mom came to bed but I open my eyes and it's day and there's a sticky arm on top of mine. I talk to her but she doesn't take any notice. I try tickling her but she groans at me and then I don't even want her to wake up anymore. I get down off the bed and the floor creaks. Pina is asleep on the sofa in the living room. I don't know where

Ana is. I find Grandma in the kitchen. She's frying bacon and making everything smell like Sunday.

'Hey, kiddo,' she says. 'How did you sleep?'

I tell her pretty good, but it's a lie. The truth is I had nightmares I can't remember anymore, and I was hot and I sweated in my mushroom T-shirt, and now that the cool air on the porch is hitting me I feel all cold in it.

'Where are my clothes?' I ask her.

'They must be in the bathroom. You want hot cakes?'

'Yes.'

'I can do you a hot cake in the shape of something? What shape do you want?'

Hm, I think about it. I want to ask her for something difficult but not too difficult.

'Can you do a tree with its children but the children aren't leaves like on a normal tree but more like mushrooms?'

'A tree with little leaves that are actually mushrooms.'

'Uh-huh, but not poisonous ones.'

'Got it. Bacon?'

'OK, but first I'm going to get dressed,' I tell her, and walk off to the bathroom.

Sitting on the toilet, it occurs to me that maybe if I do a poop and then flush and run out to the yard, just maybe I'll be able to see it passing through the pond system: one filter, then another, then another, and the water going from black to clean. I stay there for a while trying very hard but nothing comes out apart from a few wee-wees. Ana opens the door and says, 'Your hot cakes are ready.' I tell her she can have them because I'm not ready. She goes off all happy. Then my mom comes in. She takes her clothes off and gets in the shower with her ring around her neck because she never ever takes that off.

I ask her how come she's grumpy if it's Sunday and she says, 'Because of the strident, stupendous, strificant, whatever they're called mushrooms.'

I get mad at her for eating them without telling me, and she says the same thing Grandma said, 'They're just for grown-ups.'

I ask her if she got sleepy and laughed and saw things. She says she saw Chela and that she's OK and that she says hi, but she asks me not to tell Pina. I can't tell if she's crying because she's camuflashed by the steam and the shower curtain, but lately everyone's been crying over Chela, or they get mad, or put their head between their hands. I don't know what that letter she wrote said. Ana says that even Pina doesn't know, but I don't believe her. And I don't dare ask Pina.

'What did Chela's letter say?' I ask.

'That she's gone,' says Mama.

'She's always going,' I say.

'It looks like this time she's not coming back.'

'Is that allowed? I didn't know.'

'You're my Luz, my shining star, do you know that?'

I tell her I do, more or less. Then she asks me what I'm doing still on the toilet: am I sick? I explain my idea about the poop passing through the ponds and she says I can give it a try.

'But I don't have any poop,' I tell her. 'Nothing.'

She tells me to try again after breakfast. So I wipe myself and flush the chain and wash my hands standing on tiptoes and dry them too. And while I do all of that I explain to Mama about how I'm going to turn into a fish and go down to the middle of the lake to visit the Emperor Umami and make a wish for him to make me braver.

Mama goes quiet for a while. She must be thinking about my plan. But when she pokes her head around the curtain all she says is, 'Did I wash my hair already?'

ABOUT THE AUTHOR

Born in Mexico City, Laia Jufresa grew up in the cloud forest of Veracruz, and spent her adolescence in Paris. In 2001, she returned to Mexico City and discovered she didn't know how to cross a street. She's been writing fiction ever since.

Laia's work has been featured in several anthologies and magazines such as *Letras Libres*, *Pen Atlas*, *Words Without Borders* and *McSweeney's*, and she was named one of the most outstanding young writers in Mexico as part of the project *México20*. In 2015 she was invited by the British Council to be the first ever International Writer in Residence at the Hay Festival of Literature. She currently lives in Cologne, Germany.

ABOUT THE TRANSLATOR

Sophie Hughes' translations and reviews have appeared in the *Guardian*, *Asymptote*, *The White Review*, *Times Literary Supplement* and *Music & Literature*. She has worked as an editor-at-large for *Asymptote* and translation correspondent for *Dazed & Confused*, and in 2015 she co-guest edited a *Words Without Borders* feature on contemporary Mexican literature.